FORTY GRAINS OF BLACK POWDER

Previous Books by RLB Hartmann

I Rode with Cullen Baker
Floyd and the Traveling Yard Sale

FORTY GRAINS OF BLACK POWDER

Book One of the Cordero saga
Tierra del Oro

RLB Hartmann

Catawba River Press
Morganton, North Carolina
2011

Forty Grains of Black Powder

First Edition

ISBN-13: 978-0615481845
ISBN-10: 0615481841

Cover design by RLB Hartmann
Back cover photo : Ramón Garza Wilmot
Flying Hawk photo by Tom Stine
The typeface chosen for the Tierra del Oro novels is
Centaur

Prologue

Los Nogales. 1862.

Marieta first saw him across the way station dining area. He sat with two other men at a corner table, and was staring at her.

Averting her glance, she tried to listen to Papá's plans for their new home in California. She could tell that Mamá, too, was weary of hearing yet again what opportunities were to be had in the gold fields, how safe the estate in Spain would be in the hands of their sons until their return, in a few years, when he had increased their fortunes.

Suddenly the strange man stood beside her, introducing himself to her parents, taking the empty chair, offering to guide them to interesting sights in the area, which included northern Sonora and Territories of the United States.

"How fortunate," Papá exclaimed. "We must remain here for a month for repairs, a prospect which none of us desired to endure."

Repairs were vital, for the coches and wagons in their caravan would traverse desert country. Already weeks of her life had been spent on shipboard, on trains, in swaying stage coaches. She welcomed a month of hotels and the company of a man who looked at her as if she were the only woman in the world.

Sixteen and sheltered, Marieta found the attentions of Luis Panadero most enjoyable. Having brought no dueña to accompany her daughter, Mamá shared in all the excursions and meals at restaurants. "He is handsome, sí, mija, but there is a look about him which I do not like."

Marieta liked everything about Luis, from his straight black hair and broad shoulders, to the persuasive words he whispered in her ear. "It is true, I am a poor man now, but one day, I shall build a magnificent casa on my land beside the Río Sangría." In only a few weeks, his patter included an entreaty. "Querida, I wish for you to be the patróna. We can wed here in Nogales, before your family leaves for the gold lands."

He and Papá met each evening in the hotel bar, to drink, laugh and trade stories like old friends. Marieta told her mother, "I love him. He loves me. There is no reason for me to continue to California. My destiny is here, with Luis."

Riding beside her new husband on a jouncing wagon seat, one hand holding a broad-brimmed hat against the efforts of the wind to dislodge it, she pushed from her mind Mamá's tearful face, Papá's hurried hug and final admonitions to be a dutiful wife.

She looked forward to making friends in the village that Luis said lay on the other side of the life-giving river which ran through his property. "There is a small church, and shops where you can buy what you need."

It was only later that he added, "Don't get close to those people. They are not our kind."

When she caught sight of the Río Sangría and the tiny village on its west bank, she searched the countryside of red Sonoran dirt, rocks, and cactus, and asked, "Where is our house?"

Luis gestured ahead, toward a long ridge. The near side was a sheer cliff rising maybe twenty metres above the level desert floor. "It is only temporary, you understand. I have tried to make things nice for you."

Her anxious eyes finally saw the adobe hut where she was to live. One room, at most, with a thatch roof. It blended into the dusty countryside like a lizard or snake. Her heart seemed to stop, then struggle to beat again.

Inside had been whitewashed, and an unbleached cloth, securely fastened around the top of the walls, served as ceiling. It would help to keep out scorpions that nested in the thatch. Opposite the door there was a barred window, adobe ovens along one wall, a brazier, small table and two chairs, coal oil lamp, and a new shuck mattress on the dirt floor.

"I shall need to be away from time to time," he told her. "On business."

Despite her disappointment, she did the best she could to be a dutiful wife. Luis allowed her the freedom to walk over a shaky footbridge to the village, purchase items in the market, hire boys to deliver water and goods to the casita, and attend the services held in the small church. As he never accompanied her, she was able to make a few friends among those señoras who spoke a bit of Spanish, and the young priest, Padre David.

After Luis returned drunk and surly from four days in Los Nogales, she knew what he felt for her was not love, but the pride of possession. When she objected with spirit to his neglect, he slapped her and twisted her arm.

Hiding bruises under a cheap rebozo, she lingered last to make her confession. Her wicked thoughts grieved her. Alone with the priest, the tears came.

"Ah, Marieta, I am sorry." In moments Padre David was opening the booth latch, taking her into his arms. His sympathy was all he offered, for she had made her pact with the devil and there was no help for it.

Their growing friendship, both a torment and a thrill, gave her a reason to go on living. Luis's brutality made their mutual attraction all the sweeter. Luis's absences made it possible to find solace and fulfillment in another man's love. When it was certain there was going to be a baby, she feared it would be Luis's. Padre David said gravely, "It is more important than ever to keep our secret."

Her condition at first seemed to mellow Luis, but soon the drinking and business trips increased in frequency and intensity. On the night her son was born, he was not to be found. The village partera sent for Padre David, and it was he who clasped her hands, murmuring encouragements.

Christening the child, the priest said, "I baptize thee Ramón Rafael—" His eyes lifted from the sleeping baby to fasten on Marieta's gaze, sharing desperation and joy, and he finished, "Cordero." Her heart leaped, joyful.

Seven years later.

He loved the smell of the morning.

The smoky aroma of mesquite fires, drifting from beneath the eaves of chozas where his friends lived, beyond the river. The rain-scented wind, crossing the plain from the mountains to the west. The bright clear light rising behind the eastern hills.

Morning sun cast thin lavender shadows, and lit the petals of plants that had appeared dead for months. Mamá knew their names and showed him which were safe to pick, which bore thorns. There were many thorns, so he learned to love them in their places.

After a rain, brittle bush and sage, peppergrass, Indian blanket, primroses and verbena emerged out of the dawn grayness into bursts of pink, yellow, scarlet, and dazzling white. Paloverdes and mimosas and the pervasive odor of creosote bush mingled with damp earth. Pochotes and huisache bloomed, organ pipe and ocotillo swelled in their skins, and the corn and beans tasseled and flowered.

Rain brought life to the rocky desert floor, an end to the dry season and the renewal of hope.

North Sonora, 1870.

Chapter One

As he did daily, Ramón knelt beside Mamá on the packed earth floor of the village church, listening to the words leaving her mouth and ascending to God.

He tried not to look at the crown of thorns piercing the wooden forehead of Christ, where painted blood ran in thin, crooked streams. The crucifixion story reminded him of times when Panadero hit Mamá, when they were not swift enough to find shelter with friends or in their own root cellar amid the vegetables, until rage was spent and the Dragoon pistol was empty. "Luis wasn't always like this," she told everyone. "It is the tequila. Pray for him."

Alone with her in the sanctuary, Ramón's fingertips touched the faded cloth of her pink-flowered dress, seeking comfort.

She turned the pages of her worn prayerbook, but she no longer needed it to guide her. Her voice stopped, waiting for him, and he murmured, "Precioso Diosito, make my papá stop drinking, so that he will love us."

Another voice spoke softly behind them. "Marieta." Without rising, Mamá turned her head. Ramón thought there was a brief fearfulness before she answered, "Yes, Padre?"

The priest, younger than Panadero, squatted near them. When he held out a rosary, the silver Cristo glinted in a shaft of sunlight. The beads and cross were carved from a dark wood. "Please accept this as—an aid to prayer."

Mamá shrank from the offer. "I cannot. He would find it." There was no place in their hut for hiding things, just as there was no place for them to go where Panadero would not find them. He had thrown away the one Mamá had brought with her from Spain. Panadero's heart had no room for God.

The priest reached out, took her hand. Placed the rosary into her fingers. "Leave it beneath the altar cloth. It will always be here when you need it."

For long moments their eyes spoke to each other, and Ramón felt a force he didn't understand. Padre rose and went into the sacristy. Mamá bowed her head. Her fingers moved the beads, but she forgot to say the prayers aloud. In a few minutes, she crossed herself, and Ramón mimicked her gesture. He watched her hide the rosary beneath the altar cloth. Then they hurried out of the church and back into bright sunlight.

Along the single dusty lane, thatch-roofed adobes and canvas-shaded market stalls lay quiet in the afternoon. Villagers who had risen before dawn to work in garden patches and care for small goat herds, now took their rest. Distant jagged peaks rose behind the whitewashed church.

Ramón turned to walk backwards in front of Mamá, so he could see them. "Do you know what I would like for my saint's day? A caballo, that I can ride into those hills, when I'm older."

"You know Luis won't pay to feed another horse."

"But if we pray and light a candle—"

"And there is no money for candles."

He turned again, hiding his disappointment from her, and trudged ahead. They crossed the foot bridge over the

Río Sangría and climbed the tussocky slope to their hut, a one-room adobe shadowed by a rocky cliff.

"Why is our house here, and not in the village? Why is he not kind, like the fathers of my friends?"

Mamá was silent, sad. But now that he had begun, he couldn't stop. "Why does Panadero never call me hijo?"

"What does he call you?"

He heard surprise and curiosity in her tone. "Trouble. Is that a bad word, Mamá? My friends say he calls me bastardo, and other bad things. They say he will go to Hell for shooting his pistol into the walls of our casita."

Mamá put one hand to her head as if the pain had returned. "Moncho, you must forgive him. And when you speak of him, you must always say 'Papá.' We three are Panaderos."

"No, Mamá. You and I, we are Corderos."

The Corderos were her brothers who yet lived in Spain, and her parents who had traveled with her for months across the ocean and then by stagecoach, because her papá saw opportunity in the riches of California. She had told him about them many times.

They entered the casita, a room furnished with a small table and two chairs. A clay jar of drinking water, a gourd dipper. Two empty wood candle holders on the barred window ledge. A charcoal brazier, where she cooked their meals. Pegs on one wall held clothing. On a packing crate draped with a white cloth sat a coal oil lamp.

A framed painting of La Virgen de Los Remedios holding her niñito, Jesús, hung above the crate. Mary and her Son wore golden garments and jeweled crowns, and tiny figures of angels hovered on either side of the haloed brown faces. Ramón thought Jesucristo was the most fortunate boy who ever lived. "Dios is his father," Mamá had told him. "Diosito divino."

Unfair, to have not only fine clothing instead of coarse cotton but also a kind and loving papá. La Virgen and Jesusito lived in Cielo, not the barren hills of Sonora. In Heaven, no one ever rode in drunk on a lathered horse, curses streaming from cruel lips, fists ready to bruise. Once, a bullet had broken the glass from the frame. Mamá had cut her finger, picking it up. Ramón's finger just fit the hole in the forehead above La Virgen's right eye.

"When you are grown, Ramoncito," Mamá would say, "you'll understand."

He was seven, but if he lived to be as old as Mamá, as old as the priest, even, Ramón knew he couldn't understand a father who openly insulted the Indios of the village. Those men sang and played guitars in the soft evening twilight. Those men carved wooden toys for their children.

Panadero never once crossed the river to attend the fiestas, nor knelt in the plaza when the old priest from Nogales came to say a special Mass. Panadero stayed away for weeks at a time, yet his voice sometimes echoed in Ramón's ears: "Why did you name him Ramón? Why not Luis? I know why. ¡No es hijo mío!"

Mamá laid her shawl and prayerbook beside the lamp, washed her hands in the basin, then prepared their noon meal. He loved the aromas of fresh masa which she patted into tortillas, the brown fragrance of beans simmering in the cazuela, and pan dulce baking in smoke-marred adobe ovens in one corner. Pastries were a treat that came seldom and were all the more treasured for that.

Mamá promised to send him, one day, to the old priest in Nogales, to be taught. He looked forward to lessons in mathematics, language, history and geography, penmanship and commerce. He was disappointed that his teacher would not be the village priest, who ruffled his hair with a firm hand and called him "mijo" and whispered to Mamá when no other worshippers were present. The candles, incense, strange chants and responses all filled Ramón with a sense of awe and possibility.

In the afternoons, lying on his petate and pretending to sleep, he watched Mamá shell beans, sweep the packed earth floor, bend her head to pray. Often she lifted her eyes to the smoke-stained adobe wall where hung the framed picture. "Mamá, tell me again about when you were a girl in Spain."

"Our casa grande was beautiful. The patios were paved with glazed tiles, and we drank from glasses of crystal. My brothers and I used to ride to the far reaches of our hacienda for a día del campo—a picnic. Our favorite spot was near the river—"

"Like the Río Sangría? Only not so swift."

"Sí, a calm river, and wildflowers everywhere."

"Where is Spain, Mamá?" he would ask, to keep her talking, and she would tell him, "Far away, mijo. Too far ever to return."

In her family's casa grande had been many books with engravings, and at her hacienda were fine horses in the fields, and brothers with whom to share music and games and lazy afternoons beneath widebranching trees. Ramón imagined the patios, fountains, arches, mahogany chests and tables, spicy seafoods, silks, and days of sunshine cooled by ocean breezes. He tried to imagine shorebirds, and water so deep that it could cover the ridge soaring at the edge of their dooryard.

One evening he finally voiced a thought that had often kept him awake. "Let's live in California, with my abuelos. They wouldn't let Panadero hurt us anymore."

Mamá's eyes filled with tears. "I chose to marry Luis," she said. "They must never know we're not happy here." She lit the lamp, then beckoned him to sit on her lap and held him close. "It is my penance, Moncho."

Penance was what Padre made people do when they had sinned. What was Mamá's sin? Suddenly he disliked the priest for making them remain in this sunbaked hut beside the Río Sangría, where there were no china plates from which to eat their meals, nor carpets to warm their feet on chilly January mornings.

"Perhaps it will be different this time," Mamá said. "Besides, there is no money, for traveling."

There had been no money for a saint's day present, either, so she had made a cornshuck family for him. A father, a mother, a boy-child, and a tiny baby he named Marisa. As dusk deepened into night, he played with his make-believe family while Mamá read to him from a book she had brought from Spain. His eyelids grew heavy, yet he was afraid to sleep.

He felt her near him, tense, waiting, and he knew that even while her voice read the words on the pages, creating images in his mind, she was listening for distant sounds that would become hooves pounding to a halt in the yard. Listening for the bootsteps of Panadero striding into the casita, overflowing the small house with his towering presence and stunning them with terror.

Then he heard the far-off thunder, swelling moment by moment, and Mamá's voice faltered. "Dios, save us!" she cried softly, snatching up her shawl with one hand and grabbing his arm with the other. She pulled him to his feet and guided him ahead of her toward the doorway.

Leaping out into the square of light cast from the lamp, he barely dodged a plunging horse that was reeled back on its haunches, reined in cruelly by its rider. Mamá's fingers jerked his arm, then lost their grasp. Dust filled his eyes and nostrils. He stood blinking and gasping as Panadero swung down from the saddle.

"¡Demonio! You might have made my horse fall." The rough boot shot out, grazing Ramón's leg below rolled-up calzones. Panadero turned to Mamá. "Send the bastard to your friends. I have need of you."

Ramón saw the hem of her skirt trembling. "He's a child, Luis. Why can you not—"

"Not my child! My sons have huevos. He's a perra. You know what I do with perras. Maybe tonight, before he gets any bigger."

Mamá cried, "Ramón! Mijo! Run!"and he fled through the darkness, bare feet cut by gravel.

The cliff side of the ridge was too steep to climb, but at the back he was able to scramble upward, upward, until, breathless from sobbing, he had to stop. Clinging to the sun-warm rocks, he listened to his churning heart. Above that noise, Panadero's angry voice carried on the night air. He scooted forward, raised his head to peer over the edge.

Below, lamplight from the open doorway cast moving shadows over the threshold. Clay dishes, bowls, and ollas sailed out into the yard and broke. A cane chair landed on one leg and bounced before it stopped, the backrest tipped forward till it touched the dirt, like a person on his knees.

Presently there was a terrible silence. A greater fear took hold of him.

Had he not seen chickens and goats slain for the cook pot? One moment there was breath and warmth, and then by some act of knife or gun or hands about the neck, the eyes dulled and life ended.

Running headlong down the slope, he scraped and gouged his knees and palms on rocks and thorns. He had reached the plain before he heard her calling, "Ramón. Moncho, mijo, it's all right, little one. He is asleep."

Shivering, he ran into her arms.

In the morning, Panadero threw off his blanket and sat up. Eyes red and puffy from drink, yet he demanded, "I want food."

Mamá had been across the river to borrow plates and had brought back a kind señora's chorizos and blanquillos. She had swept away the broken dishes, picked up the stubs of candles and scattered clothing. Ramón rolled the petates and stacked them as usual in one corner. The casita was nearly empty, but it was clean. And Panadero had not broken the adobe ovens.

Squatting the way men did at a campfire, scooping each mouthful with a bit of tortilla, Panadero ate as if nothing had happened. Ramón nibbled the delicious food without appetite, though Mamá's healing ointment soothed the fiery threads where crucifixion thorns had ripped his legs.

Panadero wiped his fingers on his bandana, belched, and declared, "You'll see. I'm going to build a casa grande finer than any estate in Sonora." Then he went to find his horse.

While the old man was gone, Mamá sang and told stories, and Ramón played with his friends in the village. They built reed forts on the mud flats of the Río Sangría, rode their family burros, stalked and clubbed fat rabbits and roasted them in campfire coals, milked one of the goats to moisten dry tortillas at the noon meal. He raced older boys until his chest heaved and sweat ran down his bare skin. Sometimes he won.

This was his tierra, his homeland. He loved every rock, thorny plant, slant of light, and familiar night sound, with all of his being. Days stretched into weeks of peace.

But he knew peace didn't last forever. The only thing lacking was someone brave enough to free them from Luis Panadero.

Chapter Two

One stormy afternoon during siesta, there was a scuff of boots and Panadero stood blocking the doorway without warning. They started up, with nowhere to run.

His cheeks showed pale from a freshly-shaved beard. He wore a stiff new suit, and his hair shone with something that smelled good. He made Mamá sit at the table and poured wine from a bottle into two glasses. He urged her to drink. "Celebrate, Marieta. I told you one day I would be rich."

"You told me many things, Luis."

"¿Y de qué? This one has come true."

The villagers began to call him 'don Luis.' He was now El Patrón. He drank less and no longer hit Mamá.

Masons, painters, and workers in wood and iron came to talk with don Luis. They brought great squares of paper which they spread out in the sun, deciding with gestures and arguments the placement of doorways and windows, patios and porticoes.

Indios came from the village to dig a larger root cellar, which one day soon would hold bottles and bottles of fine wine. Others mixed earth for the slabs of adobe that made building bricks.

With black powder, men blasted huge rocks from the drought-shallow river. The booms filled Ramón's chest like the end of the world, but he was drawn to watch the spurts of water and listen to peónes shout with fear and prayers. Each day he ran around the rim of the foundation, dodging workers laying stone. "The casa grande is going to be very big!" he called to Mamá, who stood with her arms crossed beneath the folds of her rebozo.

While the house was being built they lived with Indio friends. He didn't know where his father slept. Probably in the old house, to keep thieves from taking the barrels of nails and wagon loads of floor boards and glazed paving. Burros arrived with stacks of curved red roof tiles. Ramón climbed the slanted mounds barefoot, like a rock lizard, the dizzying height filling him with a sense of power. No matter, if he was still 'Trouble' to the man he refused to call 'father.'

Before the workmen quite finished, more wagons came, loaded with thick colorful rugs, heavy tables and dressers, all sorts of things for the kitchen, and crates filled with glassware. Girls from the village, now Panadero's criadas, drew each piece unbroken from its nest of straw with cries of joy. Ramón wasn't allowed to touch the glass, but felt pride in the richness of Casa de Panadero. Don Luis had taste, everyone said so.

Ramón lingered in the high-ceilinged rooms, strolled along the central hallway lit by a crystal chandelier, ran up and down the wide staircase with its treads smooth under his feet, the banister like silk beneath his palm.

One of the upstairs bedrooms was his alone, and the rope bed was a novelty after reed petates on a dirt floor. He bounced on the mattress, opened the shutters and leaned out of the window overlooking the patio. Another window faced east, from which he could watch the sun rise every morning before breakfast.

For the first time, he felt safe. Panadero couldn't toss out these heavy mahogany chests and tables, dressers and cabinets. He would never break the German crystal nor porcelain dishes. Everything, from the rugs to the desk and chair in El Patrón's office, was the finest available, and the cost was dear. Nothing would ever push don Luis into destroying this great white house or its sparkling fountain.

Near the center of the casa grande, between the sala and the dining room, the old hut remained. It held unhappy memories for Mamá, too, for she urged, "Have them tear it down. Poor, ugly thing."

Panadero lined the interior walls with shelves full of ornate, leatherbound volumes. "Tear it down? Estúpido, it's my library."

"Why do you want books?" she asked. "You know you will never read them."

He laughed, though it was not a pleasant sound. "These are to impress cattlemen who must be shown my wealth and class. If you don't like this room, stay out."

Ramón was content to sleep in his own bed, thrilled to hang around the corrals with the vaqueros and peónes, to mingle with norteamericanos who lived in a 'bunkhouse' and worked the stock on Panadero's range. Happy to sit at the huge linen-draped table and have servants bring foods hot from the American cook stove which La India cursed daily in Apache.

When the piano was delivered, El Patrón was outside somewhere on ranch business. The criadas, cook, and niños who served their plates and cleaned their shoes, all gathered with excited murmurs, but as Mamá only sat slumped with her hands folded in her lap, they finally lost interest and drifted away.

Ramón laid one arm around her shoulders. "¿Qué te pasa? Have you forgotten the music you used to play in Spain?"

"I haven't forgotten."

"Then, play a song."

"My heart is empty of songs."

Something in her manner closed his lips, but he hoped that one day the songs would return. In Spain, she had worn fine silk dresses, and her black hair was draped with a lace mantilla on a silver comb. He waited for those items to arrive and be taken from their packing with a cry of joy, but, like the songs, they never came.

When Mamá requested a saint's niche, Panadero told her, "No damned saint is welcome here. Not in my house."

But Mamá longed so for a little chapel that he ordered one built in a far corner of the tree-shaded lawn nearest the village. High above the satin-draped altar was a small, plain glass window. A velvet-covered stand held her prayerbook, and cushioned her knees when she knelt with her rosary.

Two silver candlesticks held wax candles that burned night and day and smelled sweeter than El Patrón's pomade.

Now, after Padre David had given the sacraments to villagers in the church, he carried the blessed Host to the chapel and placed the wafer on Mamá's tongue. Impatient to be confirmed so he could join in the sacrament of the Bread and Wine, Ramón diligently studied his catechism. Mamá and the padre encouraged him in wanting to become an acolyte, to serve God by assisting at the Mass.

One morning Ramón was wakened before dawn by Mamá smoothing his hair and kissing his cheek. "Rest well, my son. God will take care of you."

He struggled up from the blanket and saw in the light from the hallway that she wore traveling clothes. "Mamá. Where are you going?"

"Only a little trip into the hills. Luis wishes to show me something marvelous."

Swinging his feet onto the cold floorboards, he reached for his new boots. "Wait! I wish to see it, too."

Her gentle hands on his shoulders urged him back under the cover. "Not this time, hijo. We're not taking the carriage, and the ride will be too long for you."

Swathed in his sarape, barefoot, he followed her down the stairs and onto the patio. No one, it seemed, had been awakened to see them off, to wish a safe trip to El Patrón and his beautiful wife. It was still too dark for her to see him wave adiós, and he dared not call out.

Panadero roughly boosted her onto a sidesaddle, led his mount and hers to the main gate, opened it himself. Once they had ridden away, Ramón ran to the gatekeeper's shelter and found the man snoring and reeking of liquor.

Unanswered questions thronged his mind. Had she lied about where they were going? But Mamá never lied. It was Panadero who lied. The same terrible fear he'd felt that night when he believed Panadero had killed Mamá, now gripped him afresh. None of his friends nor any servant could tell him anything.

After the longest day he'd ever known, unable to eat the supper set before him, he climbed the steps and sat on the galería. At nightfall, sick from staring down the empty road, he pushed at La India's hand grasping his arm. "I wish to stay and wait for Mamá."

Stern-faced in the flickering lamplight, La India took a firm hold and led him to his room. She warned, "If you go outside at night, Los Aires will attack you."

Was Mamá outside tonight? Had Los Aires attacked her? What had made her leave? When was she coming back? Was she coming back . . .

Now he was afraid of La India, and ate his meals and slept on a spare petate in whatever village hut he found himself when dark came. Padre David too had abandoned him, finding duties in Nogales that were more important.

Weeks later, El Patrón rode in alone. Running to meet him, Ramón cried, "Where is my mother?"

Panadero swung off the lathered horse, eyes blazing like one of La India's devils. "She's run away and left you! Forget her!"

Tear-blinded, Ramón fled through the house, across the back lawn, and into the chapel, where he flung himself down on the little carpet which had come from Persia. La Virgen and her niño Jesucristo still hung in their frame on the wall behind the small altar; the carved figures of Saint Benedict and his own santito, Ramón, stood in their niches

23

as always; lighted candles made them glow. But he could no longer trust them.

After dark, he stealthily made his way into the church and felt beneath the altar cloth.

Mamá's silver rosary was gone.

And so was she.

Talk was that the young priest left for another parish, and when the old cook sickened and died, she was buried in the campo santo by the new priest, an older man who kept out of Panadero's way. Gradually, Ramón grew to trust no one, and became so used to the nickname that he thought of himself as Trouble.

Panadero moved out of the upstairs room he'd shared with Mamá. Learning this, Trouble returned to sleeping in his own bed, which he could reach by the back staircase. He crept across the hall, and one by one rescued her books, the only things of hers that remained, scattered on the floor.

In a few days, he asked Josefa to set a place for him at the mahogany table, and sat waiting, afraid but curious to see what might happen when the old man faced him. Aromas of shredded spiced chicken and hot tortillas, soda biscuits and roasted corn, reminded him of suppers when the casa grande was first built and his heart soared in the foolish belief that finally the familia had found grace in the eyes of Dios.

Heavy boots marched along the corredor. Trembling, he held to the seat of his chair to keep from running out into the evening. Hooded eyes flicked to his as Panadero entered and took a seat. Niños brought platters and baskets of hot food, wine and frothy chocolate to drink.

Panadero lifted his knife and fork and cut into a thick piece of beef. Trouble chose the chicken and beans. They ate in silence. When the old man finished his meal, he rose and left. A criada started into the room to clear the table but, seeing that someone remained, she halted, curtseyed, and backed into the hallway.

Savoring the sweet caramel of a flan, Trouble lingered, triumphant, caressed by the night wind smelling of rain.

He was almost nine. For a long time now, he had wanted a horse but lacked the courage to ask for one, though he often stole out of the house, entered the corrals, and leaped on a dusty back. In this way he learned balance, and which hand and knee signals brought the desired result.

Outside one morning to watch the sunrise, he heard an ax beyond the willow grove, and crept forward to see what new thing might be there.

A wiry mestizo worked alone. Trouble was amazed that the man was able to lift and secure poles heavier than those used for corrals. Presently, curiosity got the better of him, and he left the shadows and squatted on his heels, waiting to be noticed.

"What is your name?" the man asked without looking around, intent on his work but in a kind manner.

"Promise not to let El Patrón hear you call me by it."

The head turned in profile, and the man's lips smiled. "Te juro." *I promise.*

"Ramón Cordero. My mother's name. I will never use his." He spat on the ground. "His name is evil." The man seemed unsurprised. "What is yours?"

"I am Manuelo Vásquez, and I come from a tierra far to the south."

25

"Why are you not called Manuel?"

"My twin, Manuela, died when we were children."

And I could not save her. The words went unspoken, but Trouble understood that the blood bond was stronger than the need to use a name that wouldn't stand out among other Mexicans.

Manuelo carried an air of assurance about him like a cloak, and his bloodshot eyes were shrewd. He had lived in the bunkhouse with the norteamericano horsemen and vaqueros for some months, but persuaded El Patrón to allow him his own hut if he could build it. This was astonishing. There was much he could learn from this man.

With Manuelo for a friend, he grew less afraid that don Luis would attack him bodily, but every time he and the old patrón crossed paths, taunts flew from the cruel mouth to wound him. Bastardo, pendejo, Trouble. When unshed tears stung his eyelids like bees, he found refuge in Manuelo's hut, where he was welcome.

One listless day when everyone else sought shade, his feet carried him along the central hallway and out through the back patio to the nearest stock barn, where he often curried the caballo padre, El Rey, and sat upon the horse's back in the stall. He imagined opening the gate and riding away from Casa de Panadero.

He'd never before climbed the ladder to the loft, a dim, sweltering space beneath a tin roof. Among bound bales of hay stored for feed, he discovered broken tools and gear, empty grain sacks, mice droppings. He'd half hoped to find a discarded saddle, or a pair of spurs.

In a far corner sat a dome top trunk, grimy with barn dust. Lifting the heavy lid, he was disappointed to see nothing but a woman's folded clothing.

Then for a moment he was playing on the dirt floor with his cornshuck family. Sunlight cast familiar shadows on the walls, and Mamá was wearing— This. Gently he touched the pink-flowered dress. If she had run away, as Panadero had claimed, why had she not taken her trunk? She must have been in a big hurry.

Using his penknife he cut a small square and stuffed it in the front of his shirt. Along the bank of the Río Sangría, he picked a handful of tall grass. Using twine to bind the strands, he fashioned a figure no taller than the handspan of a man. He made a hole in the cloth for its head and tied a strip around its waist. Smoothing the dress, he whispered, "Mamá."

From Manuelo he begged a tin document box, pried nails from floorboards in his room to create a space, and hid her there.

In only two years, Manuelo was given the position of mayordomo and a room in the casa grande next to that of El Patrón. Responsibilities were many. As segundo, second in charge, he was expected to keep accurate account books, inform the hacendado of misbehavior among the peónes, and act as emissary to other wealthy ranchers in the area.

Pleased to have his friend achieve such status, he was impressed at how Manuelo calmed tempers, tended injuries, and gave advice that others heeded. Even with El Patrón, the segundo often got his way in matters of some importance.

At thirteen, Trouble was ashamed not to own a horse. Choosing a time when the dinner meal was especially rich and satisfying and Panadero seemed unusually mellow, he spoke: "There is a pinto in the little corral that I would like very much to have."

Panadero didn't bother to look up. "Play with your toys. A shuck horse is all a pendejo needs."

For a terrified moment, he feared the patrón had found the grass figure, Mamá in her dress; then the stream of time flowed on and he began to breathe again.

He held his tongue until he and Manuelo were alone. "I will have a caballo."

"He would recognize any horse from his stock, even one from the farthest estancia."

"Not from his stock."

Manuelo's eyes crinkled at the corners. "¡Aha! You think of stealing a caballito? You will be shot."

"If I am, bury me beside my mother's chapel."

After sufficient time had passed for Manuelo to have forgotten, or think he hadn't meant what he said, he left the house before daylight, wearing moccasins and carrying a short, limber rope. A dark wool sarape and mud smeared on his hands and face would help him go unnoticed.

To avoid the gate keeper and confuse the guard dogs that trailed him, sniffing for a morsel, he followed the Río Sangría north until it crossed the hacienda boundary. The low banks always ran full, even in the dry season, but the river was not the rushing torrent it sometimes became. Presently he was able to join the road to Nogales and for perhaps an hour walking was swift.

Talk among the vaqueros and villagers had hinted at an Apache stronghold in the hills, where unconquered warriors hid their families and returned with plunder taken from Mexican towns. In some crevice between canyon walls, the camp would be difficult to find. But near water. And they would have horses.

Turning off the road, he cut a stout stick with which to discourage snakes, and to feel his way through the thorny brush. He traveled with increased caution, testing the night air for the faint aroma of a stream, the elusive odor of a hot, dry fire. He had never been so far from the casa grande before, and he trembled with excitement.

He descended the sandy bank of an arroyo and walked along the bottom, sure that it would lead to a bosque of cottonwoods, a spring, and—possibly—to the camp he sought. He followed the creek bed until it fanned out and became foothills.

Starlight revealed gashes in the chisled cliffs, aided in finding a descending path, navigating its twists. Moment to moment, he expected a watchman to send a big rock crashing down on his head, or an arrow into his back. He wondered whether, like Panadero, Apaches kept vicious dogs to drive off any intruder.

At last he emerged from the mouth of the canyon. Then scents on the wind told him he was near an encampment. He crept forward. Ahead was a level space and eight or ten wickiups. Crouching behind chaparral, he listened to the cicadas. All else was silent, save for the cry of a night bird as it flew up from its roost.

Dark shapes moved against the star-bright sky, shapes of the horse herd grazing beyond the encampment. Pulling the loop in his reata a bit wider, he held it open and went toward them, murmuring "shuu-shuu" as did the Indio horse tamer Manuelo had brought from his distant tierra, to handle wild stock.

Each time his quarry moved out of reach, Trouble changed course, keeping himself in front of them. Then, as others wheeled to trot away, one hesitated, ears tipped forward. A solid-coated colt, probably a bay. He slipped the rope over its head. Holding the soft muzzle, he blew gently into the nostrils. Manuelo had told him, "The sharing of breath helps the caballo to know and respect you."

Stopping often so that anyone chancing to be awake would not notice deliberate hoof beats, he led the pony back through the canyon. He'd been gone longer than intended, for spikes of sun reached into the sky at the eastern horizon. Bay was young and strong, an eye-pleasing color, and tame. A bit thin from being grass fed, but grain would remedy that.

He was in the barn, feeding the pony when a niño found him. "El Patrón asks for you."

Not a good sign. Fighting fear, he walked across the flagstones toward the glass doors. Light from the dining room spilled onto them, and he could see the old man seated at the head of the table, steaming dishes arranged before him, and the mozo Juan was pouring coffee.

Panadero asked, "Where have you been?"

He sat down and started to eat. There was no point in lying. "To the Apache camp."

The old man's glance shot up. Surprise slowly changed to disbelief. Sopping bread in a pool of brown salsa, he leaned over the plate to receive it, chewed thoroughly, swallowed. Then he said, "Liar."

Quelling rage, Trouble left the room, expecting to be ordered back, but was spared. On his way to the barn, lounging Indios avoided him as if they sensed danger. Not even Manuelo was around, to hear of his daring success. He had almost finished currying the pony when he heard someone calling, "Trouble! ¡Venga acá! You are wanted."

"¿Porqué?" he asked, but Juan refused to tell him. At the farthest pole pen a crowd was gathering. Vaqueros, peónes, niños, norteamericano wranglers. Among them was Manuelo, leaning on the gate. Joining the wiry little mestizo, Trouble asked, "Who's going to ride Zopilote today?"

From behind them Panadero said, "You are." He stood apart, smoking a cigarro. "I wish to admire your skill as a horseman."

Stunned, Trouble watched wranglers rope the mustang. Two vaqueros wrestled the bit into place while a third threw on a saddle and pulled the girth tight.

"Get on," Panadero urged. "A niño who can steal a pony from the Apache surely cannot be afraid."

He was afraid. He'd seen grown men injured badly by this maverick—but he cried, "¡De acuerdo! I will! "

Stepping through the gate into the billowy dust, he reached for the pommel. Zopilote lunged, tearing it from his hand, but someone lifted him by one arm and the back of his pants and tossed him up. Sorry to be still wearing the moccasins instead of his heeled boots, he grasped the reins without any hope of staying on, and prayed that when he fell he wouldn't break his neck or back. Shamelessly he clung to the mane and saddle horn. "¡Listo!" Ready.

The vaqueros let go. Zopilote bucked the length of the corral and crashed into the fence. Whirled, pitched back across, crashed into the opposite fence. People scattered, and cries of ¡Viva! from the watchers and furious squeals from Zopilote filled the sunbaked corral. The horse leaped, twisted in midair, and came down with hooves bunched. Pain shot through Trouble and with a dizzied glance at his father, he lost his grip and was thrown.

Wranglers ran after the kicking mustang, and younger boys started a game of tag. Peónes and vaqueros drifted to their morning's work. Panadero's eyes were slits, lips tight. Throwing down his cigar butt, he set his heel upon it. Then he turned and walked back toward the house.

Manuelo picked him up from the hoof-cut dirt. "Your bone is broken, chico," the mayordomo said, and for the first time he felt the stabbing in his left forearm. "Come."

They walked past the corrals to the hut in the willows and Manuelo gave him a squat brown bottle. "Drink as much as you can."

Lifting it at intervals, he sat on the cot and counted items in the dim small room in order not to faint. Manuelo busied himself in a corner, his body shielding preparations atop a narrow table cluttered with various containers. Some were glass, others clay; some empty, others holding powders or herbs in hues of brown, black, dark green, rust, cream, stark white. "I didn't think you lived here anymore."

"You know I live in the casa grande, at don Luis's orders."

"But here is your bed, and olla of fresh water."

Manuelo came to him with a shallow dish in which was a grayish mixture, full of lumps like a poorly made flan. Hunkering at his knee, the man helped him take off his shirt, then smeared the stuff on his injured arm. Before the supply was gone, the pain had begun to fade.

"Tu eres un curandero." You're a healer.

Smiling, Manuelo reached for the squat brown bottle and gulped from it. Then he sat beside Trouble and told the legend of La Llorona, the Crying Woman, who in life had murdered her children and after death was punished for it by having to wander the earth in search of peace.

"It is very bad luck to see Llorona," the segundo warned him. "If she casts aside her rebozo to show her face, there is instead a hollow-eyed skull, and if perchance her breath falls upon you, your very blood will freeze, like the crystals of ice around the rim of a tinaja in the Sierra Madre on a January morning."

"¡Vaya!" he scoffed. "That's only a story." Like Los Aires. Meant to scare children.

Manuelo laughed. "Sin duda. Only a story."

With a sudden jerk that left him no time to yell, Manuelo put his bone in place. Swiftly wrapping the arm in a cloth, the man spoke in a dialect different from the village Indios; whether a prayer or a magical chant, or merely something to keep him occupied, Trouble didn't know. The drink had made his head spin, and he sank down on the cornshuck mattress, murmuring, "Is it magic? Was it your magic that kept the Apache dogs from barking? Is this how you made Panadero choose you as majordomo?"

Manuelo covered him with a thin blanket. The kind, bloodshot eyes hovered near him. "¿Nuestro secretito, no?"

"Sí," he answered drowsily. "Our secret."

Later, while trying to explain the bandage to Padre Felix without lying, he noticed that a group of village girls seemed to be talking about him. Even if none of them had witnessed his undignified spill from Zopilote's back, they must know about it. When he sought to escape their interest, his best friend encouraged, "Hombre, it's because they like you. Don't run away."

Chuco's brother said, "Be careful, little one, who you take for pleasure. Look at those niñas. What do you see?"

Beneath fragrant-bloomed huisaches lining the street stood half a dozen girls. Most his age, some younger. Three from Apache stock. Three mestizas, with eyes and hair of dark brown. Their skin ranged from tawny to creamy. When they saw him looking, everyone hid smiles or giggles in rebozos, and one even fled behind her house, bare heels flashing. He had not considered doing more than stealing a few kisses. These girls all had fathers and brothers who carried knives and wouldn't hesitate to defend their honor.

"Six señoritas, two too young to think about, and one too shy. The others—" He shrugged.

Jesús laughed. "Open your eyes wider."

"What should I see?"

"Have a good time with the Inditas, but unless you know the mother of a sweetheart as well as you know your own private parts, leave the half-breeds alone."

"But the mestizas are pretty."

"Think hard. You're not stupid."

He thought hard. Then his jaw dropped and he felt his cheeks flush. "You mean— Panadero could be— She might be—"

"¿Quién sabe? You wouldn't like making love to your media hermana, I think."

It changed the way he looked at all his friends, not knowing who might share Panadero's blood. If what Jesús said were true, mothers had lain with Panadero while married to, or at least living with, men working in the hacienda fields. Surely Padre Felix taught that such a thing was a mortal sin. This kept him awake at night. "He is not my papá!" he told himself; but how could he be sure?

Finally he asked Manuelo whether the gossip were true.

"What choice do they have? Every family owes for supplies from his storehouses. The clothes on their backs, sandals on their feet, food that gives them strength to work. Many years' wages cannot pay a debt which grows each day from interest and purchases that cost more than can be earned. When El Patrón wants some woman, or beats a man for a small thing, why do you think that one remains? The law gives men like don Luis the right to own them, just as he owns the cattle you see there." He flung his arm in an arc over the vast grassland where the herds grazed. "Those who would flee are hunted down and returned—or killed."

"Then the law must be changed."

"Not in your lifetime, mijo. Each must live according to one's Destino."

Annoyed by his friend's lack of spirit, Trouble rode Bay for an hour, and when both returned to the lamplit casa grande sweated and hungry, he had to admit that the segundo was simply stating a truth. Panadero had the authority to rule the valley, and was ruthless enough to use that power.

While the broken arm healed, Padre Felix supplied books, paper, and pens, and gave him lessons in reading and mathematics, with the admonition not to tell don Luis what they were doing.

For minor accomplishments, the priest awarded cards with religious pictures stamped in bright colors. Ramón kept them in the document box, and could never look at them without recalling the chromolith of La Virgen and El Niño, and the bullet hole in her forehead.

Somewhere along the way, that picture had disappeared and another hung in Mamá's neglected chapel.

"Why don't you teach my friends?" he asked. "They come to you to learn the catechism."

"Indios require only the laws of the Church," Padre answered. "If they spent time reading, who would do the work?"

"Am I different because I'm the hacendado's son?"

The priest was silent, looking hard at the open book in his robed lap. Finally he raised his head and said, "Manuelo asked me to."

Trouble began to suspect that the curandero was no simple healer, but a brujo, a powerful male witch, capable of accomplishing supernatural deeds and casting spells. Just as he once had prayed for men to kill Panadero and free Mamá, now he waited for the day when the wiry mestizo would challenge and defeat El Patrón.

Chapter Three

Three years later.

Trouble woke with a start, the metallic taste of fear in his mouth. He sat up. His sweetheart leaned on one elbow beside him. "The same dream?"

He crossed a packed earth floor, unshuttered the single window. Beyond the dappled shade of an acacia, morning sun glared off the parched strip of ground between village houses. Past the hour when he should have been leaving his own bed across the river. "It's always the same."

"Tell me."

He regarded her outstretched hand, drowsy smile, the rumpled sheet and cornshuck mattress on which they made love. "You've heard it before."

"I can hear it again. The dream is sad, but your voice pleases me, Ramoncito."

"There isn't time." He pulled on his trousers and cast about her small drab room for the shirt and boots.

Wisps of nightmare trailing him, Mamá's sad voice murmuring, "God will protect you," in his ear, he passed over the foot bridge and entered the casa grande by way of the servants' patio. From the corredor he could see Panadero lifting a cup of coffee. Manuelo stood at the old man's side, ledger open, attentive.

Nothing changed. Not his dreams, not his nightmares. Not his life. Yet, seated at the foot of the table, he felt anew the bittersweet emotion that kept him bound to La Hacienda de Panadero.

No other place on earth could possibly create in him the same joy as those clear mornings when the desert bloomed brilliantly yellow, and red-plumaged flycatchers darted in and out of cactus and smoketrees. No other place could ever provoke the same unnamed yearnings whenever he saw cottonwoods silhouetted against scarlet or lavender sunsets above that rim of distant blue mountains.

He loved the wide halls, large airy rooms, inlaid flooring, and tiled patios fragrant with flowers planted in huge clay macetas. He never tired of touching the smooth banisters, heavy Spanish chests, massive carved doors of mahogany cut in the jungles of Chiapas. It all reminded him of the stories Mamá used to tell of the Cordero family home in Spain, and he often imagined her coming down the stairs, cool in the flowing pink flowered dimity, and pouring his breakfast chocolate from a silver pot.

Panadero's voice broke into his thoughts. "...sell the gelding called Bay."

Sell Bay? Had he heard right? Trouble's glance met Manuelo's. El Patrón moved on to another matter involving some small theft from a storehouse.

"Un momento," Trouble said, controlled, but the old man continued to speak to Manuelo.

"Un momentito," he said again. He pushed back his chair and tossed down his napkin with its embroidered silk P in one corner. "Bay is mine. You can't sell him."

Panadero reared back in feigned surprise. Then the black eyes narrowed. "Nothing is yours, bastardo. If I wish to sell that caballo, I will do so."

From the corner of his eye he caught Manuelo's slight frown, a warning. Any appeal to don Luis's sympathy or reason was wasted, any use of force was laughable. El Patrón struck first and hard, as many a peón or vaquero knew, and lately his temper had grown savage.

Fuming, he left by the glass doors opening to the courtyard, where wrens and sparrows twittered in the wide-branched ayales he used to climb before the casa grande was built. The peaceful fountain pattering in its tiled basin calmed him, restored clear thought.

He considered riding Bay to one of the estancias, outposts on the rim of the property maintained to ward off thieves or stray families trying to scratch out a living independent of the hacienda. Then he realized he would have to travel farther than that, to be rid of Panadero.

During siesta, while the household rested and the halls were empty, he took money from Manuelo's little cashbox.

Then he crept into the dim library, the forbidden 'old house.' The window, facing out into the comedor, admitted enough light to kindle memories as he glanced about, fury welling. Overflowing.

On a peg over a desk hung a belt gun. The Dragoon was old, discarded by El Patrón for a better weapon; but preferable to nothing. He found a box of ammunition in one drawer and filled the chambers. He buckled on the cartridge belt, tied down the holster. Heavy and unfamiliar on his hip, it gave him a sense of power he had never felt.

He would miss familiar voices, games and laughter and swimming in the Sangría with boyhood friends, riding over the vast fields of Hacienda de Panadero. He'd miss Manuelo, and girls in the village—especially Beatriz. He wished he could bring her with him. She was going to cry when she realized their pleasant frolics were ended.

And though he never went there anymore, he would miss Mamá's chapel, abandonado in its corner of the adobe wall beneath the trees.

Crossing the yard, he passed through the unguarded wagon gate to the corrals, caught and saddled his gelding. Careful not to be noticed, he entered the pen holding his father's favorite caballo padre, El Rey, and put a lead rope on the stallion.

He walked the horses up to the keeper of the main gate. "Abre, por favor," he said, dropping a small fiber sack containing ten pesos at the bare feet. With a grin and nod, the Indio unlocked the chain and swung aside half of the great scrolled-iron door. He passed through, reined Bay around, and looked back.

This was his tierra. And he must leave it.

"I am Ramón Cordero!" he cried, then whirled and spurred his mount southward. El Rey raced beside them, head high, mane flowing.

Sofía Ibarra finished putting away the things from her woven bag and closed the dresser drawer. Turning to gaze about the small room which was now hers, she noted the connecting door between it and the bedroom of El Patrón, and shivered. Her tía had finally died, freeing her from the duties which had bound her for weeks, and El Patrón had sent for her to work in the casa grande. Her heart beat fast in anticipation. Tonight, she would sleep in the same house with Ramón.

From the hallway she heard his father calling, "¡Sofía!" and she went out.

"¿Sí, Patrón?"

Don Luis motioned for her to come closer. "No more of that," he said, laying a heavy hand on the back of her neck under her braid. "You may call me Luis. Come, I want to show you the rest of the house. And—" He removed his hand in order to take a key ring from a cabinet. "I give you charge of these. La Vieja will tell you later what each one fits."

She padded alongside him in her slippers, aware of his bulk, his age, his power. He was over sixty. Well, she would find out tonight whether coming here was worth the cost.

A blur of sun-filled windows, flowering potted plants, balconies and patios; trying to take in the elegance of the house and its rich Spanish rooms, she could hardly pay attention when don Luis showed her the cocina and told La

Vieja, "Sofía está segunda ahora." He pinched her chin playfully.

The servants lined up for her inspection, mumbling their names, some known to her, a few not. Amid whispers and giggles after her back was turned, Sofía sought a glimpse of don Ramón.

In that, she was disappointed. Later, when she was going over the day's menu with the cook, she ventured to ask, "Where is the son? I have not seen him today."

She had seen him in the village, dancing with others at the bailes, eating savory foods during fiestas. Strolling with señoritas beneath the huisaches that lined the single dusty street. Perhaps seventeen, fair skinned, dark-haired and slender. She knew that while she looked older than her twenty-six years, she wasn't like the silly chicas with whom he flirted, maybe even bedded. She had ideas and dreams, which she longed to share with him. She yearned to hear his voice, feel his touch, to know every thought in his head. Don Luis's summons to the casa grande was an answer to prayer.

The cook turned a wrinkled face to her. "Have you not heard? Trouble stole the caballo padre and left. Two days ago."

Sofía's knees suddenly went limp. She braced herself on the back of a cane-bottom chair. "He's not here?"

La Vieja gave an impatient grunt. "I said he left. Patrón was furious. He sent men looking, but they have not found the boy."

The cocina was stifling, suffocating. Sofía lurched to her feet with some wild thought of running back to the village and living in her dead aunt's hut. But the hacendado would only come for her, full of questions. Perhaps even beat her, if he suspected the deep motives of her heart. Slowly, she sat down again. "Is there cool water? I feel faint."

La Vieja gestured toward a clay olla suspended from one of the patio roof beams. "There. Am I expected to bring it to you?"

She managed to draw a deep breath. "No. I have no wish to become your patróna. Don Luis is my master, too."

San Lázaro.

In the center of the knife-scarred table lay a pistol, a silver-plated .45 with bone grips. Forfeit in a game of monte, it was worth betting on.

Mingled with low, indistinct voices, someone was languidly picking the strings of a guitar. Lighted candles, despite the smell of cheap tallow, reminded Ramón of his mother's chapel, and he reached for his neglected glass of tequila. He had not yet developed a taste for it, nor for the women who hung about in the shadows. He knew enough about sangre del mal to avoid contact with them. Shrugging off the embrace of a girl leaning against the back of his chair, he placed his coins.

The dealer flipped over the cards. "Hombre," he said, "you have won."

The man who had lost blinked in disbelief and drained his greasy glass. The cantiñero brought another squat brown bottle. Ramón examined the single-action pistol.

Superior to that old Dragoon, it was slightly larger, a bit heavier, than the factory-made Colt's he'd seen in Nogales. Clearly this was the work of a master gunsmith.

The grips fit his palm and his finger curled easily around the trigger.

The loser leaned as if to reclaim it but stopped short. "It is like those guns from over the border, no? I found it in a ravine, far in the Sierra Madre, many years ago. Thinking someone had fallen to his death, I searched the brush for a body, but there was none. Not even bones. I say to myself, Who would throw away a fine gun like this? but of course there is no one to tell me." He noticed others listening. "I call it the Mexican Colt. It can kill an enemy at more than fifty paces. The loads take forty grains of black powder."

Though Ramón had no intention of killing anyone, such a weapon would give him an edge if there ever came a time when he had to use it. He could engage a saddle maker to fashion a suitable holster in which to carry it. Maybe his fortunes had changed, at last. He laid the gun in his hat on the floor between his boots.

The dealer shuffled the cards. The loser motioned for the cantiñero to fill his glass. "Be a good boy, and give me a chance to win it back."

Through the open door behind him, a gust of January wind set candle shadows to flickering and chilled Ramón through his shirt. A hand came to rest on his shoulder and a hot voice said against his cheek, "Your papá wants you home."

His first thought was of the unloaded silver gun at his feet, then of the useless Dragoon back in his room. A small hard object bruising his ribs warned him not to fight. A second man added, "Cuidado. Don Luis is paying us well."

Both of them were known to him, only slightly, as riders employed by don Luis to find peónes trying to flee their debt.

"Take the stallion," he said, as one of the men looped a reata around his neck. "That's all he wants. He cares nothing for me."

The other man tossed Ramón's sarape around his shoulders. "Oh, no, muchacho. We have orders, and those orders say you come with us."

The music and drinking had stopped. The men he had played cards with sat silent, watching. In their dark eyes he saw pity and fear, but no hint of attempting a rescue. "My stuff is at the posada—" He bent and picked up the hat, folding it over so the gun was concealed.

"We have packed everything," the first man said, "and Bay is ready for you."

The night wind whipped the corners of his sarape and rippled the tails of horses waiting beneath the street lamp. His saddlebags and blanket roll were on Bay, but he knew the rifle scabbard would be empty. One of the trackers tied his hands in front so he could control his mount in the rough country they would be crossing. The other caught up El Rey's lead.

"You hombres are damned thorough." As they swung into saddles, he managed to lift the flap of a saddlebag and slide the Mexican Colt inside. Settling his hat, he ran a thumb under the reata where it chafed his throat.

They traveled at a fast pace until the moon set, then camped in an arroyo. Joining them in the night were two others, hardened men of middle age, whom he did not recognize. At dawn they gathered brush and built a smokeless campfire. They shared coffee and cold tortillas with him, and joked about how each would spend the money don Luis promised to pay.

In three days, he found no opening for escape. Landmarks told him when they rode onto hacienda land and through a lonely guard post kept dark for reasons of security. Another hour, and it would be night. Once in the dooryard of Hacienda de Panadero, he would become Trouble again.

When they reached the Río Sangría, within calling distance of the lamplit patio, he dropped back just enough to avoid being noticed and shoved his saddlebags off Bay and into the brush. The trackers were seriously spending the pesos soon to be theirs. Supper, drinks, women. With cries of success, they plunged their horses across the river, and, sensing familiar territory, Bay carried him up the far bank.

A few peónes lingering about the courtyard gave them curious stares. Then, halting at the edge of the patio, they all dismounted, and one of them lifted the rope from his neck.

Sofía stood before the china cabinet, taking pleasure in the washed goblets she and don Luis had used at supper. Eating the meal so early, like norteamericanos, was difficult to get used to, but being here gave her a prestige that made up for the inconvenience.

A clatter of hooves in the courtyard brought Manuelo from his office with a sheaf of papers in one hand. Through the leaded glass patio doors, Sofía watched riders dismount beneath dim lanterns, puffs of steam blasting from their horses' nostrils in the January chill.

One of them was Ramón. Her heart thrilled. They had found him. "Gracias a Dios."

Don Luis, too, heard the horses. He swept aside the string curtain of silver beads that separated the sala from the dining room. She shrank back, seeking concealment behind folds of drapery bunched at this side of the doors, and peered through the gap where velvet met adobe.

Suddenly the patio seemed full of men. All bore traces of a long ride and a cold splash through the Río Sangría. Soaked to the knees, wearing neither hat nor coat but a draggled sarape, yet Ramón was unbowed.

Oh, worth it, worth everything, to be here in the same house with him. Once she showed him all she could offer, he would no longer be content to dance with others nor stroll, arms linked with someone else, along the river.

Don Luis had left the doors ajar, so she heard Ramón say, "Where is the fatted calf? I'm hungry." His voice thrilled her. His father told the trackers, "Manuelo will pay you."

As the segundo went out and presented to each of them a little sack of coins, the boy entered and stood hands on his hips. Don Luis followed him inside. They looked at each other for most of a minute. Then don Luis gripped his shirt front, struck him in the face, and threw him across the floor. Before he stopped skidding, his father had swung around to the door post and unhooked a riding whip.

She took a step forward, but strong fingers closed on her wrist. "If you value your skin, you'll come with me." Manuelo drew her away from the noise of scuffling and blows, and shut her in her room.

Cowering in the dark, she could still hear the industry of the whip and muted cries of pain.

At last the old man shouted, "Cry, damn you!"

A kick and a muffled grunt.

"That is for trying to make a fool of me."

Another kick, a whimper.

"And that is for stealing El Rey."

Silence.

Her trembling hand was on the china knob when a familiar, heavy tread approached from the end of the hallway.

She was ready to tell any lie to avoid intimacy with El Patrón, but he entered his own bedroom. Despite the pounding of her heart, she heard the plops of his riding boots as he tossed them aside, and the creak of bedsprings as he lay down. Drawing a deep, aching breath, she thanked Dios for sparing her this night and for allowing the boy to be found and returned. She prayed that his father's whip had not been too severe.

When she woke, after fitful sleep, her neck was so stiff she would have liked to call Josefa, whose lithe brown fingers were capable of easing such afflictions and who would without questions bring a tray of pan dulce and chocolate to her room. The need to see Ramón again, however, spurred her to put on a dress and try to tidy her hair.

He wasn't in the comedor, but don Luis was, his mouth already working on a bite of beef while Manuelo filled his cup with black coffee. A niño brought in a basket of fragrant hot rounds of norteamericano bread, adding to platters of carne asada, eggs, tortillas, frijoles, and pastries.

She murmured, "Buenos días," and two pleasant voices answered. Don Luis simply gave her a nod. Then he motioned the mayordomo to take a seat beside him, and began instructing him in how to conduct an upcoming cattle sale.

She noticed that the other chairs had been removed. The niño served her plate and left. Eating breakfast and giving Manuelo orders seemed the only things on don Luis's mind, yet she wondered if he were plotting further punishment. Movement in the doorway drew her attention.

Ramón, dressed in glove-tight black trousers and a fresh white shirt with rows of pleats down the front. His black leather boots gleamed from fresh polish. He was skilled in playing his role as son of the hacendado, but the set of his mouth reminded her of a child who has only lately finished crying.

He brought a chair from the sala and seated himself opposite his father. Lacing his fingers in front of him, he stared at don Luis until the old man shouted, "There's a stink in this room. Let us have some air."

Manuelo leaped up and flung open the patio doors.

On the north side of the house, the comedor quickly became uncomfortably cold. Shivering, she spilled salsa down the side of the bowl and onto the tablecloth. She made the stain worse by trying to mop it up with one of the napkins.

Worse still, Ramón got up and closed the doors. She expected strong words and perhaps thrown dishes, and dreaded witnessing another beating with the riding whip. When he came back, he leaned both elbows on the linen cloth, chin resting in one palm. *Oh, Ramón,* she wanted to say, *don't tempt him.*

Forcing down bites of eggs and bread, she couldn't help sneaking glances. ¡Diosito! how she loved him. But she lacked the courage to offer food. If El Patrón dismissed her, she might be compelled to leave not only the house, but the hacienda. This afternoon, she would go to the village church and light three candles to her santa patróna. Nothing so sweet had ever been given her, as this second chance to be with Ramón, and she must guard against doing anything stupid.

Presently don Luis shoved back his chair, and Manuelo lit the old man's cigar. After a couple of puffs to determine the quality, El Patrón inhaled deeply and blew a cloud of smoke over the table. "Any other thief would have been shot."

Without raising his voice, Ramón said, "I'd prefer being shot to living here with you."

Don Luis stood up, reaching for his hat. "Don't push your luck." Manuelo handed it to him, and they went out.

The moment they were gone, she clapped her hands to summon the serving boy from the hall and told him, "Bring dishes and hot food for don Ramón." She was sorry her voice shook, when she wished to command.

"¡Muy bien!" The niño ran from the room.

She realized with humiliation that Ramón must know what duties the patrón required of her. As she desperately sought a topic of conversation, he asked, "You were not here before, were you— ?"

Raising her eyes no farther than Ramón's collarbone, she cleared her throat. "I am Sofía Ibarra. I came last year, to tend my tía, who was dying. Who died."

"Sofía," he repeated, and his saying her name brought a warmth to her cheeks. "You're taking a big risk, being kind to me."

The niño brought a tray and transferred an abundance to the table. She drank a second cup of coffee while Ramón ate. In his position, she felt, she would not have been able to enjoy the beef and sauce, or the small cakes of hot soda bread. He was more macho than he looked. Sweet, defiant. Within reach.

"I— I am sorry—" Too soon, to tell him how deeply hurt she was by his ill treatment, how much she longed to ease his every pain. She finished simply, "I did not realize that don Luis could be so cruel."

Ramón drained the last of his coffee. "It's why I warned you."

He laid aside his napkin. "I deserved punishment."

"Oh, surely—"

"Not for stealing the horse." His eyes met hers, their directness making her pulse leap. "For getting caught." Then he pushed back his chair. "Con su permiso."

She watched him saunter across the patio and into the sunshine. He paused to hold his fingers under the fountain spray before continuing out of view, no doubt intending to relax in one of the cushioned woven chairs on the front galería. He hadn't invited her to accompany him. Did she have the courage to join him anyway?

No.

Yes.

No.

Dawdling in the hallway, hoping he would come in soon, she heard a door close upstairs. As a maid descended, arms laden with soiled clothing, Sofía was startled by the garment uppermost on the bundle. A faded shirt, streaked across the back with dried blood. Ramón's shirt. Ramón's blood. The criada held it up. "Señorita— Señora, what shall I do with this? It is full of holes."

"Give it to me," Sofía told her.

When the maid was sorting laundry in the servants' patio, she went to her room and hid the shirt in the bottom drawer of her dresser. It might prove useful, if her other strategies failed. There was a bruja in the next town who knew spells. He had run away once. If he should decide to do so again, she meant to go with him.

Trouble pretended not to notice Sofía watching every move he made. While she was distracted by a criada with a basketful of laundry, he slipped away, crossed the foot bridge, and went downriver, searching for the broken chaparral that would mark the place where he had tossed his saddlebags last night. The horse handler tending Bay would have taken the silver gun to Panadero, and that would have been the last he saw of the Mexican Colt.

Locating the gear, he tucked the pistol out of sight beneath his sarape.

Last night, after Panadero left him beaten and bloody, he had gone to Beatriz. There was a scuffling in the room before she opened the door to him, but she let him in, leaving the door open to the full moon rather than light a lamp.

"Do you have any of that salve your grandmother makes?" He took off his shirt. Her sound of pity told him the wounds were as bad as they felt.

"Pobrecito. You must have known he would find you."

"The old man is afraid of me. But I don't know why."

She unstoppered a small clay jar. Tending the raw lash marks, she said, "There will be scars, querido."

"There are scars already, that no medicine can heal."

Her fingers lingered on his shoulder. "Ramón. Why did you not go to Manuelo for his healing herbs?"

"He did nothing to help me. I'm not sure I trust him anymore."

"Of all the people on this hacienda, he is the only one you can trust."

A faint scuffing, like a mouse, beneath a pile of clothing in the far corner. Her face was in shadow, and he realized she had not expected him to return. His question held no emotion, for he felt none. "Does that include you, mi amor?"

As he stepped out into the cool night, he had heard her say, "Go with God, Ramoncito."

That fiasco with the old man at breakfast might have been worse. Checking to be sure Bay was still in the barn, Trouble was returning to his room with the concealed Mexican Colt, when he came across Sofía in the back patio, untangling a lapful of embroidery yarn.

She said, "In the evenings, don Luis enjoys a drinks in the sala, and Manuelo reads aloud. Will you join us there?"

He answered gently, "Forgive me, but meal times with Panadero are enough." Sitting in a room with Panadero while the segundo read to him held no appeal, and being the focus of Sofía's attention made him uneasy.

Her lips crimped in obvious disappointment before managing a smile. "As you wish, don Ramón."

Moving the foot of his bedstead, he raised the loose floorboards and took out the tin document box which held boyhood treasures: arrowheads used for birds, centavos won from friends playing patolli, dozens of merit cards awarded by Padre Felix for excellence in mathematics and language, favors in the form of hair ribbons from sweethearts in the village.

Carefully he lifted the lid. He hadn't touched "Mamá" for a long time. The grass had become dry and fragile. He supposed the scrap of flowered cloth was no more faded now than it had been the morning he found it. A cheap dress, packed for a trip, then left behind.

He shut the lid and picked up the silver-plated pistol. Who had lost—or thrown—it into the ravine? How many men had been killed with it? Wrapping the Mexican Colt in a silk dresser cloth, he placed it beneath the document box, and replaced the boards and the bed.

When he opened his door, Sofía sat waiting on the top stair, still working on the tangled yarn. She looked up and smiled. Against his better judgment, he gave her a friendly nod. What lure or threat had the old man used to bring her into this godforsaken house? Strong, whatever it was.

Luis tossed his narrow-brim sombrero at the hat rack and reached for his new bottle of Beaujolais. The médico had warned him long ago against spirits—advice he had heeded—but lately many of his cherished wines also sat ill on his stomach. He dreaded giving them up, particularly after an hour or two in the saddle spent inspecting his fields and stock. "Where's the bastardo?"

Sofía stood in the corredor, wringing her hands.

Irritation stirred. "Damn you, mujer, speak!"

She gasped. "In the village. Why do you want him?"

He stared at her. For someone so timid, her question seemed bold. "It doesn't concern you."

The excellent midday meal left him feeling drowsy and sluggish. He hoped he would be able to sleep.

In his room, he removed his boots and lay down on the bed. The glass doors had been opened earlier when the day was warm, but now a stiff breeze wafting the filmy white curtains sent a shiver along his spine. Trouble's theft of El

Rey had upset plans to return to La Nariz. *He's become too cunning*, he thought. *I never should have let him live.*

His mind drifted back to the night he and his men robbed the pack train. Only four of them, but practiced enough to wrest a fortune in gold coins and bullion from ten armed guards. In the dim light of an evening, they had attacked while weary men and heavily-packed burros were moving toward supper. Full-throated yells, sharp reports of handguns, squeals of frightened animals, and, over it all, the acrid smell and taste of black powder smoke.

"Drive the burros into the hills," he told the others. "There's a cave where we can hide the gold. When we have need, we come again. Like drinking at a fresh spring."

Once the bulk of the treasure was cached, each took a sack and started over the Sierra Madre toward home. A quick knife, a fall from a cliff, disappearance under the waters of the Río San Pedro.

His partners had not spent much. He used what was left to purchase land around his shack, including the village across the river. To build the casa grande and stock his range, he had returned once, taking half a dozen of the bags. Twenty were still there, in the cave at La Nariz.

Making that damned map had been a mistake. He knew the way as well as he did the road to Nogales. Yet he had enjoyed making it, keeping it, deeply thrilled each time he entered his library, knowing it was safely hidden. Like the gold. Until Marieta picked one of the leatherbound books he'd never expected anyone to read. She held the bit of folded paper before his face, asking, "What does this mean?" her tone revealing dangerous suspicions.

"I'll show you," he had promised, masking his fury. And his fear. At the height of his success, he couldn't afford to have authorities questioning him. "Pious fool," he thought. She would have ruined everything he had schemed to acquire.

Marieta. He hadn't thought of her for years. Avoided looking at the child who resembled her in every way. "He's not mine," he muttered, and turned on his side for a more restful position. That the bastardo would take the caballo padre and leave the hacienda surprised him. Trouble. No longer a child to be ignored, taunted, shamed. Now he must be guarded, beaten. Mastered.

Throughout siesta, Luis worried over his next move. Finally he put on his outer clothing and boots and started for his office. "Send Manuelo to me," he ordered the niño whose job it was to open the patio doors.

The segundo did not seem surprised when he said, "I want men watching Trouble every minute. If he goes beyond the estate grounds, make sure he is followed. Should he pack supplies and try to leave again, see that he's stopped."

Manuelo bowed. "As you wish, Patrón."

That night, after he had finished with Sofía, he told her, "I want you to watch the boy. Whenever he leaves the house, alert the men Manuelo has assigned to follow him. Do not fail me, Sofía."

He needed time to decide how he might rid himself of Trouble without causing suspicion. Giving freedom to one like that would be a bigger mistake than keeping the map.

Well, that problem had been taken care of, years ago. Unable to bring himself to destroy the symbol of his cunning, his triumph, his treasure, he'd found a new hiding place for it, close at hand in the house but more secure. He liked knowing the map was there, his secreto.

His thoughts returned to planning the trip to La Nariz. Twenty more sacks, and three times that amount in bullion. ¡Dios! such wealth. He would never live long enough to spend it all here on his estate. He should take a journey, a tour. Increase his holdings. Perhaps buy fine horses. Ideas churned through his mind, keeping him from sleep.

"May I go to my room now?" Sofía's meek voice came at him in the dark.

"Remember what I told you. Watch that pelado."

"I shall," she promised.

Every time Trouble took Bay for a ride along the river, or went for a walk down to the grotto where someone had long ago placed benches before a plaster statue of the Virgen de Guadalupe and there was shade and grass for picnics, a peón shadowed him.

When he rode to Nogales to see what was new in the shops, someone followed. Each time he visited señoritas in the village, another man stepped in his tracks, waited patiently in a sheltered doorway until he had finished and returned to Casa de Panadero. He was a prisoner, and could only suspect El Patrón's motive. It went beyond the fear that he might repeat his theft of a caballo padre. It even went beyond unreasoning hate.

"What is he hiding?" he asked Manuelo. "What does he think I'll find?"

Manuelo answered, "Quién sabe?"

Trouble cared little for the village dances or drinking pulque and aguardiente, revelries which often ended in a knifing; but he welcomed anything that would fill a few hours. He frequently sat on the balcony or in one of the patios with Sofía, drinking horchata or juice from the oranges grown on bushes near the wall. She was so shy that conversations were difficult, causing him to limit topics to simple household matters, news from Nogales, incidents among the peónes, and things he had read. Gradually, she began to ask about his childhood.

He told her about going to the Apache camp and stealing Bay.

She leaned toward him in apparent fascination. "Were you not afraid? My father used to tell how the Apache raided our towns and killed our people." She shivered. "Don Luis must have been proud of your courage."

He poured himself another glass and offered her the pitcher. "He hated me for it." Leaving out the part about Manuelo's healing salve and his own belief that the wiry little mestizo was a brujo, he related the perilous ride on Zopilote.

"It was then," he added, "that I knew El Patrón really wanted to kill me."

She grasped his forearm in both hands. "Oh, don Ramón, you cannot think so. He is harsh, but to—kill you? Why would he wish to do that?"

Slowly, he answered, "I cannot guess. But if he could do it and not get caught, I am certain that I'd be dead."

Trouble spent many hours in the village but continued to sleep in his room upstairs, which had gone undisturbed in his absence. He also took most meals at the casa grande, partly because the food was superior, chiefly because he knew his presence irritated the old man.

"You think, when I'm gone, you'll get your paws on this place," don Luis charged. "I'd burn the casa to the ground first. I would take it apart, piece by piece, with my hands, before I let you become patrón."

"Who said I wanted to be patrón?" He sipped the supper wine. Port, too heavy for his taste.

"Only a fool would not." Don Luis gave a guffaw that made Sofía cringe. "¡Ja! True, you are a fool."

"If I am, it's your blood which made me so." Trouble jumped up from the table, making his chair tip over and crash to the floor, making Sofía start as if shot. He threw it into place and strode out to the barns to cool off.

Currying Bay helped his anger evaporate, yet he wanted to cry, something he couldn't do with a vaquero leaning in the doorway. For years he'd kept Mamá pushed out of his thoughts, except for a reminder once in a while, like the grass doll.

What had her life been like, all this time? He wished he could see her again, hear her say that Panadero was not his father. That his father was the padre who had mysteriously disappeared, as she had done, or some peón from the village. Anyone but El Patrón.

New thoughts paused his breath. Maybe Panadero had told some of the truth—she had run away. And met the young padre! Maybe that's what the old man was hiding. *He knows where she is. Where they are.*

Excitement ran through him in great waves. He sent the currycomb over the horse's coat in long arcs, until tears and sweat mingled. There must be some clue, something he could find that would tell him what he yearned to know. Someone knew. The old man knew. He would shake El Patrón until the secret fell out. The idea of that happening was so ridiculous, he sank down beside Bay and laughed wildly until the vaquero approached, asking, "Don Ramón, are you all right?"

"Vayase," he said, muffled. "Leave me alone."

The guard retreated but didn't leave. He stood in the darkness outside and rolled a cigarette. The wisps of fresh smoke reminded Trouble of crowded cantinas in little towns to the south, of campfires on the trail. He had no desire to accept the patrón's responsibility for the hacienda, nor for the villagers who were dependent upon it. But if thinking so irritated the old man, then let him think so.

"There's no will," Manuelo had once told him. "Only a deed."

"Y de qué?" he remembered saying. "He'll burn the place to the ground before handing over anything to me." *Soon*, he thought, *I will leave this place, forever.* As soon as he learned Panadero's secreto.

Until then, at least the roof over his head was grand.

Tired of the amusements available across the river, and his suspicions growing that Beatriz was intimate with one of his best friends, Trouble more and more often spent time with Sofía, beneath the shade trees with a pitcher of juice, hardly speaking, enjoying the quiet, she doing embroidery, he pondering what Panadero's secret might be. He wondered if she knew.

One stormy afternoon, she seemed particularly anxious for his company. "Let us sit in the west sala. Josefa has prepared chocolate, and the chairs are more comfortable."

Windows shuttered against the rain and wind, the long, narrow room felt steamy. Plants responded by flowering, their perfume heavy in the still air. He sank onto a down-filled cushion and accepted the drink. Sofía pulled a wicker seat close beside him and seemed to ponder the contents of her cup, her plain little face thoughtful. "Ramón. Do you ever have dreams?"

"Sometimes they are nightmares."

"No, I mean—dreams of being somewhere else."

"Anywhere else," he declared.

"When you—went away—" Her eyes were intent. "Where did you live? What was it like?"

"San Lázaro. Magdalena. I was free in those places."

"Ramoncito, do you think—"

Whatever she meant to ask, he never learned, for out in the cocina La Vieja gave a wail, and Sofía jumped to her feet. "¡Madre de Dios! What now!" She hurried to see what had caused the cook's distress.

He stood up, stretching. Mingling with flowers was scent of burnt beef. While she was busy setting matters right in the kitchen, he stepped into the library.

He often played this game of hide and seek, to tease her into a blush when he reappeared suddenly. Aware of El Patrón's decree to stay out of the old house, she would never think to look for him there. Then he heard her tell La Vieja, "I shall select a wine for dinner," and slippered footfalls descended the steps to the cellar.

As he waited in the dimness for her to complete her task, he remembered Mamá's stories and the pastries she used to bake for a treat. Was she happy now, bitter tears replaced by laughter?—or did she still miss him, as he did her . . .

He crossed the room to where the ovens had been, before Panadero's workmen walled them over. Running the fingertips of one hand lightly over the plaster, he noted that a couple of jagged cracks marred the surface. Idly chipping off several small pieces, he was intrigued by the corner of a paper nestled between two bricks.

He began easing it free.

Chapter Four

A quarter sheet of letter paper, ripped cleanly, folded once.

His thumb flicked it open. Not a letter. In Panadero's neat script were three names, each crossed with a single line, and an X next to a small circle labeled PT. The letters must mean something, though he didn't know what. A series of *MMMM*s running roughly north-south had to be the Sierra Madre; winding lines with branches must be rivers or streams. Or trails.

Disappointed that the clue apparently did not lead to Mamá, Trouble calmed himself and studied the diagram. 'La Nariz' penned beneath a shape like a reclining man's nose appeared to be an important landmark. The presence of a map explained why the old rascal so jealously guarded this room. The map likely meant that the thing he was hiding was a treasure.

La Nariz. Beyond the Sierras, possibly a month's journey eastward by horseback.

When he had memorized the map and believed he could find the place, he wiggled the folded paper back into the narrow crack and picked up the fragments of plaster from the floor.

He bumped into Sofía as she came out of the wine cellar. "¡Siento!" he said. "¡Perdón!" and ran up the stairs.

She called after him, "Where are you going?"

"Visiting!" he called down.

"In the middle of the afternoon? In this rain?" She sounded dismayed.

Safe behind his door, he selected under garments, two shirts, and another pair of jeans, all of which he put on in layers. His boots would not fit over more than one pair of socks, so he arranged the extras in the front of his shirt. Over everything went his rain-proof poncho. Movement was somewhat hampered, but if anyone caught him carrying a bundle or saddlebags, his plan failed before he started.

Satisfied with what he saw in the mirror, he tightened the chin strap of his hat, moved the bedstead, and knelt to retrieve the document box and the Mexican Colt. He replaced the boards and, taking a final look around, turned the china knob and peeped into the hall.

Empty. Sofía must have gone to alert one of Panadero's men, so his first stop in the village was the hut of La Vieja's son, where he removed the extra clothing, stowed the tin box in his saddlebag, and made up a bedroll. "I'll return for it at midnight."

Luis entered the comedor anticipating his supper wine and a savory roast. Several hours a day, now, he rode his saddle horses instead of using the carriage, preparing his legs and back muscles for the trip to La Nariz. The bullion was a problem, but he felt confident that he could work out a method of converting it to spendable currency.

As Sofía took her chair, he said, "Don't make me have to ask."

"Ask what?" She looked distracted and almost upset her wine glass as she unfolded her napkin.

He shouted, "Where the goddamned pelado is."

She touched the napkin to her forehead. "In the village. Visiting."

"Who is watching him?" He drank some of his port.

"I sent Gerardo."

"Gerardo is a fool." He cut into his meat.

"Manuelo selected him."

"Then Manuelo is a bigger fool." Yet he was relieved not to have the despised face present at his table. The pleasure he used to feel at goading the little bastard had palled over the years.

Gagging, he emptied his mouth of burned beef and shoved the plate away. Too tired to do more, he allowed Sofía to appease him with baked chicken. Tomorrow he was to meet with a horse breeder from the United States. If the man's stock proved worthy, the gold would buy finer blooded mares than those he'd been using with El Rey, and his reputation among other ranchers in Sonora would be enhanced.

He lay awake much of the night reviewing his assets, planning his strategy. Everything was going well, yet he felt uneasy and found himself listening for Trouble to slip back into the casa. One of the treads on the stairs always creaked under foot. Toward morning a storm swept in from the mountains, blotting smaller sounds in a fury of wind.

At daylight he dressed and went up to the boy's room, where he found the bed undisturbed. Uneasiness increased. He continued out to the kitchen patio, where Gerardo huddled in a ragged sarape, waiting for La Vieja to unlatch the door.

At the sight of him, the niño jumped up, forgetting to bow. "Buen día, don Luis."

He let the familiarity pass. "Give your report."

"Trouble spent last night at the house of the señorita Beatriz Ochoa."

"He is still there?"

Gerardo shrugged. "I did not see him come out, señor."

"¡Cabrón! Go back and watch until he does."

The niño set off at a run and Luis went to his office to review the contract. He planned to have this meeting in the library, where rich furnishings and shelves of expensive books lent an appropriate air of prosperity. The old house was a novelty, providing a topic of conversation, a necessary ritual before getting down to business. He paused in the doorway.

Darker than he remembered. The small, uncurtained opening into a hallway beyond had been the single window in the casita. Yet even in the dimness he could see a haze of neglect on everything. Had it really been so long since he'd finalized a contract here? On the other side of this wall was the comedor, pleasantly bright because of the French doors. Inappropriate. Men of stature did not cut deals in the dining room. The sala? No. The Spanish furniture was uncomfortable, as evenings spent there had proved, and that damned piano haunted the room with its silence.

The library, then. Fumbling to light a lamp, he called, "¡Criada!"

A girl appeared at his elbow and he sent her for more lamps, more cushions. He supervised the arrangement of the articles.

While she went about with a feather duster, he watched to be sure she didn't snoop. The incident at La Nariz was uppermost in his mind, now that he'd decided to return. He felt a resurgence of the old fear that, some day, in one of the hundreds of books, a prying eye might find a half-finished letter, written by Marieta to her parents in California, telling them how she was treated, her suspicions about the source of his great wealth.

The criada suddenly called out, "Mi patrón, there is a crack in the wall here," and bent for a closer look.

The ovens! His heart lurched. "Get away! You've done enough."

"But señor—"

"Go tell La Vieja to send Josefa with refreshments." Josefa was prettier than this girl, and less curious.

"What sort do you desire, señor?"

"Several kinds of pastry and the best red wine in the cellar. She knows where to find it. We shall have coffee afterwards."

After the criada left, he stepped to the plastered wall and examined its surface. The hairline crack which he had known was there now seemed wider, edges chipped. He could see something. That was never possible before. Was it only a bit of straw, sunk in the adobe? Or was the map visible? Chills crept along his cheeks and the back of his neck.

A light footfall creaked the floor behind him and he whirled on Josefa. "Who has been in this room?"

She nearly dropped the tray. "No one, Patrón! Only yourself, and Celia." She gave a frightened look around. "What is the matter?"

"No importa. When Señor Campbell arrives, seat him in the patio until I am ready."

"Sí, don Luis."

In his office, he unlocked the liquor cabinet and poured himself a brandy. Fortified, he returned to the crack. Not his imagination—he could see the folded edge. He bent to examine the polished oak floorboards. Clean. Bits of loose plaster must have fallen, to reveal the map. Someone had removed them. Someone other than the lazy criada.

Suspending breath to steady his hand, Luis grasped the paper with his fingernails, heedlessly breaking off more plaster, and slid it free. In the sala, he took down the framed painting from over his wall safe, and locked the map inside. No one could get at it there.

Negotiations with Campbell took little more than an hour and a few drinks, some jokes, a couple of Havanas smoked in the cool patio, a final handshake. The man had scarcely passed through the front gate when one of the peónes approached. Given permission to speak, he said, "Trouble is not here."

Luis chewed his cigar and studied the villager whose face he knew but whose name he'd never bothered to learn. "How can you be sure?"

"Two geldings which were pastured by the river are also gone."

"The caballo padre?"

"Safe, Patrón."

"Send me Manuelo."

When the mayordomo heard the accusation, he said, "Do not blame Gerardo, por favor. Beatriz swears that Trouble was with her until one hour ago. He cannot have gotten far."

"Those geldings that were pastured by the river. They were near your casita."

"Sí, Patrón."

"But, of course, you know nothing of this matter."

"No, señor. I have not used the casita for years."

Trouble's escape coming on the heels of the discovery of the chipped plaster made Luis tremble. What if the boy had been in the library, seen the paper, and removed it? Realized what it meant, and was at this moment on his way to La Nariz? "Send the trackers to me."

After two days the riders returned, only to admit they had lost the trail less than twenty kilometres south of the hacienda boundary. "We circled the entire rancho," one of them whined. "A chingado wind destroyed all the tracks. It is not our fault."

Not Gerardo's fault. Not Manuelo's fault. Not the fault of the best trackers in Sonora. Oh, no.

Chafing under this fresh problem, Luis slept poorly. If he did nothing, in a few weeks Sonoran authorities, and officials from Chihuahua as well, could come knocking at the gate with warrants for his arrest. Little bastardo would be with them, gloating.

Stopping Trouble meant hiring a professional.

Sofía lay on the cot in Manuelo's old hut among the willows by the river, healing leaves bound with a strip of linen against her throbbing temples. Over the last months, though she had never so much as touched Ramón's hand, she had stopped expecting him to run away again.

A huge mistake. Had she been bolder in declaring her love, she would be with him now. Had it not been for the crisis of the burned beef, she would have confessed her desire there in the cozy intimacy of the west patio, while the rain fell.

México was a vast country, and the north border near at hand. Whatever direction he chose for escape, she had lost him, and the bitterness of being left behind hurt more than an awareness of all those nights he'd spent across the river, in someone else's bed.

Stealthy, she returned to her room, opened the dresser drawer and took out his rumpled shirt, all of him that remained. Edging the rips, the smears of dried blood had browned, a powerful reminder. Burying her face in the mustiness of old sweat, she toyed once more with the possibility of finding a bruja who could work a spell. Not to bring him back, but to find him so they could be together.

Manuelo was driving him home from a cattlemen's luncheon when Luis noticed the ridge. It lay outside the adobe wall that surrounded the house and lawns, a landmark guiding wealthy men to him for the closure of a contract. Now he realized what a vantage point it provided, rearing stark and sheer, towering over the casa grande. A man good with a rifle could pick off anyone he chose, from that ridge.

Unconcerned about safety then, he'd been satisfied to have the wall constructed too low for real defense, and the top kept bare of broken glass, a usual feature on such estates. But high walls topped with shards of glass would be no defense against an armed man on the ridge. An armed, vengeful pelado, who had been to La Nariz and discovered its secrets.

Masking his fear, he dismissed Manuelo and drove the carriage out to the storerooms, where among the dry goods, baskets, ollas, tools, and discarded saddles and harness, he located three small kegs of black powder. Left from the work on the casa grande, it was used in making ammunition for hunting.

Later that night, he moved the kegs to the wine cellar beneath the house until he could study out the details. To keep the servants from gossiping, he told them the kegs held wine which needed to be aged, and he put his wax seal on each lid to discourage sampling. During the building of the casa, he remembered, a man had been killed while blasting out those river rocks. Leveling the ridge would be hot, heavy, dangerous work at best, and almost immediately he came to the realization that the house was too near.

Never should have built so close.

He knew why he'd done that. The old house was there, kept as a trophy, like the map, a tangible sign of how far he had come, how much his cunning had accomplished.

No great explosions to knock the damned ridge down so it could be carted away, leaving no place for an enemy to hide. No. A hundred tiny charges, chewing away at the rock, cracking, loosening, but not forceful enough to throw boulders down on the casa. Such a job would take months.

Trouble could return in a few weeks.

Three days later, Luis met with a mestizo notorious for eliminating his own enemies. "Five hundred pesos if you can do the job," he promised. "And keep your mouth shut."

La Nariz.

Trouble veered off his southerly course and turned east toward the Sierra Madre, a distant range stretching left and right as far as the eye could see.

He had played blackjack with Juan and Enrique and shared their supper of tortillas, frijoles, and tepache. Afterward, he'd spent a pleasurable hour with Beatriz. It was tempting to tell her of his discovery and suspicions; but caution kept him silent. By the time he was ready to leave, the rain had stopped and a gusting wind, ushering in the dry season, shook the shutters and whipped the chaparral.

The geldings carried clothing, a groundsheet, a blanket, enough supplies to last a month, and four full canteens. He would water his stock and replenish his supply at springs or tinajas along the way. The few trails led to villages, which he avoided in case others were following who would ask questions.

Traveling alone invited curiosity as well as a risk of attack, despite the Mexican Colt stashed in his saddlebag and a Remington bolt-action military rifle in the scabbard. He'd traded a pair of silver cuff buttons for that rifle, and practiced shucking it from the case until his awkwardness passed. Grizzlies could be aggressive, and he had no way of guessing how long he might be camping in the mountains. Unsure whether the treasure he sought consisted of cash, jewelry, or some other form of wealth, he postponed making any plans for its disposal.

Growing confident that the rain and wind had assured his escape, yet he kept a wary eye on his back trail and continued to conceal cook fires. When none of El Patrón's men appeared to be following, it occurred to him that he was on a fool's errand, as the old man likely had spent the fortune long ago. How else could the casa grande have been built, the ranges stocked, the finery bought? No matter. The promise of La Nariz beckoned from across those forbidding peaks, those haunted canyons. And he was free.

He liked the lonesome grasslands, bleak ridges, and nights made desolate with coyote singing. Glimpses of mule deer, striped ground squirrels, and hundreds of colorful twittering birds sent tremors of pleasure along his spine. Wending always eastward, he skirted impenetrable stands of chaparral and forded steep-banked arroyos still running full of muddy water.

The scrub brushland of yucca and prickly pear gave way to ocotillo, smoke trees, and paloverde. Frequently a wall of towering rock forced him to retrace his route. As the trails climbed, piñon pines changed to oaks, oaks to fir. He woke cold and stiff in the mornings, and needed the wool sarape Chuco had made him accept.

From a pinnacle he scanned the plains ahead for any landmark that resembled a nose. He realized that the angle of approach could make a difference in how the mountain appeared to a traveler

Descending the slopes, he rode through other stands of firs, oaks, paloverdes, and more thorny grasslands. Soon, the rugged Sierra Madre lay behind him. Camping near the headwaters of the Río Casas Grandes, however, he sensed that his quest was nearing its end. Again he heard the cry of a night bird, the same as when he had ventured to the Apache camp and taken Bay. Though it comforted him, he slept fitfully through the long night and packed up without making coffee.

Alternating mounts, stopping only to let them blow, he pushed onward. Then he saw, half a day's ride away, the unmistakable shape on the horizon, like the only visible feature of a long-buried giant. His heartbeat quickened.

In the evening he reached the base of the mountain. Smaller than he'd imagined. He untied a short-handled spade from his saddle and gazed up at the silent ridge. The map had offered no clue as to where to dig. How little he knew the old man, not to have any notion of what kind of place Panadero would choose for burying a treasure.

The afternoon of the third day, near the bridge of the 'nose,' he came upon a suspicious pile of rocks and dead brush. Pulling aside the debris, he found a low, narrow opening, like the mouth of a cave. Cautious of snakes and scorpions, he poked about with the spade and lit one of his candles before crawling into the passage.

It widened almost at once. He stood up. The space was large enough for perhaps three men to walk around. A shelf of dirt ran along the back wall, similar to the adobe benches called asientos which peónes used for seats or beds. He fixed the candles in a clump of wax dripped on a flat stone, knelt and began breaking up the dirt, which came away in chunks. Dry soil sifted down in a cascade. He tossed aside the tool and used his hands.

Leather sacks, laid in two rows. The small, heavy bags closed at the drawstring end with rawhide strips. The kind used by packtrain traders. Now the letters *PT* on the map made sense. He struggled with the first knot. At last it loosened, and he tipped the contents into his palm. The sheen of gold in the candlelight filled him with triumph.

There were twenty sacks, and he opened them all. Each held between thirty and eighty coins, the smallest valued at ten pesos, the largest, fifty. Of Mexican strike, old but still acceptable in any transaction. The total must be more than $200,000 pesos.

He took up the spade and resumed work. In moments the metal clanged against something solid. Pulse racing, he uncovered bars of bullion, six of them, each weighing more than he could lift without leverage. He guessed them to be worth as much as the coins, but only an assay could determine the value.

No wonder Panadero had grown increasingly vicious. He was over sixty, his weight punishing on any horse he rode, and plagued with a weak stomach. He had to know that to redeem this cache, he must do so soon or not at all. He could be on his way here, now. Alone, for he would never trust outriders to accompany him on such a mission. Suffering the inconveniences of travel, but determined. Armed. Ready to kill.

To be sure nothing was overlooked, Trouble excavated here and there. His remount could manage the sacks, but he'd need mules to carry away the bullion. If he took it to Ciudad Chihuahua—

A stroke of the spade uncovered dirt-encrusted bones. A small hand, an arm.

Recoiling, he allowed a cry to escape. "Ay, Dios mío." He stopped digging. Three names had been crossed off the paper on which the old man had drawn his map. Doubtless partners, killed for their shares.

Shaken, Trouble was about to leave when a gleam of something not gold, but shiny in the glow of candles, made him kneel and brush away the sand. Entwined in the fingers was a necklace. No—a rosary. The beads and cross carved from a dark wood, the Cristo on the cross finely crafted by a silversmith.

Grasping the icon so hard that its corners gouged his palm, he leaned back against the cave wall, stunned, images thronging his head. Images of Mamá, bowed over her prayerbook. She had not run off with some lover, leaving him behind.

Hot tears spilled over his cheeks. "Lo siento, Mamá." Sorry, for believing the old man's lies. For doubting her love for her son. His heart flooded with rage and his first thought was to return to Hacienda de Panadero and avenge this evil. In his room at night, he had practiced with the Mexican Colt until its leap from holster to hand was more natural than an eye blink, and as fast. He could shoot Panadero without a shred of guilt. His second thought was to camp nearby and simply wait for Luis to come in range of the saddle gun.

Slowly he wiped his face with shaky fingers. Resting on his heels, considered the scattered bags and bars. He could take the coins. Travel anywhere in the world, do whatever he pleased. California, to seek out his mother's parents, if they still lived. Ciudad de México, with its cathedrals and commerce. South America, Europe, places he had read about in the books given him by Padre Felix because Panadero had forbidden his use of the casa library. Forbidden because it hid the truth. Only Dios knew how many others had stained the red Sonoran earth with their blood.

"Greedy old devil," he muttered. "I refuse to become like you." Using his penknife, he opened the silver link that attached the crucifix. He put the Cristo into his pocket and, placing the sacks in their proper rows above the bullion, covered them with loose dirt and smoothed all traces of his visit. He took up the spent candles, turned over the rock with its telltale wax drippings, picked up the spade. He blocked the entrance with the rocks and brushy debris. This time, he meant to disappear so completely, Panadero's trackers would never find him.

The squat adobe seemed to have sprung up on the edge of the plain like a rain-watered desert plant. In the distance Trouble could see a few chozas of poles and thatch. The faint trace of road he'd followed out of the sierra continued southward through a narrow valley rimmed with dry hills. Above the open door of the adobe hung a bullet-pocked sign: Cantina de Mateo.

He put his horses in the rock corral, noting that the water in the trough was fresh, and carried his saddlebags across the dusty yard. Stepping over the threshold, he allowed his eyes to adjust. Unshuttered windows left and right, the bar straight ahead with two shelves behind it. On a petate, a middle-aged fat man snored while flies buzzed about an open pulque jug.

"¡Cantiñero!"

The bartender stirred, rubbed his face, and squinted toward him. Clean-shaven except for a mustache, short black curls clinging damply to the forehead. He rolled over on his face, so the word was muffled against the mat. "Siesta, hombre, si por Dios."

Trouble dropped the saddlebags and went to stand over him. "A drink, por favor. I'll pay double."

From an inner doorway, a girl's voice said, "You sound very thirsty, señor." She stepped through the curtain closure and approached them. The neckline of her white blouse drooped in front just enough to tease. Her hair was the same chestnut color as one of his horses, and cut different lengths to frame smooth cheeks. Her lips parted, revealing small, even teeth. "Are you perhaps hungry, too?"

"A drink, first." Since leaving La Nariz, he had felt no desire to eat, only a gnawing helplessness and indecision.

Each day found him farther from Casa de Panadero, less sure of what revenge he meant to exact.

The girl went behind the counter and set out three empty glasses. "Una copita de aguardiente, fifty centavos. Mezcal, twenty-five. Pulque, ten." She turned to a shelf behind her for a bottle. "Dos pesos buys you this much Americano whiskey."

"¡Dos pesos!"

She shrugged. "You said you will pay double."

"I didn't realize you are a bandit."

Grinning again, she touched the tip of her tongue to the corner of her mouth. "Oh, we always give good value."

He had no doubt about that. Glancing at the snoring man on the floor, he fished centavos from his pocket. The cross scraped his knuckle, wrenching the knot in his stomach. "I'll try the mezcal."

The girl poured an exact amount into one of the glasses. She pushed a small clay bowl heaped with tostadas toward him and stood back, watching. The mouthful of liquor burned all the way down and momentarily shut off his breath. A crisp tostada failed to soothe the flame and he couldn't hold back a cough. "Damn! That is vile."

"¡Ay!" she cried, and peered at the container. "I think I gave you the aguardiente instead." She laughed, the jug poised, and asked, "Another?"

"Not today," he said, and had to clear his throat.

"Then you look ready for siesta."

"How much for a room?"

She seemed to assess him before saying, "One peso, which includes a bath."

He became aware of the sweat and dirt and stubble of sparse beard. He fished out three pesos. "A room, and Americano whiskey, por favor."

Picking up the bottle, she led him behind the curtain and down a short hallway to a room pleasantly cool from an open window. Instead of the reed mat he expected, there was a low bedstead with a shuck mattress and a soft pillow. A small table held a basin and pitcher like the ones pictured in the catalog from Chicago which had made the rounds of Panadero's wranglers until it was in tatters.

"I shall wash your back."

He sat on the bed and started to take off his boots. "I want to sleep." He couldn't remember when he had slept through the night.

"You'll feel better if you wash first."

"Later."

"You need a bath."

"I need," he explained with more patience than he felt, "to get very drunk, and then to sleep. ¿Comprende?"

Pressing her lips together, she flounced to the door. "You pay for having the linens washed, then, hombre!"

He settled against the pillow and filled the glass. When it was empty, he filled it again. And again.

Groggy from whiskey and the deep sleep of exhaustion, sprawled across the bed on his stomach, he became aware of a soapy rag tenderly cleansing between his toes. Rinse water splashed in a tin pan. A soft towel dried his foot. Then hands pulled at his shirt, uncovering his back. "¡Pobrecito!"

He caught her forearm. "What are you doing?"

"Giving you the bath, señor." She gestured toward the window. "You have slept for hours." Her voice softened. "Lie down. I have not finished."

He resisted her hand against his chest. The evening sun slanting across the room brought a sadness that made him want to cry, to hit his fist against the wall, to break something. He took the rag from her and held its coolness against his aching temples.

"Leave me alone, por favor."

She caressed his hand. "Don't be downcast. Tinita will give you something happy to think about."

He looked at her over the rag. "Tinita…that's your name?"

Watching him, she nodded, hopeful. She reminded him of smoky-eyed women in the cantinas of San Lázaro and Magdalena. But pretty, and younger than he'd first thought; maybe sixteen.

"And Mateo—?"

"Tío. Apaches killed mis padres when I was five years old."

"Lo siento." He slid off the bed and tucked in his shirt.

"How did you get those scars?" She sounded curious, but not unconcerned.

He put on his boots. "I prefer not to talk about that."

She held out her hand. "Then, let's go outside. The cool air will make you feel better."

In the hallway, words of a song— "Perdoneme, esposa mía, perdóna mis aventuras,"—came from the small cocina, mixed with the clatter of pans and the aroma of frying meat. Trying not to retch, Trouble hurried her along the passage and they emerged onto a small patio.

Unaware, she said, "Tío Mateo is a good cook. You will eat with us, will you not?"

The fresh air didn't seem to help either his head or his stomach. He would feel better soon, or die. "Perhaps."

"And sleep here tonight?"

In the corral his horses dozed with hanging heads. He'd pushed them hard, and they could use a bit of grain from those sacks in Mateo's stores. Too, the bed had felt good after nights on the ground. "Perhaps."

She led him to an outcrop of boulders nestled in a thin grove of cottonwoods bordering a stream. Climbing onto a large, flat rock, she beckoned him to join her. He did so, and fought off a flash of memory of another lifetime, when he had stood on a stack of roof tiles to oversee the building of La Casa de Panadero.

Leaning back on her palms, drawing attention to her breasts, she examined him appreciatively and reminded, "You haven't told me your name."

"Ramón Cordero."

"Where is your tierra, Ramón Cordero?"

He hesitated. He no longer knew.

"Are you a bandido?"

"No, of course not."

She narrowed her eyes. "¿Hacendado?"

He was silent. What gave her such an idea?

She spat over the edge of the rock. "That is what I think of hacendados."

Amused, he asked, "You know a few, do you?"

"Those gachupínes took all the good land and left nothing but arroyos for true Mexicans."

"Mestizos, you mean."

"You look and speak like one of us, though you dress like a gringo. Worse than hacendados."

"I am a true Mexican," he declared. "To prove it, I must tell you, I own only what you see and the two horses in your corral."

She leaned against his shoulder. "Then you are rich." The warmth of her breasts engulfed his arm through the sleeve, and the fingers of one hand slid into the hair at the back of his neck. Her lips touched his cheek, parted, and the wet tip of her tongue traced a circle against his skin. "I would see more."

Sparkles before his eyes beat in time with his heart. He wasn't sure if it was the whiskey or her nearness. "I cannot afford supper, a room, and 'more.'"

"Ah, 'more' will be payment enough." Her breath was hot in his ear. She grasped the inside of his thigh.

"Mateo might not think so."

"You're not dealing with tío."

"This rock is not very comfortable."

"Pues, the grass is."

She jumped lightly to the ground, pulling him after her, and they lay down in the shade of the boulder, sheltered from view of anyone at the cantina, its barns or corral.

Dizzy from drink and desire, he allowed her to push aside his shirt and fondle his chest; but he knew her hunger was impersonal, satisfied by any man. While he was trying to justify taking advantage of her need, she drew back enough to ask, "What has made you so sad, joven? Tell me. Was it a woman?"

His spirit was sore, like a bruised sinew needing massage but wincing at a touch. Worse, this lonely outpost, on a vast plain that was not his tierra, was too near La Nariz. "I can't."

"You can." She unfastened more buttons. "Trade. My secrets, for yours." Arms and legs wrapped around him, she whispered, "Stay here forever." Her tongue explored one corner of his mouth. "With me."

He halted her hands, gave them a little squeeze, said, "We'd better stop. My head is pounding like thunder."

She hugged, then released him. "After supper, then."

The cantina had no dining room for guests, so Trouble sat at the table with Tío Mateo and the girl, sipping beer chill from a cellar and listening to stories about Tío's boyhood in Durango.

After the beer stayed down, he ate an enchilada and felt better, talk diverting his mind until the cantiñero yawned and stretched and excused himself.

"Ramón," Tinita said quietly, "what is bothering you?"

He felt exhausted, yet knew he couldn't sleep. She left her chair to sit on his lap. Putting her arms around him, she snuggled her face in the curve of his neck, and he surprised himself by telling her everything—childhood terrors, the theft of El Rey and the beating which left scars, finding the map and the place where Panadero had murdered his mother—everything except the enormity of the treasure and its location.

Her lips tickled his collarbone as she mused, "Don Luis Panadero. Will you kill him?"

He considered. "No. I never want to see him again."

"Then, stay. I can make you forget."

She inflamed him anew with practiced caresses. He longed to trust her, lose himself in lovemaking, give her children, spend evenings listening to Mateo sing and tell stories. But almost against his will, he stood up. She clung to him. "Por favor, Ramón. Tonight. One night."

He peeled her fingers from his wrist. This girl could not heal the damage begun in childhood, damage made unbearable at La Nariz. "Forgive me." He was relieved when she didn't follow him to the corral, and he rode out into the moonlit night. Nothing ahead but the emptiness of the unknown, nothing behind but memories.

Following the easiest routes southwestward across the Sierra Madre, he camped where he found water, moved on when he grew restless. He lost track of the days.

Finally he rode down out of the last foothills into a well-watered valley. On his right, to the west, lay a vast grassy plain; beyond the plain, a border of distant blue mountains. In the distance ahead, he could see scattered thatch-roofed chozas and a few adobes huddled behind mud walls.

Coming upon a lightly traveled road, he followed it.

Chapter Five

Beyond a fringe of paloverdes, a mission church glared stark and white in the sun. In the campo santo behind the church, chopping cactus with a hoe, was a small plump figure in the brown robe of a priest. Thin, wispy white hair blew about in a light breeze.

The road veered sharply to the left and turned into the dusty main street. Weary from days of aimless travel, tired of roasted quail and rabbits for every meal, Trouble walked his horses to the public fountain, where he removed their bits to allow them to drink.

The padre called cheerily, "Buenos días," and came toward him.

A gourd dipper hung from a cottonwood branch. Trouble filled it under the flow. "Beats water out of a canteen."

Though the priest's round face held few wrinkles, his jowls sagged; he appeared to be about sixty years of age and well fed. His eyes were the blue of the Spaniard. "We are blessed with few travelers in this part of the world. I am Father Navarre."

"What village is this?" He hung the dipper back where he'd found it. Father Navarre. Not 'padre' followed by a Christian name. Did the villagers not like this man? Or was the aloofness the choice of the priest himself?

"It is called Los Pobres. The Río San Miguel lies that way." He gestured to the west. "The Río Sonora, there." He gestured to the east.

Fields had been planted in corn and were ready for harvest. Down the street, he could see a plaza bandstand, a few shops, a few houses. Acacias and paloverdes shaded dooryards. Perhaps a hundred inhabitants, counting infirm grandmothers and babes wrapped to their mothers' backs in rebozos. On the south side of the street, a large rock casa appeared deserted; probably it had once belonged to an hidalgo dead in the last revolution.

"Seems pleasant."

"There is nothing here to disturb. Have you hunger? I can offer estofado, and today Señora Hernández gave me a large flan."

"Mil gracias." He followed the padre along the wall of the church to a small room connected to the building by a covered walkway. A basin of water for their hands, a pot of stew simmering over a brazier. "What kind of people live here?"

Father Navarre filled two bowls, and they sat down. "Most are Opatas. Shy, backward, inclined to drunkenness and gambling, but no real evil or cruelty like that found in other tribes, such as the Coras and Huichols. There are also five mestizo families."

"You speak Opata?"

"Oh, yes. The English, the Spanish, the Opata, and of course the Latin of the Church. It is my gift, languages."

Though they finished the meal in silence, he sensed a keen curiosity in the old cura.

"I noticed your rifle," the man said at last. He got up and reached for a bottle of wine and two glasses. "I trust you have not come here to use it."

"No, Padre. For game, only." Trouble sipped the port. He was far from ready to pour out his pain to anyone, least of all a priest. Had not a man of God allowed Panadero to murder Mamá and go unpunished? At last he understood why the young priest had vanished from the hacienda.

"Tell me more about Los Pobres," he said, and the cura refreshed their wine.

In all such towns, the Indios sold chiles, beans, herbs, tortillas, and handcrafts from blankets in the plaza. Mestizos owned shops supplied by traders whose routes ran from the borderlands to the coast. Across the street from the mission church stood a sprawling, two-story stone house called the Borda casa, enclosed in a high rock wall with an iron gate, old trees and neglected bougainvillea. Long ago the family had left ; the place was abandonada.

What would happen to Hacienda de Panadero when its patrón was gone? He pushed away the thought. Forget the north, the people, the life he had lived there. He could not forget La Nariz, for the Cristo in his pocket reminded him daily of the old man's treachery. Yet he clung to it, a part of Mamá he'd never expected to find.

That night he tossed his trail gear down in the extra room at the end of a hall remote from the priest's quarters. A little window faced west, so he could see through the paloverdes to the moonlit road that had led him here.

At the base of low cliffs topped with oaks and pines was a spring-fed pond, willow-fringed and inviting. Above the dark stillness of its water, some landslide had created a level space barely large enough for a casita, a small house, with a shed for storage. A thicket of chaparral grew on the north side, from which an enemy could approach, but it could be burned off.

During breakfast with the priest—corn tortillas, beans, and the strong coffee of the region—he asked, "Who owns that hillside above the pond?"

Padre stared vaguely through the open door of his cocina. "There? The Church. But no one uses it, nor the plain beyond."

"Would I be allowed to build a casita?"

"I have no objection. Of course, this town is very poor, so . . ."

"I can pay a reasonable price for materials. Who makes adobes? Are there tiles? I prefer them to thatch because of the scorpions."

"The adobe maker died last year, may his soul rest. Tiles come by burro from Blanca Rosa. But, the saints are with you, for my good friend Francisco deals in wood and nails. Might I suggest a tin roof? If you make a loft for the passage of air, the casita will remain cool."

Trouble suspected that 'good friend Francisco' had unwisely bought sheets of tin from a trader and would be willing to part with it for almost nothing. He was right, and satisfied since it was the quickest way to have a roof. If the sun's heat became unbearable, he could always throw dirt on the surface. He traded his roan for a mule to haul heavy beams, and Padre sent two agreeably silent Opata boys with strong backs to help with the labor.

After days of rearranging melon-sized rocks, the hill leading up to the shelf became passable. Located near the spring, shaded by an ancient mesquite, the dwelling had a shed at the back, where a grassy slope overlooked the plain and the distant blue mountains. Prevailing west winds had planted wildflowers and a dozen young walnut trees in a grove only a few paces from his house.

The room measured four long strides in each direction, barely large enough to hold his narrow rope bed, a table, two chairs, and the stand on which he kept a wash basin, all of which he fashioned himself; and a cast iron stove ordered from over the border and transported by rail to the Llano station and thence by mule back.

A wooden tub served for bathing, and an olla of drinking water hung from a rafter near the front door. A shuttered casement beside the door opened to the east. Beneath a glass-paned window facing north, a flat-topped trunk held linens, clothing, books, and the document box containing boyhood treasures and the grass doll.

Open shelves along the back wall stored dry beans, corn meal, salt, chiles, goat cheese, and coffee. Each day he walked down to the market and bought fresh aguacates, tomatoes, and squash. Señoras made horchata, enchiladas of shredded chicken, pastries, and salsas. Occasionally there were fruits imported from the tropical lands father south along the coast.

He fell into the habit of exercising his horses along the base of the cliffs, then spending long evenings under the priest's thatch ramada, drinking unconsecrated wine from cases brought by burro to supply the communion chalice. He prepared a small plot of ground, planted seeds.

At night by lamplight, he read the few books brought from the north with the stove, and occasional newspapers that Padre lent him. He slept with the silver Colt holstered near his pillow. Though as the days passed, nightmares of La Nariz came less frequently, and except for Father Navarre's urgings to attend Mass, which aggravated heart wounds beneath invisible scabs, he lived well, contented. This was his tierra now.

One morning, as he unpacked items from his baskets, the glass window exploded in a shower of shards pelting his back. Before a hornet-like *whizzz* ended in the *thunk!* of a slug embedding in a plank on the opposite wall, he hit the floor on one palm and his knees.

Heart racing, he scooted under his bed and lay tense, ears straining for any movement. The door to his right, and the front door opposite it, stood open.

Sweat tickled his temples, trickled down the curve of his cheek, dried cool in the hollow of his throat. He stretched to reach the Colt in its holster, and felt better when it was ready in his hand.

It would not be Panadero himself, but a hired gun. The old bandit still packed a punch that would stun a mule, but he wouldn't risk being shot. Had he been to La Nariz? Trouble was sure he'd smoothed over every trace of his digging. Yet, the absence of the Cristo would be more damning than an errant footprint.

Faint scuff of a boot just outside. Someone crouched beneath the east window...hoping that bullet had done its work. Trouble held the Colt in both hands, focusing on the doorway despite the sweat stinging his eyes.

A shadow advancing over the threshold gave warning before two hasty shots lodged somewhere in the wall behind him. He squeezed the trigger, firing from the frame of table legs into a figure that threw up its hands and pitched forward into the room.

A twitch, like a slain buck, the scrape of boot sole, gasps for breath. Silence.

Trembling, alert for others, or signs of life from the man sprawled half in, half out of his house, Trouble cocked the pistol, and waited.

Flies drawn to the blood circled and lit and circled and lit. Dust-motes riding air currents sparkled in the sunlight.

He slid from beneath the bed, stood slowly, walked to the broken window and looked beyond the bit of garden to the thicket of prickly pear and crucifixion thorn which he had neglected to clear. How much had Panadero offered?

After a couple of minutes, he decided that one bounty hunter was all. Close enough to the body to nudge it face up with his moccasined foot, he saw a man about forty— twice his age—dressed in the clothing of a mestizo farmer.

He hoped the man had not left a pitiful little family waiting for someone who was never coming home.

From outside, a shout. "¡Amigo!"

Father Navarre panted up the hillside, hampered by his fat belly, robe, and sandals. "Are you hurt?"

He holstered the Colt. "No." Searching the pockets and saddlebags, he found nothing to identify the hired gun, nor link him to Panadero. The horse was unbranded. He arranged for the cura to sell it for him.

With Padre's help, Trouble buried the body in an unhallowed corner of the campo santo and tried to ignore the taste of fear, like rust, along the edges of his tongue. He leaned the shovel against the back of the church and, after leveling one of the chairs on the uneven ground, collapsed onto the leather seat.

For a long moment they sat listening to the laughter of children playing and curs barking in the streets beyond the wall. Inside closed eyelids, he saw himself at five, running barefoot, nostrils tingling with aromas of sun-cured grass and dappled shade. Mamá walked to her chapel, carried her tattered prayer book, wore her pink-flowered dress.

Wiping his dust-streaked face, he said, "I suppose you don't keep anything stronger than wine."

"The cantina is open. But I trust you will not try to solve your problems in that manner."

A smile touched one corner of his mouth. "Solve them with the Colt instead?"

Mamá had been dead for more than a dozen years. He could still feel her cool fingertips against his forehead, brushing back his sweat-damp hair; could still hear the terror in her cry, "Ramón, run! Run!" and feel the fiery thorns rip the tender skin of his legs as he fled Panadero.

Sipping wine beside the priest, Trouble's mind worried at the situation. Panadero must have gone to La Nariz. Must have recovered the sacks of gold coins, maybe even the bullion, and was using the wealth to pay men more skilled than his own trackers.

"When this one fails to return," he mused, "he will send another."

Padre's eyes blinked rapidly. "Then, you know who desires you dead—and why?"

He read the man's thoughts as easily as if they marched across the forehead. Killing, even in defense of one's own life, posed danger to the peaceful Opatas who came to Mass, bringing their tribute of crops and articles of leather and cloth made skillfully by their brown hands. He was not welcome here, if his presence meant one of them might die from an errant pistol shot. He had not been welcome at Casa de Panadero, either.

His fingers were stiff from the digging, the shape of the shovel handle echoed in their relaxed curve. He flexed them. Those hours of practice with the Mexican Colt had accomplished merely a postponement, an exchange of someone else's future for his own.

"Ramón." Close, the voice jarred him out of the past and into the sunlit afternoon. The cura leaned toward him, Spanish blue eyes searching. "That pistol. You are very good with it?"

He felt a pleasant giddiness from two pourings of the wine, and was working on a third when the words came out of his mouth and lay like cigarette smoke on the evening air. "Damn right, I am."

He drained his glass and set it on the ground beside his chair. At the edge of the campo santo, a crow lit on the fresh dirt, hoping for a morsel.

II

Hacienda de Panadero lay in a wide valley in northern Sonora, bordered on the west by a range of distant blue mountains and marked on the east by a wagon road, where Walker now paused, reining in his black gelding.

Last night he'd been in a Nogales saloon when a young Mexican appeared at his elbow, sombrero off, murmuring something. "Dammit, speak up."

In heavily-accented English, the muchacho repeated, "You are Señor Walker, of the gun?"

He looked up from the pair of queens in his hand and grinned. "You got it, amigo. You want to hire?"

The eyes looked puzzled. "High-er? Señor, escuche, por favor. Mi patrón—boss—want you. You come?"

Down to his last silver dollar, and likely to lose that to a full house, Walker asked, "Who's your patrón? I don't come cheap."

Leaning to whisper in his ear, the boy said, "Don Luis Panadero. Muy rico—rich." He pronounced it 'reech.' Rich was appealing. Rich was what Walker needed.

"I'll be there in the morning."

Spread over the valley of the Río Sangría, the hacienda justified the rumors he'd heard. Willows and cottonwoods lined the banks of the river. Corrals, barns, bunkhouses, stores, and other outbuildings were scattered across the upland to the north, where cattle and horse ranges pastured many herds. A long ridge lay on the southern plain, ending in a cliff overlooking the casa grande. Circled by a low adobe wall and half hidden in a grove of broadleaf trees, the two-story rock structure gleamed with whitewash. Roofed with dull red tiles, it was a fitting home for a wealthy man.

Walker rode forward to the wrought iron front gate. A peón armed with what looked like a Remington Creedmoor jumped up from the shaded bench where he'd been dozing. "¿Qué quieres, gringo?"

Walker flipped his lit cigarette butt against the dingy cotton shirt. "¿Dónde es su patrón, pendejo?"

The rifle came up, threatening. It was a Creedmoor. Maybe he could make it a part of the deal. He'd always wanted one.

The guard demanded, "What is your name? Say it quick."

"Tell your jefe that Señor Walker, of the gun, is here. He sent for me."

Suspicious, but lowering the rifle, the guard called to a niño playing in the dirt and ordered him to fetch Manuelo. The child ran off and in moments returned with a Mexican of a higher class, judging from the embroidery on his clean bleached linen shirt and polished boots. Probably the foreman. Men in that post took their superiority seriously. Walker stepped out of the saddle, and the guard opened the gate.

The foreman with the bloodshot eyes beckoned with one lazy gesture. "Señor, come with me."

They went up the gravel walkway and into a long, cool room, its low ceiling held up by thick vigas. Bright woven rugs, cabinets with carved doors, chests on thick-legged stands. In a corner, a grand piano.

Doors of black wood opened onto a center hall lined with oil paintings in gilt frames. Wide stairs led to the upper story. A curtain of rawhide strings studded with silver beads the size of hickory nuts hung over an arched opening. In the dining room was a banquet table, a silver service at the center. Worth stealing.

"Wait here."

Three side chairs along a wall looked as though they had never been moved and were not meant to be used. Through a half-open door, he saw a large desk piled with account books, a glass-globed lamp, silver paperweight, carved ivory letter opener, and a cigar box.

Behind him, the silver beads rattled. He swung around, surprised that he hadn't heard footsteps approach.

Don Luis Panadero. Mean-eyed. His straight black hair was thin to the scalp on top and full of gray at the temples. Paunchy stomach beneath a brocade vest. He removed a cigar from between fleshy lips and said, "Unless you are better than the last, you waste my time."

"You got a hardcase, I can handle him." In the last ten years he'd killed a dozen men, all on the run from the law. He'd never accepted a private bounty before, but on a streak of bad luck, he'd take whatever showed its head.

Don Luis moved to the next room and placed his bulk into the chair behind the big desk. He leaned back.

Waiting in the doorway, Walker hid his impatience with an effort, at last having to ask, "Well, what's the job?"

Don Luis reached for a fresh cigar, snipped off the end, lit it. He puffed a few times, blew out a stream of smoke. "Get Trouble."

"Trouble. That what you call him? He got another name?"

"Ramón Panadero Cordero. Maybe only Cordero."

The eyes didn't waver. Walker studied them. "He kin, or something? I don't want to mix in a blood feud."

"For one thousand American dollars, I think you will." From a tin cashbox, don Luis took a packet and held it out, but withdrew when he reached. "When you come back."

"Don't worry. I'll find him."

"Were you not listening? He has been found. You make him dead."

"That's how you'll get him."

Don Luis abruptly called, "Manuelo!" and when the foreman appeared, said, "Give him directions," and stood up to leave.

"Hey, wait a minute." The hacendado halted, nostrils flared in thinly-veiled arrogance. He went on, "I usually get paid half before, half after. For provisions."

The old man muttered, "Go to the devil."

The curtain hadn't stopped rattling when Manuelo spoke at his elbow, startling him afresh.

"You do not want to do this, señor. Don Ramón is his only son. He is angry now, but if you harm the boy, Madre de Dios—" Bunched fingers drew the sign of the cross over his heart.

Walker lit a cigarette. "You think when he's cooled off, he'd change his mind?"

"I know this man, and he does not intend to pay you. El Patrón is—¿cómo se dice?— How do you say, loco. Leave now, and do not come back."

Fighting confusion, Walker collected his horse from a peón. In the Mexican part of Nogales, he soon learned that don Luis Panadero did indeed want his son dead, had already paid to have the job done; but the gunny had got himself killed in Los Pobres. Some said, two men had been sent, and neither had returned for the reward.

"Los Pobres," he asked. Where is that?"

In a few days, he found the plank shack on a rocky hillside, on the north point of a pine-clad ridge overlooking a sorry huddle of thatched adobes, separated by mud or living cactus fences. One sprawling rock place looked like nobody had lived there in fifty years. Midmorning shadows played among paloverde branches through which he could see the upthrust of a mission church bell tower.

He guided his black gelding close to a stand of cholla and other chaparral which offered good cover. It also blocked the view. Leaving the horse ground-hitched, he wormed his way up the thorny slope until he could see a clearing in front of the rough board cabin. On two sides, window spaces were open. Door, too. A bank of rocks rising beyond a big mesquite was marked by the wet fan of a spring where he'd fill his canteens before starting back.

He hadn't quite made up his mind how he'd deal with that damned segundo, Manuelo, for lying to him.

The scuff of feet approached on his left, coming up the road from town. He slipped the thong on his .44.

A dark-haired young man, wearing moccasins, faded Levi's, and a shirt so old it no longer had a color. Brown eyes, half-breed skin. Girls would probably think him handsome. He carried a full market basket in each hand and wore a belt gun on his hip. When he was well into the open, Walker called, "¡Alto!"

The boy stopped.

Less than twenty, he seemed too young to be the son of that old don, and the way he stood obedient to the command made Walker add, "Yo busco un hombre, llamo, um, el llama de Trouble."

He suspected his Spanish wasn't exactly by the book when a faint smile touched the boy's lips. Then the mouth said, "Well, you have found him."

It was hard to believe this one could kill. He looked like the kind that ought to be romancing the señoritas with a guitar and flowers. The kind that got himself knifed by a jealous rival. "You know some English."

"Some."

"Learn it up near the border?"

"Yes."

"Set down the baskets."

Trouble did as he was told.

"Take off the gun."

He unbuckled the belt and offered it.

"Lay it on the ground and move back."

The boy stepped away a few paces. "Are you going to shoot me?"

His calm question rattled Walker a little, but he'd heard Mexicans were like that. When your time came, that was it. Destino, or some such shit. "Man up north wants you dead."

"I should like to talk with the padre first." He nodded toward the church.

"Well, hell, why not, if that'll make you feel better. But le's get my horse first. He hadn't had a drink since last night." This was the end of the dry season and tinajas and streams all the way down had been nothing but sand and rock.

96

Pointing with his .44, he made Trouble go ahead of him, around the thicket to where the gelding waited. Carrying the boy's gunbelt over his shoulder, he noted that the weapon inside was a silver-plated Colt with bone grips. He could hardly wait to examine the pistol, try it out for balance and accuracy.

"You don't tie him," Trouble said, seeing the horse. "He is a nice caballo, not to stray."

"Trained him. You use a rope. Let him step on it long enough to make his nose sore, and he'll learn to stay put."

Trouble started to stroke the gelding's neck.

"Don't get any ideas about my rifle." He shucked it out of its boot and motioned back the way they'd come.

After the gelding was satisfied, he unhooked his canteens. "Fill these up."

Kneeling at the rocks, Trouble said, "I have made fresh coffee. Would you like some?"

He took a dripping container and gulped some of the cold water. It reminded him of the spring back home. Years since he'd been there. "The Mex coffee I've tried is thick enough to float an iron wedge."

"Norteamericanos try to drink it without milk. That is not the way."

"I like mine black. Listen, if you want to clear your conscience, best get at it."

"This came from over your border. Arbuckle's."

"No kidding?" Hiking the rifle to a comfortable position under his arm, he used his hat to beat the Sonoran dust off his pants legs. "Guess I could stand a cup."

Scanning the dim room for other firearms, Walker saw only a bunk spread neatly with a Mexican blanket, open shelves stocked with tins and boxes, a flat-topped trunk under one window, a water stand and basin beside the other. There was a small table and two ladderbacked chairs. And something he'd never seen in a Mexican house—a two-lid cast iron stove with a warming shelf. "Where the hell did you ste— get that?"

Trouble set two cups on the table. "Chicago. Came on a train, then by mule back. I had to put it together."

"Heats the place up like an oven."

The young face hardened, but all he said was, "We can go outside," and nodded at the back door, which opened beneath a shed.

Beyond mesquite poles holding up the roof, a grove of slender walnut trees drooped in the still air. In the rope corral stood a mule, and tied out on a patch of grass at the bottom of a slope was a bay saddle horse.

The boy reached for the steaming coffee pot, but Walker said, "Let me."

"Don't trust me?"

"Oh, hell no." He poured coffee, picked up his cup, sipped. It was good. He toed out a chair and sat down, motioning for the kid to do the same. "What got the old man so mad at you?"

Trouble sipped his coffee and didn't answer.

Curiosity stirred. A Mex half-breed usually didn't carry a gun, own a horse, or wear cowboy clothes. Some knew a little English, not enough to carry on a conversation. It must come from living so near the border, being from a wealthy Spanish family. Though that tough old patrón sure had all the earmarks of being mostly Indio.

"My old man used to get riled at me," Walker said, "but he never meant it." He glanced at the boy. "You ain't answered my question."

98

Trouble stood up, rubbing his palms over his jeans in a nervous manner. "I am ready to talk to the priest."

"Suit yourself." He gulped coffee, almost burning his mouth, put on his hat, gathered his weapons. The holster over his shoulder gave him a surge of anticipation. The boy didn't own anything else worth taking, but if that horse carried the Panadero brand it might be advantageous to return it to El Patrón. The old don wasn't going to get that silver gun back any time soon.

"Listen, put together a bedroll and some tortillas. I ain't going to do it here, and it'll look better if everbody thinks we're just riding off together."

The dark eyes cut sharply toward him. Then Trouble readied a knapsack with a change of clothes and dried beef. He filled a canteen at the spring, saddled the bay horse.

From the door, the church was within calling distance at the bottom of the slope. They walked down, leading their mounts.

The cool, dark building didn't have benches, though a wooden floor was an improvement over the packed dirt of most Mexican buildings, and a row of lit candles dripped before the altar. A white-haired priest was marking his book with ribbons as they entered. The fat of a settled life bulged the folds of his brown robe. As he came toward them, his greeting sounded friendly but anxious. "Señores, que sea ustedes bienvenido. The Mass will start—"

"I came to tell you I shall be away for awhile," Trouble said. "I give you the mule as a gift. Also, there is the matter of—" He nodded at the confession box to one side.

"Ah, of course. Please come." The padre glanced over his shoulder as they walked down the aisle.

Walker looked for something handy to prop his boot on and wondered if it would be disrespectful to roll a smoke.

Crouched in the confessional, Trouble left the narrow door ajar so he could watch the bounty hunter. The man had unholstered the Mexican Colt and was turning it this way and that, hefting it for balance.

"Amigo," Padre murmured, "has this one also come at the orders of your father?"

Already two men rotted beneath the dirt. The second had found his way to the casita a few weeks earlier and fired at him while he knelt at the spring, filling a large olla. One bullet sprayed water into his face, another smashed the container, numbing his hand. He fell as if dead, and when the man approached to view his work, Trouble shot him with the Colt still holstered.

Now he was faced with killing again. "Perhaps it is God's will for my life to end this way."

"I cannot believe that. You must stop the evil."

"Panadero pays well." The gold at La Nariz would last for as long as it took to find someone to complete the job. "He has taken the Mexican Colt. I was careless." In other circumstances, they would have gone out on the slope behind the casita, set up targets, and riddled the afternoon with harmless competition.

"If we found another gun—"

"There isn't time. He talks much, but soon his patience must wear thin."

"Some of the men in town have rifles, for hunting. I will summon them."

"To be killed? No, Padre."

There was a thoughtful silence. Behind the grating he saw the old priest's pale eyes darting here and there as if searching the crannies of his brain for a solution.

"Why is he waiting?" the cura mused. "Perhaps he does not truly wish to do this deed."

"The money will make him try."

Father Navarre uttered a little groan. Then his back straightened and he leaned closer. "Do you know the place called by the godless Indios, 'El Cátedral'?"

"Sí, a couple days' ride on the road north. Everyone knows that haunted place."

"In three days, I can have men there."

"In three days, I shall be dead."

"They must overtake you. Delay him. It is a long ride back to your father's house."

Walker slid the boy's pistol into its holster and put the loop in place. Trouble came up the aisle alone, unarmed.

"Give that old man an earful?" The half-breed was too young to have many sins needing forgiveness; too handsome not to have a few. Good times with the girls. And, maybe killing that other gent who tried to collect the reward.

"Where'd you get this?" He lifted the shoulder carrying the silver gun. "I never seen one like it."

"How much is Panadero paying you?"

The blunt question caught him off guard. "Plenty. Get on your horse. We've wasted enough time."

Los Pobres dropped out of sight behind them as they rode north across the dusty plain. He chafed at an uneasy feeling he'd noticed earlier. Trouble wasn't like the other men he'd hunted down for money. Educated. Quality bloodline. Likely innocent of any wrongdoing. Under better circumstances, they might have been friends. Going to be damned hard to kill him, him now being without defense. Never should've taken his gun. Ought to have shot it out with him right there in his dooryard.

Dark was coming on and still they rode stirrup to stirrup, stopping only to drink from canteens and let the horses blow. He quit asking questions that didn't get any answer; but they kept scrabbling round and round like a chipmunk trapped inside his head. Only the promise of a thousand American dollars kept him to his task. He'd do it tomorrow.

Trouble wearied of expecting the sudden blast of a pistol, the hot thread of death cutting through his chest. He wondered if the bounty hunter would use the Mexican Colt. The man seemed fascinated with it. At least Panadero would never get his hands on the silver gun.

Knowing of a spring that would provide ample water, he earned a grudging "Gracias" from his captor. They camped there for the night and, as dark had fallen, chewed dry tortillas and pieces of jerky rather than risk a supper fire. He missed the comfort of his bed, the peace of hot coffee and an old newspaper before sleep. He wondered what Padre had done after their departure. Would there be any response to the call for a rescue party? He thought not. Needing solitude, he'd made no other friends in Los Pobres.

Listening to rustlings in the brush, creatures that came to the spring to drink, Trouble let his mind drift back to other times, other places. People he'd known, some he'd loved... Mamá, Beatriz, Manuelo. Some he might have loved... Tinita. Even Sofía.

Destino, he thought. *Maybe it is my time to die.*

And maybe not.

Chapter Six

The boy made a good trail companion, even helped gather fuel for their breakfast fire. Rode well and knew how to care for his horse. Didn't talk too much, or complain when his wrists and ankles were tied at night. Didn't try to sneak a weapon in the darkness, or beg to be let go. Walker cinched up his saddle with a growing sense of frustration.

They left the shelter of a clump of paloverde, picked as a camp spot because the limbs scattered the smoke of the fire, and rode for half an hour. The farther north they went, the less he felt like closing this deal. The boy's bay carried the Panadero brand, so maybe it would be enough. He could claim he lost the body down some ravine.

Hell. The old man would never believe that.

Out of habit, Walker turned his head to check their backtrail and saw riders following. Twenty, give or take a couple, bunched in a desert-wise lope that spared horses and raised little dust. "Friends of yours?"

Trouble glanced at them without joy. "Whoever they are, I do not want them killed."

Grabbing the bay's rein, wheeling westward, he set out for the only cover within a mile. He'd noticed it on the way south, recognized the place everybody called 'Cathedral Rocks.' El Catedral del Diablo.

Reaching the giant sandstone fortress, he found corners chisled by the wind and unexpected passageways inside. Promising cover, vantage points.

The riders followed. Little doubt now that he and his bounty were their quarry. If they were smart, they'd stop beyond range of a saddlegun. They wore gray shirts and trousers, and the red saddle blankets were the kind used by Mexican rural police. "Take a look," he said. "They look like Rurales to you?"

"They might want our horses."

He didn't want to be left on foot. "Get down and take the horses in with you." He prodded Trouble and their mounts upslope to a point where openings like windows overlooked the plain. He took a position at one of them and watched the riders mill around as if undecided about what to do next. The men dismounted and scattered to shelter from the sun under thin-branched mesquites. They squatted in little groups and smoked, occasionally laughing. He counted nineteen.

"Any reason they'd be after you?"

"¿Quién sabe?" the boy shrugged. "Maybe Panadero is also paying them."

Well, the old man probably had the capital to do that. Minutes before, Walker had been almost ready to let this one go free. A posse complicated things. If he sent Trouble out to them, he'd get no reward. If armed to help fight them off, likely the brat would turn the gun on him.

Walker's sweat ran in streams, wetting his shirt. And the day was young. It could only get hotter. "They won't collect a damn peso without a fight."

"They will keep out of range."

"I'll get 'em tonight when they come to steal the horses."

He tied his prisoner's ankles, then shucked his rifle and stuck the boy's gun into the front of his waistband. The bay and Blackie were getting snaky, but he didn't dare loosen cinches or remove bits, so he separated them. Had to be ready to move fast if those hombres tried to attack.

There was plenty of ammunition for defense, so long as he stayed awake; but nineteen men taking turns could outlast him. And they had nothing to stop them from easing their thirst at the nearest spring. Gathering the firearms in case Trouble got snaky, too, he went to look for a back door. Maybe a tinaja. Any water would be welcome by afternoon.

El Catedral was honeycombed by wind and rain into odd-shaped rooms with uneven footing, winding paths, and overhangs like ceilings that provided some shade with bits of sky showing through. No water. And no way out but the one they'd come in. "Damn it all," he said softly. "I've done it now."

Returning to where he'd left Trouble, he uncorked his canteen and took a drink. "Here," he said, tossing the other one to the boy. "Best go easy on it." Then he hunkered down with his back against the wall and fanned himself with his hat. He'd been in a few tight spots before, but none had ever given him such a feeling of doom.

The sun finally moved to the other side of the rocks. The heat stayed. From time to time he checked and found the bandits or Rurales, or whatever the hell they were, still there.

When the sky turned an evening blue and the air cooled, he opened their food sack and they suppered on strips of jerky and a couple of flour tortillas. The dry, salty taste remained on his tongue while he fed the horses, but he decided to save the rest of the water.

Down on the plain, campfires and the sweet brown smell of roasting meat mingled with reedy tenor voices raised in one of the songs popular on the ranchos. Sounded like a fiesta getting underway. Next thing you know, they'd be setting off fireworks.

Unpacking blankets, he said, "Guess we'll camp here."

Far into the night the spurts of song and laughter kept him awake, and toward dawn coyotes yammered far out across the hills, echoing and lonesome.

In the gray light, he woke groggy, surprised he'd slept, and saw that the boy's eyes were open. His own eyes felt grainy, and his back hurt from leaning against the rock.

Stiffly, using the rifle to balance, he stood up. Coffee aroma drifted to his nostrils. If he wasn't sure he'd get his head shot off, he'd go ask those greasers for a cup. "Does it ever rain here?"

Trouble smiled. "In a few weeks, it will rain torrents, and wash everything away."

"Wish I was back in Tennessee. This is the damnedest poor excuse for a country. Don't know why I ever came west, anyway."

"How long, since you left home?"

He pondered. "Must be twenty years. Up in Dakota. It's a hard country, too. Winters are bad. Summers are—"

"¡Señor!"

At the shout, their eyes met. He couldn't tell what the boy was thinking.

"¡Señor! We deal. ¿Bueno?"

He edged to the opening and peered over. One man, just a couple of wagon lengths beyond the entrance. A large-bodied Mex with a thick mustache, and a bandolier across his chest. The fires were out and the men stood beside their mounts. Everybody looked ready to leave.

"I'm listening," he called down.

The heavily-accented words came with spaces between them as the man strained to talk English. "You give...us boy...we go."

"And if I don't?"

"We...wait." A pause. "Señor...you have...water?"

Walker chipped off bits of rock with his boot toe. The fat capitán held all the cards. "Hell," he said, and untied Trouble's ankles. "Go on!" He made a threatening motion with the rifle. "Go rot in some Mex jail." Men caught by Rurales rotted, but not always in jail.

Wiping nervous palms on his jeans, wrists still tied, the boy disappeared down the winding path. And with him went the thousand-dollar reward.

Trouble saw their leader, whom he did not know, waiting in the shade at the base of the rocks, and bit down hard to keep from shouting, Get out of range! But, low enough that only the man from Los Pobres could hear, what he said was, "He has a saddle gun that can kill us both from up there, and he might be desperate enough to shoot."

Sweat already stained the man's armpits and fresh fear widened his dark eyes. But he nodded to a jumble of rocks at the base of the sandstone spire. "Padre said if we leave a gun for you, you would know what to do with it. Francisco put a pistol there in the night."

"Then you have done enough. The man with the rifle believes you are Rurales. Let us try to walk out of range before he decides you're not."

They started toward the little company of riders, who looked like decent family men, farmers. Trouble felt caught in a new nightmare. The men with their horses seemed to retreat before him in the shimmering distance. He glanced back at the rock window, where the bounty hunter stood, watching.

Walker leaned his elbows on the rock ledge, rifle cradled. He'd never let anybody just walk up and take his man before. It galled him to let this bunch beat him out of that reward. But if the boy had to die, just as well let them do it here, now. "Hey!" he yelled, and everybody stiffened, like a bird dog catching the scent of quail. "What you going to do with him?"

The big man made a wide gesture, palms upturned. "Some we hang. Some we shoot."

"Let me make things easy for you." He fired a couple of rounds into the dirt near the capitán's feet. The Mex leaped into the air and started to run, but two more rounds just in front stopped him. "Now. Line up your men and le's have a little show."

There was a brief exchange between the capitán and Trouble. "What do you mean, show?" the boy yelled.

"I heard Rurales like to use firing squads to get rid of prisoners. Anybody got a blindfold?"

Another brief conference. He supposed the capitán didn't understand the word 'blindfold' and tried to think what the Mex might call it. He made a motion like tying something over his eyes. "Bandana! Bandera!"

When it looked like there was going to be more discussion, this time involving the distant men with the horses, he fired a round near the capitán's foot. "Hurry up!" Then he added, "Pronto! Pronto!" and reloaded his rifle.

Someone trotted forward, bringing a black bandana, and trotted back. In no hurry, the capitán twirled it by the corners and tied it over Trouble's eyes. He said something to the boy, smiled, then stepped aside and shouted orders to his men. Jumping as if surprised, several of them drew rifles from scabbards and formed a ragged line.

The boy stood facing them, chin high and shoulders straight. A sudden gust of wind ruffled his hair, fluttered the tails of the bandana.

The capitán fumbled in his pocket and finally came out with a white handkerchief, which he held over his head like a little truce flag. He yelled out something else, and half a dozen men clacked shells into their weapons. Walker's belly muscles tightened. Here and there a hand flexed to a better grip, a cheek sought greater comfort. There was a long pause. "Get it over with, you sons-of-bitches."

The arm with the banner swept downward as the big man's voice rasped out the order. Rifle fire crashed against the rock walls and echoed over the plain.

Trouble's body slammed backward, twisting slightly as it fell.

Calling for someone to help, the fat capitán started to pick up his bounty. Walker drove him off with a spray of bullets. Expecting a return volley, he ducked behind the column of rock and swore softly.

"I got more where that come from. Clear out. You're finished here." If they didn't understand the lingo, they sure as hell would understand his intention.

From what he'd heard of Rurales, most were bandits, thieves, or murderers, and he didn't mind taking out a few; though what made him bait them like that, he didn't know. If they wanted to tree him, nothing was stopping them, and if they took it into their heads to rush him, likely he wouldn't get them all before one got lucky.

He chanced a peek out, saw the boy where he'd fallen, curved away, head resting on upflung arms almost as if he slept. The capitán and several of his men seemed deep in some disagreement. Three or four spotted him at the window and raised their rifles but nobody seemed willing to risk coming close enough to be hit. So long as they kept out of range, neither could they hit him. He rested his ass on the ledge and rolled a smoke. Another lengthy argument, which he couldn't hear.

The ragtag Rurales began mounting up. Suspicious, he watched them slowly ride away southward, occasionally looking back.

When he was certain they were gone, he skidded down the path to the rough-hewn doorway, and stopped. Glee faded. "Poor kid." If that bunch hadn't showed up, he might've gone through with turning the boy loose. Taken the bay horse to the old don and lied like a trooper to collect that thousand. He could still do that. First, though, the least he could do was throw some rocks over the body.

Hunkering to untie the bandana knot, he felt a sudden queasiness in the pit of his stomach and sat back on his heels. Something about the body bothered him. Something, on the rim of his consciousness——

No blood.

"What the devil!" He ripped off the blindfold and both leaped to their feet, facing each other, fists ready to strike. The ropes hung loosely from the boy's wrists.

Trouble rubbed his palms over his chest. "My santito must have kept the bullets from harming me."

"Santito, hell. Them bastards just can't shoot. And no wonder. Their guns must be a hundred years old." He turned to where their mounts waited. "You stay put while I get the horses."

Leading them back, thinking about finding water soon, he was surprised to see that the boy had moved. Not only moved, but held a gun down by his side. From his lips came a warning: "Hombre, throw out your weapons."

Walker's hand snapped down to his pistol, fumbled at the holster thong. Should have left it unfastened, but he'd heard of a gent who got shot by his own gun doing a fool thing like that.

Another shout, "Amigo, do not shoot!" as he switched his draw for the silver gun he'd tucked under his belt. Not there. Where the hell was it?

He couldn't see for the black haze in front of his eyes. Church bells filled his ears. Blinking hard, shaking his head, shivering, he thought: *Sun's getting to me.*

Through the haze, Trouble's shadow came closer like a dark, wet blotch moving across the sand. The crunch of boot heels stopped and the boy knelt, and Walker realized he, too, was on his knees. *God, I'm hit.* With an effort he raised his head. The haze was lifting, because he could see a drop of sweat beginning to trickle past Trouble's eyebrow.

Earnest words sounded muffled through the ringing. "I tried to warn you. You must have heard me."

He remembered those moments lost in reaching for his own gun, then not finding the Colt. He moistened his lips, wanting to ask about it, but he couldn't speak. His eyes wouldn't stay open. Fingers gripped his shoulder so hard they pinched.

"Here. This will help a little."

The rim of a canteen worked its shape between his lips, and warm water flooded his mouth and ran into his beard. He swallowed. "Where'd you—get—it?"

"You had some left, remember? Let's go over by the rocks, in the shade."

Not water, he wanted to say. *The gun. How'd you get the silver gun? I had it in my waistband.*

He felt himself being lifted to his feet, felt his knees buckle. Swaying, he grasped the boy's arm and was surprised by the firm, wiry muscle. He watched the legs of his jeans, full of dust and sweat, and his worn boots, stumbling as though they were not a part of him. The wet shirt front was cold where it clung to his skin.

Then he saw the blood. Not a lot. Against the white cloth, the splotches were bright, alive, though the edges had already darkened and looked like rust.

"We're here."

The ground came up at him too fast. Dizzy, he clung to the arm as a strong hand supported his head, strong fingers eased him onto his back, and the world steadied. Far above, the dome of blue sky. Sky, white clouds. Maybe it did rain here sometimes.

Not today. Those weren't rain clouds. Droplets on his face would feel good, cool, like when he was a kid in the summertime. He could almost smell the damp dust of the road in front of his house.

Trouble was leaning down, looking concerned. "Do you wish me to send a message to someone?"

He shook his head. His family wouldn't care.

After another couple gulps of water, he managed, "You never did—tell me—" Drawing breath was difficult. "why Panadero—" Coughing hurt his chest. He struggled to sit up, and Trouble helped him lean against the rock.

"He murdered my mother, and fears my revenge."

"I've been—shot before," he said. The soaked shirt sticking to his back meant the slug had gone through. "Did you get—the blood—stopped?"

Then he remembered the boy had no reason to try. As soon as he felt like riding, he'd best head for Magdalena. Closer than Nogales. Even a Mex town would have a doc of some kind. Somebody to sew up the holes, give him a draught for the pain that now filled his ribcage.

"Lo siento mucho," the boy was saying. "Believe me, I meant only to stop you, but the damned gun pulled too far."

The genuine regret scared him. He wasn't going to make it. Even if they could stop the blood flow, this was where he'd cash in. In the shadow of Cathedral del Diablo, under a too-blue sky.

He plucked at Trouble's sleeve. "Where is...your gun? I lost it." That sweet silver pistola didn't pull, he'd bet his life on that.

"It fell beside you, when you were hit."

His eyelids drifted shut, but the sound of unloading brought a smile. Cautious devil. *Don't trust me, even flat on my back.* A few more days—hours, really—without that posse interfering, and they could have been amigos. *I was going to let you go free. Honest.*

Then Trouble was fitting his numb fingers around the familiar shape. A bit larger, a bit heavier than the company Colt's he'd seen. No engraving. A mysterious, silver gun, carefully made by a master silversmith. "Bet it shoots true. Not like. . . that damn relic . . . they brought. You wouldn't've . . . killed me with this. "

Sips of water, blood-warm from a canteen, quieting words, scant shade. Not much to offer someone you'd killed. Trouble knelt and put a folded blanket beneath the man's head. "Forgive me."

The bounty hunter almost smiled. "I—don't blame—you."

Blame Luis Panadero, and his tempting offer of gold. "What else can I do?"

Fever-bright eyes sought the distant jagged mountains. The bounty hunter coughed shallowly and didn't answer. Some minutes later, he took a deep breath and said, "I'm called—Walker." After another pause, he added, "Don't put me up no—marker, though. That's not my name."

Sun shadows crawled to the east, sprawling across the plain like purple ghosts, and overhead the sky softened with streamers of wind-blown clouds. The black gelding had disappeared, but Bay dozed in the shade of the rocks. Harsh breathing and low moans, born of pain and fever, grew quieter, then ceased. In the stillness, Trouble heard his own heart beating, the rustle of wings as a wren flew into an upper crevice in the sandstone. Nestlings twittered excitedly, being fed. Then the bird flew away.

A small sound at his back made him turn. Walker's arm had relaxed, and in the dust beside him, his fingers loose around the bone handle, lay the Colt.

The bounty hunter's head rested at an angle, eyes half closed. There was no pulse. Grateful that it was over so quickly, Trouble murmured, "Gracias a Dios." He wished he might have shaved the stubble of beard, but carried no razor in his pack. In the man's pockets he found a folding knife and twenty pesos. Panadero didn't pay traveling money.

Silence…except for the wind moaning around the spires of El Catedral. Even in the shade, sun-baked air found him as he loosened tumbled rocks to make a shallow grave. He stripped the bloody shirt from the body and exchanged it for his. A little small in the shoulders, a little short in the arms, but Walker was past caring. When the rocks were mounded, he stood back, dusting his bruised palms and roughened fingertips, looking for chinks a coyote might investigate. Sweat trickled down his face; he wiped it with his sleeve. He said a short prayer. And left no marker.

Satisfied that he had done all he could, he bent to pick up their weapons. Wearing the bounty hunter's hat—he'd lost his in the race to the spires—he put himself into the saddle and began tracking the black gelding northward across the plain. There was a spring not far from here, he knew from the last time he came this way, fleeing La Nariz.

About sundown he saw the trees. Moistening his lips in anticipation of a clear, cold drink, he spent long minutes sitting and watching the brush-covered hills and gullies. Bronco Apaches sometimes escaped norteamericano jails, crossed the Río Bravo, and raided deep into Sonora. A few still lived in the wilder parts of the Sierra Madre.

Movement in the chaparral tensed his stomach, before he glimpsed a black mane twitching away an insect. He rode through the brittle brush and into the grassy clearing.

Dismounting, he drank, filled the four canteens, then watered the bay. He unsaddled and picketed his stock, making friends with the gelding with soft talk and caresses. "Just like a woman," he joked. Not for the first time, he thought of Tinita. Would she still be angry that he'd left her unsatisfied? Though months had passed, he hadn't forgotten her hot kisses, the silky skin of her breasts. If he kept traveling northeast, he could be there in a few days.

He noticed the worn places on the stock where Walker's hands had grasped his rifle. Going through the man's mochila, he found a battered coffee pot with half a bag of Arbuckle's stuck down in it, a small pan, a half kilo of jerky and a box of hardtack, and a kilo of corn for the horse. One saddlebag contained a couple of dirty shirts and a pair of jeans, two pairs of socks with holes in the heels, and a razor.

The other yielded an extra bandana, about a hundred rounds of .44 ammunition for the walnut-handled gun, and a black leatherbound book. Faded letters read *Holy Bible.* He stared at it a long moment before picking up the last item, a small leather account book. Pages were filled with what he took to be the bounty hunter's writing. He put it in his pocket to examine later.

Traces of old campfires spurred hunger, and he would have liked making some of the coffee; but, with the evening, a breeze had sprung up and he wouldn't risk the smoke and fragrance of a fire. A freshening breeze meant rain later tonight, so he spread his bedroll beneath an overhang and stretched upon it, weapons within reach. Chewing on a strip of jerky, he pondered what he must do.

Going back to Los Pobres would solve nothing.

Going to Hacienda de Panadero meant seeing people he knew, people who knew him. Some of them would try to kill him, for a reward. He missed his sweetheart, Beatriz, and would have liked bringing her to his casita; but she probably was with Enrique or Chuco now. None of the others, and no woman in Los Pobres, had set his blood to racing the way Tinita did.

Jumping up from the blanket so abruptly that he startled the black horse, he rummaged in his knapsack for matches. The notebook, which fit in the palm of his hand, was filled with names, descriptions, villages, the best routes to those villages. There were figures, prices, ranging from a hundred pesos to five hundred dollars. In the flickering light, he read the final listing: 'Panadero.' Is that who Walker thought he was? Or did the bounty hunter record the name of his employer? One thousand dollars, United States currency, and the only one not marked 'paid.'

Rain drops began whispering in the grass. He put out the light and lay back on one elbow, fingers slipping gently around the silver Colt. He drifted into a doze.

...Tinita smiled, beckoning. Her amber eyes and tousled hair lured him on, the low-necked blouse slipped off her silken shoulder, he caught her to him...

Tremors of thunder made the horses stamp and snort uneasily. He shook off the half-dream and covered his head with his sarape. Names in the notebook shimmered behind his eyelids, 'Panadero' gleaming in the dark like roman candles at a fiesta.

When dawn came, he readied his stock for the trip. Not Los Pobres, where men would find him. Not Casa de Panadero—that would come later.

It had to be La Nariz. He must see again the pitiful, unhallowed grave, feel again the killing rage. Then he could face Panadero with murder in his heart.

II

Luis sat in his cool bedroom, smoking a cigar and gazing out the window at the walled patio beyond. Walker was due in days ago. Still, he had not given up hope. The man had gained a reputation of being efficient, effective.

When he was certain that Trouble was dead, he could go to La Nariz and recover the entire fortune. Campbell had delivered five blooded mares and was becoming a nuisance, demanding payment. Once the gringo had the money, he'd be ready to deal again, this time, a magnificent caballo padre. El Rey was getting old.

There was a secret place down on the Sangría where Luis meant to stash the gold, permitting him to dip into the sacks whenever he wished, fearless of discovery. It was a fortune, and worth all he had done to make it his.

In the matter of travel, an ocean voyage appealed most, for it would allow him to be seen in ports all over the world, and gain recognition as the wealthy hacendado from Sonora. Manuelo, with all his faults, nevertheless was capable of taking charge of the workers for a few months.

Luis stubbed out the cigarro on the window ledge. To his right was the door connecting his room with that of Sofía. He listened a few moments, but apparently she was in another part of the house. He went into the corredor. "¡Sofía!"

When she failed to answer, he called again with more force. "¡Sofía! ¡Venga acá!"

The slip-slop tread of sandals came from the direction of the cocina, where she spent her time gossiping with La Vieja and drinking teas or sampling empanaditas. She peeked around the doorpost, forehead puckered. Her timid "¿Sí, Luis?" irritated him. He had never been rough with her, and the way she dodged him was insulting.

"Find Manuelo. Have him send a couple of riders out the south road to meet someone. I'm expecting a man called Walker."

Sofía retreated to the main hallway. She never knew when don Luis was going to lash out, with words or fists. Yesterday he fired a pistol into the hanging flowerpots, and she'd had to clean up the mess, since he'd sent the house servants back to their village last week, leaving only herself, La Vieja, Manuelo, and the lavandera. Such an action made no sense to her, but she had stopped trying to make sense of the things the old man did.

On a hot afternoon like this, she was sure Manuelo would be down at the horse barns, taking a siesta. When she rattled the heavy door back on its metal rollers, he sat up, a bent wisp of straw sticking through a black curl. "Hola," he said, smiling and reaching for her hand.

She gave it to him, but resisted when he tried to pull her down beside him. "Don Luis wants two riders sent out to look for a man named Walker."

Manuelo beckoned with his eyes. "Señor Walker is in no hurry to be found."

When she hesitated, then shook her head, he turned over in the straw and pretended to sleep. After another moment, vexed with indecision, she went out and closed the door. She had not allowed Manuelo any liberties yet, but occasionally considered doing so. Something about him attracted her strongly, and he avowed that he loved her. Sometimes she half believed him.

She was recrossing the wagon yard when she caught sight of a solitary horseman approaching from the south. Should she inform don Luis of his arrival, or run back and tell Manuelo there was no need to disturb the scouts? As the guard at the gate let the man enter, she hurried for the shelter of the back patio; but he saw her and spurred his horse across the grass. Don Luis would not like the damage to the lawn.

"Buenos días," the rider greeted, reining in. "¿Dónde está el señor de la casa, don Luis Panadero?"

This was no gringo named Walker, but a Mexican taller than Manuelo and ten years younger, with a trimmed mustache and sparkling eyes. She resented the bold way he looked at her. "I shall tell Luis that you are here," she said, trying to go around him.

Jumping lightly from his horse, he came close, grinning. "Tell him I'm here for his reward."

"Reward? You are mistaken—"

"Señorita, it is you who is mistaken. Indeed, there is a reward, and I, Felipe García, have earned it."

"You lie!"

She whirled, startled by don Luis's harsh voice and his sudden appearance on the patio. He came down the two low steps, saying, "Leave us."

Glad to do so, she fled, but stopped beyond a dense hedge where she could watch and listen.

"I assure you, señor, I am entitled to your money. The man you hired is dead, and so is your Trouble."

Sofía's heart thudded painfully, seemed to stop, thudded hard again.

Luis was firm. "Show me proof."

The stranger tilted his sombrero and gave the old man a cool appraisal. He drew a small object from the inside pocket of his vest. Taking it, don Luis looked at the object for a long while. Then he said, "Bueno. Come with me."

Faint, ears ringing with shock, Sofía stumbled down the hall to the sanctuary of her room. In a house where in the day time, doors were left open according to custom, she hesitated even now to close either the one leading to the hall, or the one connecting her cubbyhole to the bedroom of El Patrón.

But tears were overflowing, so she shut herself up in the bleak little room and tried to cry away her grief without making any noise.

In the sala, Felipe García continued, "Your man was shot in the gut. This hombre called Trouble is very quick with a gun. Fortunately, I am better."

Luis took his cashbox and began counting out pesos equaling one thousand American dollars. Then he stopped counting and glanced up sharply. "Who told you about the reward?"

"Every professional in Sonora knows of your desire to have him out of the way."

He handed García the money.

The man's bright eyes held a question.

"It is all there."

"No drink, to celebrate? It was a long ride—"

"Buy your own drink."

When García had gone, he sat down heavily in his chair and gave a long sigh. "Finalmente."

Riders had assembled in the yard and were leaving as García mounted and rode away. He cast a half-curious glance at them before loping his tired horse toward Nogales and the nearest cantina. Damn the old man. Stingy with his liquor. At least, that silver Cristo had persuaded don Luis to pay up. He'd thought it would, broken from its chain, exactly as if someone had jerked it from the neck of a dead man. Overhearing the hired killer asking questions was luck; using his wits to follow and wait was skill. Joining the rescue party was inspired. Going back to search the dead boy's deserted casita was genius. García laughed aloud, the sound making his horse shy. He dug in his spurs and they leaped forward.

Sofía lay on her bed, her feverish face muffled in the soft linen of Ramón's shirt. Her chest ached with the need to wail, and her head throbbed with the need for a stiff drink. She should have gone instead to Manuelo's old hut. Whenever she needed to escape for a few hours, the room by the river was heavensent, and so far there had been no objection to her using it. But even that was not sufficient. She must leave this place. Tonight. As soon as—

"¡Sofía!"

Leaping up, holding her breath, she listened. As don Luis's footsteps neared her door, she stuffed the garment beneath her pillow. She could not risk having her only link to Ramón taken from her now. Hastily she wiped her face and blew her nose on her soaked handkerchief, and was still trembling when El Patrón flung back the door and demanded, "What are you doing, lurking here in the dark? I was calling you."

He took her arm above the elbow and guided her into the hall.

A snuffle escaped her, and he peered around the curtain of hair that had come loose from its pins. "What is wrong? Are you ill?"

"No, I— My head hurts. I think I shall go to the abandoned casita and rest."

"Rest after you have done this errand."

"Errand?"

"Sí. Bring everyone back. The criadas must give the house a cleaning. It's unfit for pigs." His palm sent a cloud of dust from a cushioned bench. He gave an unnatural smile and playfully pinched her cheek. "I have a surprise for you. A fiesta grande. What do you say to that?"

He could not have shocked her more if he had taken one of the crossed swords from the wall and run it through her.

"Wait," he said, and she did, but through the door he left ajar, she watched him take down a gilt-framed painting, behind which was a metal door. A safe, like one she had once seen in the Nogales bank, only much smaller.

In moments he was back, saying, "Here's money. Food, fireworks, a band—three bands! And dancers. Have dresses made for a dozen of the prettiest girls who can sing and dance for entertainments. Have Manuelo use the account books to make up a guest list of the wealthiest and most influential ranchers, and send word to those chosen, to be ready. We'll begin the day after I return, and celebrate until all are ill with rich food and wine, and deaf from music and fireworks."

She cupped her hands to receive the coins. "Where are you going?"

"Don't concern yourself."

Catching sight of Manuelo crossing the yard, he left her standing bewildered and wounded.

Choosing three of his strongest horses, Luis told the segundo, "I'm going to be away for a few weeks, perhaps for as much as a month."

Manuelo appeared surprised. "A journey? It is not fit season. Perhaps you ought to wait until after the rains."

"No. I have decided. See to my gear and rations."

"Patrón, I shall choose a courier, or go myself."

"You'll attend to the accounts and keep these lazy pelados from stealing or shirking." He felt in a pocket to be sure cigarros were there. "Consult with Sofía about what is to be done in my absence."

"Muy bien, don Luis."

In his room to pack a valise, Luis searched his bureau drawers but found them empty of items he would need. He muttered a curse at the delay. His blood was fired with the knowledge that at last Trouble could no longer harm him, and he looked forward to displaying his wealth, attracting quality women. Young, hot-blooded mestizas whom he could bed without misgiving. He went into the central hallway and called, "¡Sofía!"

She came out of her room, face pale and blotched as if she had been crying. He was tired of her moods, and dallied with a half-formed decision to send her back to her own tierra. "Why are there no socks nor handkerchiefs?"

"The lavandera has them drying. I shall fetch some." She hesitated. "Manuelo says you intend to make this trip alone. What if you should fall ill——"

A shudder shook ash from his cigar. "¡Imbécil! One does not speak of such things."

"But, at your age——"

His flat-handed shove knocked her forehead against the doorpost. "I don't need you any more."

He planned to purchase mules at a settlement along the way, where he was not known. This time, he would leave nothing at La Nariz except what belonged there, lying half forgotten under a few inches of dirt. His hand slipped into his pocket, encountered the Cristo which García had given him as proof. He'd leave it, too. He had no use for it.

Chapter Seven

Don Luis rode out of the yard and through the ornate iron gate, sitting his palomino like a conquistador, with two fine bays a lead.

Sofía groaned in relief, lying in the patio hammock with a cool cloth held to her forehead. He was too old to start out like this, carrying only saddlebags and a satchel on the pommel. All his assurances that he would provision himself along the way did nothing to calm her forebodings.

With no Patrón, what would become of the place? Of her? "Ah, Dios, I wish I had never come here."

Manuelo sat nearby in a cowhide-seat chair, brooding. She wondered whether he merely waited to discuss the preparations for the fiesta, or meant to press her further to sleep with him.

She touched careful fingers to her forehead. The lump was shrinking, though her lavender-soaked handkerchief failed to relieve a different pain. Images of Ramón stalked every room in the casa grande which she had once loved, unfulfilled desires tormented her at every turn. Words burst forth, "You were Ramón's close friend. How can you go on living here, when you know don Luis paid to have him killed?"

Manuelo's body didn't flinch, not even his eyes. Only his lips moved. "Leaving will not bring the boy back."

Fresh tears spilled over and ran down her cheeks. She turned away to keep him from noticing, but he reached to take her hand. Some vital force seemed to flow from him into her. He didn't excite her in the same way as Ramón, nor frighten her as did don Luis with his appetites; yet beneath a silent, sleekly moving form, like the glowing eyes behind a Pascola dancer's mask, lay powerful secret knowledge which kept her from entirely trusting his outward kindness.

She set about deciding what needed to be done. Strong, willing workers, to clean the house. Girls who could sing and knew dances. Dresses. Food. Flowers and decorations. Lanterns to hang in the trees. A band, for the music. The guest list. Business ties extended across the border to Bisbee, Tombstone, and Tucson, as well as points all over

Sonora. Most were family men, highly regarded, and their wives would accompany them.

Manuelo broke into her thoughts. "Shall I tell you the names of the girls I think you should select? Why don't we go now and settle that matter?"

"You don't need to bother," she said, rising. His hand continued to clasp hers.

His teeth gleamed in a smile. "Are you afraid if I go to the village I might find a reason to stay?"

"That is your right." She avoided his attempt to chuck her under the chin. His teasing made her uncertain. So far he had been patient, even considerate. However, the men she had known could be sweet one second and violent the next, if things did not go to suit them. All except Ramón.

She started moving away, but Manuelo stepped in front of her. He took her arms above the elbow and kissed her cheek lingeringly. He had aimed for her mouth, but she dodged, warning, "Someone might see us and report to don Luis when he gets back."

"There is only La Vieja, and you know she will say nothing. Berta is with the other women, washing clothes in the stream." He took her hand again, fondled it. "Sofía—"

"Let us go," she said gently. "Much is to be done."

In the village, señoras sat in their dooryards, grinding corn on their metates. The men and older boys were scattered about the hacienda, tending crops and cattle. Wranglers and caballeros worked in corrals with new stock. Children and half-grown girls ran out from houses as soon as word spread that she and Manuelo were in town. They stopped in the plaza and people gathered round them.

"El Patrón has gone on a trip," she announced. "And wishes the casa to be cleaned."

Immediately voices cried out, eager to be chosen. She knew that even the prospect of beating carpets and draperies with wire whips was appealing, so long as they could freely examine everything in the house without fear of meeting El Patrón around some corner. Most had never set foot across the river, and until this moment only dreamed of doing so. Reports from those who had filled posts there in other years had sharpened expectations.

Manuelo called out names and, in minutes, a dozen young girls trooped across the footbridge, chattering their pleasure and disbelief, leaving behind younger or older sisters, and friends who were, regrettably, not so fortunate, lacking beauty or talent or both.

"Show us everything," the chosen ones urged, and would not be satisfied until she led them in exploring from pantry to cellar. Ending the tour on the back patio, she realized, somewhere along the way Manuelo had deserted. Inhaling, she blurted, "The reason you are needed is that El Patrón wants a fiesta, and—"

Cheers of "¡Viva!" and "¡Bueno!" and "¡Maravilloso!" Girls hugged each other, exclaiming and jumping around like children. Fiestas were common in the village, but for El Patrón to sponsor such an event was astounding. They would be telling grandchildren about it, years hence, they assured each other.

As soon as she could be heard, Sofía continued, "La Vieja is in charge of the food. Josefa and Lencha shall assist her." Others would accompany her and the mozos into Nogales to purchase dress materials not to be had in the storehouses. Still others were skilled in making decorations, lanterns. One by one, tasks found hands to execute them.

Then Rosa said, "Must we go home at night? I would give anything to sleep in so fine a house. Sofía, dear little friend, please say we may!"

That sparked a clamor which brought Manuelo to her rescue. "¿Cómo no? That is what rooms are for."

Some fiestas lasted only a few days, others as long as a week or more, depending on the occasion and resources of the one paying. She had no idea exactly what don Luis had in mind, except to be ready as soon as he returned. She was not even sure which of his associates she was supposed to invite, much less the length of their stay. A pounding behind her left eye sent her to bed, while a dozen señoritas moved into the servants' quarters, bringing meager clothing, personal belongings, and excited chatter that penetrated her closed door.

Supper was late, timed to their custom rather than the one to which she had grown accustomed; the second night she put La Vieja back on schedule, amusing the girls by having the last meal of the day at six o'clock. Her fitful sleep was further disturbed as they roamed the halls with lamps, giggling and complaining of hunger.

Her grief over Ramón was still sharp, dreams ravaged the sleep of exhaustion, and having people in the house again set her nerves on edge. When she snapped at someone for ripping a lace curtain, Manuelo overheard and took her aside like a misbehaving child. But there was no rebuke, only concern. "What is distressing you, querida?"

Dependent on him, she didn't dare admit that, though the boy was dead, her feelings were not. "The lavender does not seem to be helping my head."

He glanced up and down the hallway. Then he guided her into his room and closed the door.

II

The closer Trouble came to La Nariz, the more he dreaded reopening old wounds. Maybe he should just take a couple sacks and disappear off the face of the earth. The best trackers would never find him in the City of México, or Chihuahua, or Durango.

Something led him on. Merely a refusal to run any more? A curiosity about whether El Patrón had visited the cave? Did the old man realize how difficult such a trip would be, for a man his age? Wait too long, and the treasure would remain in its secret place forever. Or, a deeper, baser motive. He supposed that he would never rest until his mother's murder was avenged.

Riding back through the wild Sierra Madre, he began traveling in the early mornings and the cool hours before nightfall. Days passed without the heavy rains that would give relief from afternoons on the llano, where summer burned the countryside like a fever.

Mateo's place lay on this route.

His sweaty palms darkened the leather of the reins. He was unsure whether to stop, though he needed supplies. If he went on to La Nariz and then to Hacienda de Panadero, he might never taste the delights Tinita offered. He knew she had lovers, and despite his fear of sangre de mal, desire struggled against caution. If he fell victim to the disease, and wasn't killed by some hired gunman, Manuelo's herbs surely had the power to cleanse.

When he came to the fork in the trail, he hesitated several moments, and then took the broader track toward Mateo's cantina. It had been a long time since he'd lain with a woman.

From a nearby hill, he saw that two horses were tied to a post at one corner of the building. He hadn't counted on other guests, and was in no mood to make his presence known to strangers. He found a place in the brush where he could remain hidden until they left.

Waiting was tedious. Pebbles seemed to eat through the seat of his jeans and into his flesh. Leaning on one elbow, he broke off a harmless twig and idly chewed it. Once this business with El Patrón was finished, he could consider a commitment. He might even marry her. Padre had frequently cautioned him against any sinful union. He smiled to imagine what the old cura would think of Tinita if he took her back to Los Pobres.

One thing was certain: once he chose someone to share his life, he meant to be faithful. His sons and daughters would never be denied the love of their father.

Half an hour before dark, voices roused him and he leaned forward to see two men not much older than himself tightening cinches, making ready to leave. In moments they had ridden away toward the west.

Trembling from uncertainty and a little sick from days of going without proper food, he untied his horses and went toward the cantina, aware of dirt and sweat and a growth of beard. This time, he would let her wash his back.

Before he reached the house, she came out, carrying an empty olla. "¡Ramón!" she cried, and dropped it with a crash. But she didn't run to meet him. He drifted to a halt, and the thirsty horses, remembering the trough in the corral, tugged at the reins.

Outwardly, she had changed little. Her curly hair was caught back and tied with a ribbon, and she wore a faded brown skirt and white blouse. He noted that this neckline would not be so easy for exploring fingers to enter as last time. Coming close, eyes wide, she murmured, "Santa Madre, what has happened to you?"

"What do you mean?" he asked sharply.

She reached out and touched the front of his shirt. Walker's shirt, which he had forgotten he was wearing. "Is it blood? Are you hurt?"

"Blood, sí—but not mine."

"¡Gracias a Dios!" She made the sign of the cross.

He'd expected more. Joy. Anger. Something impetuous. She continued to stare, seeming perplexed.

"Will a couple of pesos still buy a bath and a drink?"

"And supper if you're hungry."

"I am starved."

He followed her into the cantina, and she called, "Tío, a guest for supper."

Mateo emerged from behind the bar to embrace him. "¡Hombre, bienvenido! Come this way."

When he was seated, Tinita gave him a plate heaped with spicy beef, frijoles de olla, and flour tortillas, and poured a cup of hot café con leche. Scooping up the food with his bread, he cautiously tested his stomach with a few bites. "How have you been? Is business good?"

"Things are going well," Mateo told him. "And you, señor?"

He shrugged. "I'm alive."

While he ate, Tío left to tend his horses, and Tinita busied herself with kitchen chores. When she brought a flan for desert, he caught her wrist. "You're different." She didn't pull away and the contact aroused him, but she wouldn't look him in the eye.

"You were gone for a long time."

"I'm here now. And I've changed, too."

She bit her lip, then asked softly. "Why did you come back?"

He caressed the inside of her arm with his thumb. "I wanted to see you. I thought you might be happy, seeing me."

She tilted her head, staring at him with half closed lids. "I dreamed about you. Every night, for months after you left. I looked for you to come riding in, every day. Do you know what it's like, dreaming and hoping for something that never happens?"

"Yes," he admitted. He tried to pull her down on his lap, but footsteps approaching made her wriggle free.

Mateo stuck his head around the doorpost. "Señor, you may have your bath whenever you are ready."

Trouble went down the hall to the dimly lit room where the cantiñero had a tub waiting. Stripped, he lowered himself into the tepid water. So she was angry. Stubborn. He wondered if she would get over it before he fell asleep. The heavy meal, and the events of the last week, had left him exhausted. Still, his loins ached in anticipation.

He stepped from the tub, relieved his bladder, toweled himself dry. When she didn't come knocking at the door, he used the bounty hunter's razor to shave. Then he put on clean clothes from the knapsack and went out.

Mateo was absent, but in the full moon light he saw her sitting beneath the thatch ramada. At his step, she rose and held out her hand.

They strolled without speaking toward the cottonwood bosque where they had almost made love the last time. Climbing onto the flat surface of the boulder, they sat near each other, arms around knees, and she asked, "Where were you?"

"South, beyond the mountains. There is a town called Los Pobres, where I built a casita."

"Do you like living there?"

"Yes." When she was silent, he added, "It's peaceful."

"¡Ay, Dios! It is peaceful here."

Her scorn pricked him with misgiving. "You would not be contented in a little town, with a few shops, and a priest?"

"Never. I want a big house in a city, where there are many people and much to do."

The gold at La Nariz could make her dreams possible. Yet he resisted mentioning it. If Tinita were unwilling to live with him in Los Pobres, how could he be sure she loved him, and not the things he could buy? Too, his mother's death was connected to that blood money.

"Don't be angry with me," he murmured, drawing her to him. She slid her arms around him, nestling her face in his open shirt. She was pleasing to hold, not thin, not plump, and her skin and hair smelled clean. "Did you dream about doing this?"

Something between a sigh and a moan was cut short by his mouth, finding hers. Her fingers tightened in the tangle of uncut hair at the back of his head, and her skin was soft and moist as obstacles of clothing gave way.

III

Though Agua Prieta was nothing more than a spring around which had sprung up a handful of miserable chozas,

Luis easily found a family willing, for a small price, to let him sleep in their room and eat their supper of roasted blue quail. Throwing his blanket over the stained covering, he stretched himself on the shuck mattress and lit a fresh Havana.

Almost halfway, and everything was going well. He had three horses and enough provisions, and had closed a deal for three mules. Packing the bullion should be no problem. He would stay off the main roads, to avoid thieves and murderers who lurked in wait for lone or poorly armed travelers.

The nearer he came to La Nariz, the more eagerly he anticipated handling the gold again, using his wealth in the ways he'd always intended. As he gained prominence in the upper circles of society, he would search out a beautiful young creole and buy her jewelry, gowns, and bonnets such as were pictured in magazines. With a respected daughter of good family for a companion, he could hold his own with any of the so-called gentlemen who had made fortunes in railroads and silver mining.

Confident that his casa was being aired and scrubbed by a swarm of busy chicas, he drew deeply of the cigar smoke. Sofía had to go. Lately, Manuelo, too, had begun to irritate; something undefined in the segundo's manner bothered him. The man was efficient, but spent too much time in the village.

Marieta had been pretty. Beautiful, even. Had she not been blind with youth and inexperience, and enticed by promises, he never could have managed to get her away from that old Spaniard she called Papá. His mind drifted among faded images of her, of himself with her. He regretted that she'd driven him to eliminate her, regretted that his suspicions of her infidelity had tainted his love for her. After she found the map, what choice was there? He knew her too well to trust her to keep silent.

Drowsy, he snubbed out the cigar.

Somewhere far to the south, Trouble's bones were scattered, picked over by coyotes. Felipe García was not the sort of man who buried his victims. Luis expected the fortune hunter to return, making unreasonable demands. Once the fiesta was done, and Manuelo dealt with, he'd see to it that García joined the others. Then he would be free.

Days passed, villages came farther and farther apart, the mountains grew wilder and more dangerous. Luis feared meeting a bear or cougar on one of the narrow precipices, and carried his rifle in the crook of his arm. Doing so made his shoulder ache, but a holstered pistol was almost useless.

His back hurt from sleeping on the ground and every knuckle was skinned from contact with metal parts of the harness. Used to being cared for by servants, he found it a burden to think of everything, do everything. He missed La Vieja's hot meals. Even Sofía's whining. However, he had come through countless kilometres of cliffs and ravines, and was almost to his goal.

Stopping in Bavispe to rest and purchase coffee, he caught the stares of idlers and attempted to smooth his unwashed hair and wipe the grit from dirt-lined wrinkles.

The lure of a meson persuaded him to ease his pains by soaking in a tub of hot water and to treat himself with a hot meal. From next door wafted the smells of pulque, men's sweat, smoke from cigarillos.

In clean clothes, he went over for a drink. The dark interior with its low voices and greasy packs of monte cards felt gratifyingly familiar. He'd missed such places, being isolated for so many years on the hacienda, playing the genteel patrón. He laid a coin on the bar. "Tequila."

Two men, not of his class but a rank above the peón, leaned on the scarred wood, drinking. "¡Salud!" he said, and gulped down what should have been tequila but was mezcal. Neither man returned his toast, but thinking they hadn't heard, he raised his voice. "Let's play cards. For drinks."

The nearest man didn't look up. He was small, dirty, dressed like a campesino. The corners of his mouth were surly. The one beyond cautioned, "Careful, my compadre is drunk." The speaker appeared to be the worst kind of mestizo. Unfit for work. The surly man spoke. "If you want to drink with us, you must buy."

Luis turned in disgust to look for better prospects. He'd come in expecting to spend an hour playing cards, savoring the drinks forbidden by that goat of a doctor, smoking and exchanging bawdy stories. He might have paid for the liquor had they shown themselves worthy of his generosity. He clenched a fist. "I buy no man's friendship."

The borracho eyed him, spat on his boot, and muttered, "Puerca vieja."

Luis's fist shot out, the man's nose spurted blood and he sprawled against the legs of his compañero, who lifted him to his feet and steered him outside. Luis ordered another drink. His knuckles stung, but the satisfaction was worth losing a little more skin.

IV

"There is a thing I must do," Trouble told her, "but when that's over, I will come back."

Tinita clung to him, face against his chest, breathing in long shuddering sighs from their lovemaking; so it was with shock that he realized she was crying.

"What? Did I hurt you? Did I say something wrong?"

She shook her head, unable to answer.

He grasped her chin, forcing her toward the moonlight. "What's the matter? Don't you understand? I want you. I want to marry you." Dios, he hadn't meant to say that, not yet, but her tears wet his hand and he didn't know what else to do.

The rain of tears became sobs. Words came out in a wail, "You're too late. Too late."

"What do you mean?" he cried, even as the hair on the back of his neck prickled.

She wrenched away and began pulling on her clothes. "I am already married."

For a stunned moment he felt nothing except the cool night wind drying the sweat on his skin. Then anger swept through him in a torrent and he leaped off the rock. Throwing on jeans and boots, he started for the cantina.

She ran after him with the shirt. "Where are you going? He's in Janos with friends and won't be back for days."

He fended off her efforts to give the shirt to him, to catch hold of his arm. "You should have told me!"

"I wanted to make love with you. Was it not fine? It was, for me."

He stopped so abruptly that she went on a few steps and had to turn to face him. "I don't take another man's wife to bed."

Tinita's eyes blazed in the faint light and her words were fierce. "I never would have married him if you had stayed when I wanted you to stay."

Shame and pity and defeat left him drained. He took his shirt and said, "Forgive me." But when she threw her arms around him, sobbing that she loved him and would go anywhere with him, he grasped her wrists and held her away. "No! You belong here, with your husband."

When he let her go, she slapped him across the mouth. "You damned gitano! I will tell Pablo how you forced me, and he will beat you senseless." She whirled and ran into the house.

Reluctant, lips stinging from her palm, he followed.

The shadowed patio hid someone whose presence he sensed even before he heard Tío's quiet invitation. "Señor, here is a comfortable chair."

He felt his way to it and as soon as his eyes became used to the gloom beneath the ramada, he saw that Mateo held a sleeping baby about five or six months old. "This is Lucía," Tío said.

"You heard?"

"Some."

"I did not force her."

"I believe you, señor. She says things to get her way. I do my best, but it's not easy, a girl-child growing up without a mother. Maybe I should have gotten married again myself, long ago, but the women, they don't like a fat man."

Slouching in the chair, Trouble leaned his head back and drew a slow, deep breath. He was far from sleep, but lacked the will to select provisions from Mateo's store, or saddle his mount and ride out. Three days, if he pushed, to La Nariz, and then the trip back over the mountains to deal with Panadero. He regretted coming here. The sweet release he'd enjoyed had turned bitter, sickening. Had he remained, last time, he might be married to her, might have accepted her child as his own.

Or he might be dead, shot or stabbed or poisoned by a jealous lover. "Tío, do you believe in destiny?"

"¿Destino? Sí. Otherwise, we must take responsibility for what happens."

Trouble felt the burden of responsibility for everything that had happened since leaving Hacienda de Panadero. Perhaps not feeling responsible was the kind of thinking which caused the evil that beset on every side. Yet Tío was not an evil man, while Panadero was. It was too confusing. He closed his eyes.

From beyond the patchwork of black shadows and pale light came the far-off sound of thunder. He started up, his belly knotted in fear before he realized he was no longer five years old and none of the riders coming was his father.

Foolish, to suppose they could be from Hacienda de Panadero. There was almost no chance that anyone had tracked him this far. Still, it was time to leave. "I need ammunition, corn meal, coffee."

Tío said, "I took the liberty of packing it for you. No charge. I wish you well, señor."

"Gracias, Tío."

He went along the hall to the room to retrieve his food sack and saddlebags, Walker's knapsack, rifle and hat. He carried them out to the corral and began saddling up. He was fastening the last buckle when Tío came around the house with four horses belonging to the riders. The moon had set, so he didn't bother to check what brand they carried.

"Vaya con Dios," the cantiñero said.

V

Sofía lay in the big hammock in the shade of the main patio, soothed by the music of the spring-fed fountain. A dozen kinds of butterfly flitted among the blossoms of the orange trees, and flycatchers and orioles called back and forth in the towering pochotes and ayales inside the wall.

Through the open doors she could hear the chatter, chatter, chatter, as the girls sewed cloth into dresses, prepared and sampled dishes being considered for the fiesta, and washed their long black hair. Bursts of laughter and shrieks cut into the pleasant sounds around her and she groaned in annoyance. The casa grande had been cleaned, true, but dry winds left a layer of dust over everything each day, and dishes and platters and glasses were left from one meal to the next. Her polite suggestions to pick up after themselves were ineffectual, her demands met with hostility.

"Oh, don't be so bossy," Charita complained. "We have time. Manuelo says the old cabrón will be gone for a month or more."

She had given up trying to control them, and turned her thoughts inward, to the raw wound of losing Ramón. Sometimes, though, her musings strayed to the comforting remembrance of the lean, naked body of the segundo, in

141

bed with her in his room, his hands which left no skin untouched, his mouth which whispered in a dialect she had never heard and brought responses never thought possible.

Dizzily, she sat up and tried to shake off the spell of Manuelo's lovemaking. He wanted to marry her, but hinted at complications having to do with the village priest. The problem of don Luis did not seem to bother him very much.

When she questioned, "Then, we would leave? Go to your tierra? Or mine?" he was evasive on that point.

"No one has to know," he kept saying. "We can bring a priest from far away, in secret. I am not ready to leave La Hacienda de Panadero."

VI

A few hours past dawn, Trouble found grass for his stock in a narrow valley and allowed them to graze. His anger at Tinita surged and cooled, surged and cooled. He was glad he had not stayed.

In a bosque of mesquites to diffuse the smoke from his fire, he made pozole from the cornmeal and used water from a canteen to make coffee. If he wanted meat, he would have to shoot a rabbit or sage hen or quail, and in Indian country he was not prepared to risk that. After a brief rest, he packed with care, leaving behind only confused tracks that disappeared over a rocky area. Anybody trailing him would have to work at it.

Desires that had lain dormant for almost a year had been reawakened, turning his thoughts to Beatriz. He could be with her in a few weeks. She would desert whomever she was with, even Enrique, for him. What if she were married? With a child? Entirely possible. Probable.

Unbidden, Sofía crept into his musings, like a maltreated cat into a safe lap. After her usefulness faded, Panadero would want rid of her. Manuelo would guard her, so long as he remained a part of the household; however, the alliance between the mayordomo and the patrón could be severed in any number of ways, and Trouble wouldn't be surprised to find the post deserted.

Over the years, Manuelo had disappointed him by never using or even revealing any of the powers he'd once believed his friend possessed. Taking Sofía from the casa grande might save her life. He pondered the complications of such an act. He didn't care to be linked with her permanently.

To the north, gray clouds were forming for the first hard rains, but they would miss him unless the wind changed. Without gold from La Nariz, he was limited in how far, and how fast, he could travel, whether alone or with a woman. He wished he could turn southward, forget it all.

But Los Pobres would never be safe, so long as Luis Panadero had his range and the money to pay men to kill him.

Chapter Eight

Trouble had been asleep for several hours, judging by the relaxed state of his muscles, when a noise woke him.

Walking hoof beats, of more than one horse.

The Mexican Colt came into his hand like something alive as he cat-footed past his stock. The gelding snorted, and a quiet voice out of the dark, about a wagon-length from his bedroll, said, "Alto."

The scuffle of horses, stopping.

In the dark of the moon, he could see nothing but heard riders dismounting. Putting the bole of a mesquite between him and them, crouching, he called, "¿Quién es?"

The flame and crack of a pistol answered, spraying dirt into his face, and someone else yelled, "Naldo, damn you!"

More scuffling as they hung onto reins and sought cover. "¡Amigos! ¡Amigos!" cried another voice. "¡Estámos amigos!"

"Amigos, hell!" He fired into the sounds, ran sideways, collided with the rump end of one of his horses. Shielded by the animal, holding his breath, he waited.

There was a groan.

Someone said, "Dios mío, está muerto."

Someone else pleaded, "En el nombre de Dios, yo no disparen." In the name of God, don't shoot any more. A match light glowed, like a tiny flag of truce.

"Light a fire," Trouble said, and the man touched the flame to a tinder-dry smoketree.

As it blazed up, he saw there were three of them. All roughly-dressed mestizos, though one had the features of a gringo. The man on the ground was younger, cleaner, more handsome. And dead.

"Give up your arms," he ordered, and they tossed away guns and knives, including a couple of machetes. "His, too," he added, and when he had collected their weapons he said, "Keep the fire going." He wanted them in sight.

They fell to gathering brush, cursing when thorns ripped flesh and clothing. Soon they had a waist-high pile, and another match sent tiny orange tongues licking along the loose branches.

"Who is he?" he asked, sensing that he knew.

"Pablo Renaldo," the man beside him answered.

"Who is Pablo Renaldo?"

They shrugged. One finally answered, "The husband of old Mateo's niece."

"You followed me from Mateo's?"

They cast silent, uneasy glances at each other and at him. He cocked the Colt again. The man who had struck the match nodded, "Yes," while the other cried, "No, no!"

"You followed, and you meant to rob me, didn't you."

More glances. "Tinita said you might have money."

Somehow, that didn't surprise him. "Mateo was not a part of this."

Both denied the cantinero's involvement.

He nudged Pablo Renaldo with his boot. "Bury him." Backing away, the Colt loose in its holster, he checked his picket ropes. The bay's had come loose, so he retied it. When he glanced up, the men were standing on either side of Pablo, doing nothing. "Bury him!"

"We have no shovel. How are we to—"

"Quit whining and dig."

On their knees, the bandits began digging like coyotes after a jackrabbit, and for a time loose gravel flew. "Dios mío, give us a machete, señor, the ground is hard."

"Dig," he said.

Their weapons in a row before him, he lay on his blanket and watched. Every now and then one would stop to rest, flex bloody fingers, feed the fire. The night crawled toward daybreak. He thought of Mamá. Had Panadero used his bare hands to dig her grave? Or had he taken a spade along for the job.

He thought of Walker. "You hombres are lucky. It takes much longer, when there is only one working."

The sky line was gray when the men straightened a final time, asking, "Is this deep enough?"

Trouble shrugged. "Es su amigo."

It satisfied them. Taking opposite ends of the blanket shrouded body, they lowered it into the hole and in a few minutes, Pablo Renaldo was buried and his friends were riding back toward Mateo's.

Trouble broke camp without delay, his anger at Tinita overshadowed by rage. If not for Panadero, there would be no fresh graves in the red Sonoran earth, end of the journey for men silenced forever by his hand.

He longed to plunge into don Luis and beat him to a pulp, but he was sure he couldn't whip the old man in a bare knuckle fight. Until recently at least, El Patrón packed a punch that would stun a steer. He'd seen it used more than a few times on peónes and disorderly horses. Even so, a beating would effect no lasting cure. Taking authorities to La Nariz, showing them the bones, would be no proof of murder, only his word against that of a wealthy hacendado. Stopping Panadero meant using the Mexican Colt.

Kill, or only maim? He still had no plan for exacting revenge, yet he must go on. Whatever waited at Casa de

Panadero, he would not flinch from making an end to the evil.

As La Nariz loomed closer, his heartbeat quickened. He dreaded having to enter the death chamber once more, where under a thin layer of earth were the pitiful remains of the mother he had loved so well, missed so dreadfully, and almost hated during all those years when he believed Panadero's lies. Yearning, boyhood years, when he still believed somehow he could earn his father's respect.

"Ah, Manuelo, could you not have saved me from this?"

Manuelo, offering aid for his bruises, seen and unseen. How long ago it was, that he'd dreamed of the day when his friend would strike Panadero down and bestow his inheritance, allowing him to live free in the house he loved.

Then he saw the lonely landmark. Higher than either the ridge shadowing the casa grande or the one beside his casita in Los Pobres, the distinctive peak reared above the horizon. A haunted place, cursed by treachery and violence.

For Mamá's sake, he would find a local priest willing to bless the cave.

Dismounting once more in the bosque of paloverdes, he waited, scanning his back trail in case the bandits had gathered their courage and decided to avenge Pablo's death.

All around him the sand and rocks, dotted with clumps of droughty chaparral, stretched to a hazy horizon. A trickle of sweat traced a crooked path down his chest, his belly, wetting the rim of his jeans. He blotted it with his shirt, wiped his face. No sounds, except an occasional rustle of wind in the paloverdes, the distant call of a dove, the stamp of a hoof.

Half an hour, an hour.

Satisfied that no other soul was here, he crossed the open space and walked up the hillside.

Nothing had disturbed the cover he'd replaced there himself. Panadero had not returned. Maybe he never would.

II

Everything was ready for fiesta, inasmuch as Sofía could tell by the items crossed off her lists.

Most of the food she planned to serve was in season, grown on the hacienda or one of the estancias. Tropical fruits had arrived from the south: avocados, pineapples and mangoes, coconuts, tamarinds and mameys. Paper lanterns were ready to be strung and placed in the high branches of the pochotes and ayales, and along the portico roofs.

Musicians were on call, on payroll so they could rush from Nogales at an hour's notice. The village band sulked because mariachis from a distant city were to be honored instead of them. Announcements had gone out with the date left blank, with a notice assuring that a messenger would bring word as soon as the patrón returned and had rested.

For rest he must, after so arduous a journey. How could it be otherwise, on horseback at his age? Sofía racked her memory for anything that might hint of what drove him, but other than his ruthless hiring of a gunman to kill Ramón, she found nothing.

Halting in the hall outside the cocina, she listened to determine whether the girls were gossiping about her.

"This is a strange fiesta," someone said, with a giggle.

"No wonder. Look who is giving it."

"I heard he paid five thousand pesos to have a man kill Trouble."

"Are you loco? It was ten thousand. El Patrón has always hated him."

"Old Lencha says it's because Trouble is not his son."

"Marieta—the mother—ran off with another man. No one knows who."

"The priest who came to say Mass in the village at that time left shortly after she did. I think he was the father."

"I wonder where the old man went? He's staying away for a long time."

"Ah, he's never coming back. He probably got afraid the policía would find out he had Trouble killed."

"Let's have the fiesta without him. We can eat all the food ourselves, and dance the dances we like instead of showing off for ricos and gringos."

A burst of cheers and laughter.

Sofía's fingernails cut into her palms. How could they be so carefree, when they were in bondage to a murderer? How could they laugh and eat and make cruel jokes, when Ramón was dead? Some of these same girls, she knew, had known the sweetness of his touch, the ecstasy of union with him. How could they call him by the hateful nickname given by a vicious old man, a name some gringo might use to label a cur.

When she first came to Hacienda de Panadero to tend her aunt, and heard him answer to 'Trouble,' she had asked Manuelo, "Why does he endure such an insult? Even his friends use it."

"There is more than one meaning to that word," Manuelo had told her. "Think about it."

She had thought, but not about that. If she had managed to run away with Ramón, would the gunman who found him have killed her, too? She preferred death to this present misery.

As promised, after she agreed to marry him, Manuelo had brought a strange priest from somewhere to the south, and in the sheltered grotto where the Virgen de Guadalupe stood in her bower, they pledged undying devotion. He had been gentle, passionate, even grateful. She had been full of guilt, first that she wanted Ramón instead, then that Manuelo made her forget—briefly—that she did not love him, that their marriage was not what he believed.

Backing away from the cocina, Sofía left the girls to their merriment. The headache that never quite let go had started to pound again. Manuelo had been in the village since departing her room under the secrecy of the morning darkness. She wished they could stop pretending for the sake of people who meant little to either of them, stop waiting for she knew not what, and begin living peacefully somewhere far from Hacienda de Panadero.

In time, she hoped her feelings for him would change.

Whenever she tried to rest anywhere in the house, the girls came knocking, to tell on each other for misbehaving, or to ask her opinion about the new dresses or how to wear their hair for the party. Even during siesta someone always thought of a way to disturb her; so she slipped out of the house and through the back gate, across the wagon yard and past the barns, down to the willow-bordered river, where Manuelo's old hut offered solitude.

As she approached, slippers soundless on the thick wildgrass, she saw a male figure beyond the casita, turned from her, kneeling, as if lighting a campfire or placing something small on the ground. Stopping to catch her breath, she realized he was Manuelo.

What was he doing? He stretched both hands in front of him, palms down, head bowed. Then he slowly turned his palms up, lifting his face to the sky. In front of him, a thin stream of smoke curled upward.

The afternoon was hot. Why did he need a fire?

While she watched, he changed his position with a fluid motion, so that he sat, one ankle tucked behind the other, hands resting on his knees, shoulders erect. Faintly, she could hear him singing—chanting—in the dialect she didn't understand.

She noticed other thin columns of smoke like the first, coming from the litter-strewn ground behind him. Her mouth opened to call a warning, yet no sound came from her throat. The smoke streams formed a circle around him. She expected to see flames leap, running outward in greedy tongues, consuming the dry grass and twigs. She expected Manuelo to become aware of what was happening and shout for help in stopping the blaze before it raged out of control.

She tried to rush forward, but her slipper caught on a fallen branch. A whirlwind of dust and dead willow leaves leaped and swirled towards her, and she blinked against the pelting, shivered in a sudden chill. Moving shadows, as if a storm threatened, mingled with flashes of sunlight. The wind did not touch the thickening columns of smoke which continued to rise.

But there was no fire, no shout. Only the gusting wind and the bright sun and the smoke.

She was looking at him when he disappeared.

III

Leaving the cantina, Luis went to check on his stock before going to bed. In the waxing moonlight he peered at the pole corral where he'd left them in the charge of a mozo. There were no sleek bays, no palomino. No mules, save two that did not belong to him and whose condition bespoke advanced age. One small saddle mare turned to snuffle at his sleeve as he leaned on the gate and cursed.

He pounded on the door of the mozo's hut and shouted until the man awoke and opened it.

"¡Caray, hombre! It's the middle of the night. What do you want?"

"It's barely past midnight, and already someone has stolen my horses and the mules I left in your care. You must pay me damages, you scoundrel, or I shoot you where you stand."

"Dios mío, think of my wife and little ones. Stolen, you say? Let me see——"

Shutting the flimsy door and swathing his face in his sarape to ward off los aires, the mozo led the way back to the corral and stood scratching his head, making his hair stick up in an unruly thatch.

"What are you looking for! They're not here. Did you see anyone earlier? Two hours ago? You must have heard the thieves. Unless you are one of them——" He grabbed the man's throat with one hand, shoved his pistol in the ribs with the other.

"Spare me, señor, I am honest. If someone took——"

"You watched me turn them into your corral."

"Direct the matter to the alcalde. He will know what to do."

"You are coming with me."

But the alcalde was harder to get out of bed, and when he did answer the summons, all he said was, "What do you expect of me? Take your complaint to the Federales in Arispe."

"Arispe is three days' ride over the mountains!" Luis's ears felt on fire and he could scarcely breathe.

They gaped at him while he described the men in the cantina. They both talked at once, saying nothing that would aid in finding the thieves or bring back his stock. Incensed at their stupidity, he shouted, "I know who took them." He described the men in the cantina.

Then they shrugged, and the alcalde repeated, "Take your complaint to the Federales. Those men do not live in my district." He shut himself inside his house, and the mozo started to walk away.

Grabbing him, Luis said, "Mark me well, pendejo, you shall suffer for this."

He returned to his mesón and his own bed, but rage kept him pacing the floor and smoking the rest of the night. The thieves had stolen his stock, food sack, canteens, grain for the animals, rifle, even extra ammunition. He'd brought into the room the satchel with his clothes, and the saddlebags with his handgun. At least they had not gotten those items, or a wallet of money.

Nor the map, in the wall safe in his office at Casa de Panadero. Comforting to think of what that little piece of paper represented. How cunning he had been, how daring. Living on the hacienda, he'd grown soft. Careless. He vowed to be more alert.

In the morning he tried to find stock suited to his purpose. Already the alcalde followed him about as if he were the bandit, so he was unable to use threats or force on those who owned strong animals but refused to sell even at double their worth. Grim, he returned to the damned mozo who was responsible for his plight, and purchased the two ancient mules and the saddle mare. He smelled the thievery used on him and swore to get even on his way back.

Three weeks of rough country and trail rations had trimmed his fat, so he put himself into the mare's stirrups with confidence. In almost twenty years, new settlements must have sprung up between here and La Nariz, mining outfits which kept better stock. This sort of obstacle was nothing.

He had ridden for perhaps an hour, glancing over his backtrail frequently, as stopping to cover his tracks posed delay and required much effort, when the mare balked. He spurred her. She bowed her back, and he gouged her flanks with the rowels, but she only shied first left then right, refusing to go forward.

Thinking she saw a rattlesnake or gila monster—he was out of bear country, though pumas often ranged over the plains; and the land now was too level to conceal anything larger—he scanned the ground before them, eyes raking the parched earth for any danger.

About a hundred paces ahead he was surprised to see a man standing, hatless, arms to his sides. He wore the shirt of a campesino, but not the loose calzones. The shirt was bleached white, the trousers dark brown, like those favored by his mayordomo.

By God, it *was* the segundo. The shape of the head, the cut of the hair, the set of the shoulders—there was no mistaking him.

Panadero blinked, and the man was gone.

Only rocks and cactus. No pueblo nor rancho from which he might have walked in this blazing wilderness. Of course, there had been no one there. A coyote, standing on its hind legs, staring at him. The white underbelly could resemble a shirt. The thing had stared at him, he was sure of that. Then it must have dropped on all fours and blended into the tawny sand, ghosting behind a bush or rock.

But coyotes had pointed ears.

IV

Everything at La Nariz was just as Trouble had left it. Swallowing against a dry throat, he set aside the rocks and brittle smoketree branches, tugged away the two flat stones.

In his haste to leave Mateo's, he had forgotten candles, and because he never smoked he had few matches he must save for supper fires. Yet his eyes adjusted to the gloom, and light from the outside showed him the shelf of earth beneath which lay more gold than he could count. Showed him the unhallowed place his mother had been, the whole time he was growing up, wondering about her.

"I keep your cross in a little box at home," he said softly. "My casita is in Los Pobres. That's my tierra, now."

On his knees, he could feel minutes moving from the future into the past, measured by his heartbeats, by his breathing. He remembered sitting on Mamá's lap, his head resting on her shoulder, listening to her heart, her breath. Stilled forever on this earth by a greedy old man who had robbed them all.

One day, maybe soon, one of them would join her. But neither would be buried here, unless he told Manuelo or Sofía what to do if he were killed. "Mamá, I know you wouldn't approve of what I am planning. Padre says we must forgive, in order to be forgiven."

Gently brushing at the loose dirt, careful not to disturb her, he searched for and found the chain that had held the Cristo. "Perhaps one day I shall accept all this as Destino. But not today."

Drawing the circlet to him, he examined it. A religious symbol, an aid to prayer, it was perhaps three handspans in length, with small wooden beads at intervals. Fashioned by a silversmith, given to her by the young padre.

He remembered the secret hiding place under the altar cloth in the village church. Remembered searching there for it after she disappeared, and not finding it. Now he knew it was not his mother who had taken the rosary, but her husband who found and used it as evidence against her.

Wiping away the dust with the tail of his shirt, he placed the chain around his neck. If he survived his return to Casa de Panadero, he would re-attach the Cristo left in the tin document box in Los Pobres.

"Would you forgive him, if you could?"

He lingered, wishing for an answer, a sign. Mamá had been dead for fifteen years, but his images of her alive were vivid. The long-dreaded burial chamber seemed peaceful, even blessed already.

"I can't! I can only try to stop him from murdering someone else."

The men he had buried weighed on his conscience, though in every case he had acted to save his own life. He wished he might make amends. He thought of only one way, one person.

He scratched out one of the leather sacks and tucked it into the front of his shirt. Tinita needed it, to free herself and her child far from the lonely outpost at the edge of the desert, to start anew in a city where there were many people and much to do.

V

Luis watched dark clouds roil over the mountains, and breathed deeply of the cooling air. The mare had to be rested often, but she was holding up; and neither of the scrawny mules had died. In fact, the grain he had been giving them put new life in their mangy carcases—enough so that he had to take care not to get bitten by the larger whenever he strapped on its pack.

Tomorrow, La Nariz. He anticipated the soothing sheen and silkiness of the coins, the promise of the bullion. His first plan of taking everything to the hacienda had to be changed. Once the coins were removed, dig up the bones and toss them into the nearest arroyo. Take no chances of stirring up an investigation. Then, in one of the Mormon settlements, or one of the larger towns, find someone willing to buy the bars where they were cached. The coins, along with what he accepted in payment, would be enough to provide the sumptuous life he meant to live.

That afternoon thundershowers raced down out of the Sierra Madre and over the plain behind him. As he could not reach cover, and missing his own coat which had been stolen, he dismounted and rummaged in his pack for the new canvas waterproof. The stiff material frightened the animals, but well-placed blows got them under control and he mounted and spurred eastward.

Gusts of wind tore the corners from over his knees, and the downpour, overtaking them, wet his legs. Rivers ran inside his collar whenever the rim of his sombrero blew up. The cord under his chin kept the hat on, but the buffeting soon chafed his skin, and the shifting wind flattened the brim over his eyes in an annoying manner.

Rivulets bounded off a hillside in front of them and the mare's hooves slipped in the mud. He cursed the rain, the wind, the sombrero, and the mules that pulled on the lead until his hand was numbed. Heavy clouds foretold early dark and the probability of night storms.

At an overhang of rocks, he reined in and dismounted. High and not likely to be flooded. Room for himself and his gear. He didn't expect to find a better place to camp. The animals were used to weather. Besides, a good soaking might rid them of bothersome ticks and would clean the raw spots in the mule's hide where the pack had rubbed. No dry wood for a fire, so no supper. He rolled up in his blanket and tried to sleep.

...the cave was just as he remembered it. He removed the rocks and brush and crawled inside along the narrow passage until he could stand up. The lit candle gave off only a dim glow and he blinked and stretched his eyelids in an effort to see clearly. From the corner where the shelf of dirt concealed his treasure came a shimmering gold swirl that slowly gathered into a shape. His cheeks and the back of his neck prickled and a shudder ran though him.

Images shifted, confounded him, made him dizzy. At first the shape resembled that damned segundo, but the next moment it was not Manuelo, but Trouble who sat on the shelf of dirt, grinning. . .

"¡No! García killed you— You are dead—"

He woke, shivering. Wind-blown rain cascaded off the roof of his shelter, spattered on his face. In his sleep, he'd threshed about, knocking aside the canvas, and his clothing was drenched. He struggled upright, blood racing, nerves twitching along his arms and legs. Fumbling in the dark, he found the pack, the coal oil, the lantern, a dry space to set it. Matches were harder, but at last he had a light. His dry mouth cried out for a drink. Even a little jar of pulque would calm the susto, the crippling fear. He uncapped a canteen and drank deeply of the stale water.

While he watched, the lantern flame flickered and died.

VI

Trickles of water in Mateo's irrigation lines under the noon sun blazed white, shocking the eye. Trouble left his stock drinking at the trough and crossed the yard. Only the cantinero's horses dozed in the shade of their ramada. No thirsty drifters, none of Pablo's friends.

The barroom was dim. Silent. Among the bottles of tequila and aguardiente, jars of mezcal and the skins containing pulque, he found a bottle of whiskey, half full. Tilting it, he took a swallow, then another.

He pushed aside the inner doorway curtain and stood looking down the hall. From a partly open door came the snores of a middle-aged, overweight man. Farther on were other doors, also open. He leaned against the wall and finished the whiskey. His eyes burned from lack of sleep and the glare of gypsum. He was dirty, bearded, sweating. His unwashed hair was in need of cutting.

Drawing a long, shaky breath, he set the bottle on the floor, stared at his dusty boot toes. Then he carefully put one foot in front of the other until he came to her room.

She sat cross-legged on the bed, skirt pulled up to take advantage of occasional breezes, the child cradled in her arm, nursing. Her wide eyes were not surprised at seeing him. Maybe she didn't know. He wet his lips. "I—" He had to clear his throat. "I bring bad news."

Her gaze was calm, but her fingers nervously played with the curls on the baby's head. "They told me."

"They came into my camp at night, shooting."

"I don't blame you."

That was what the bounty hunter Walker had said. Feeling awkward, he wasn't sure what came next. Watching her slip the drowsy baby's mouth off her nipple and adjust her blouse brought arousal. She laid the child on the bed and held out her hand to him. "Hold me," she whispered.

He didn't move. He wanted to tell her he was sorry for Pablo's death, but clearly she didn't need an apology. He fought the urge to slap her for sending them after him, but it went against his principles to hit a woman. His pity and anger struggled against a stronger emotion.

"You wouldn't be making love to another man's wife, now." Her saucy smile showed she had not missed the effect of her bare skin and the invitation.

"I didn't come here for that," he said, aware that the tone made his words unconvincing.

"But it is what we both want." She beckoned with one outstretched hand, while the other moved lazily on her inner thigh.

Taking the leather sack from his shirt, he tossed it between her legs. "This is what you want."

Startled, she watched him as if she expected him to pounce on her while she unfastened the rawhide thong. When she saw the coins, she gave a little shriek and tipped half the contents onto the bed. Her face lifted, glowing. "¡Ah, Madre de Dios! We can go all the way to the City of México—"

"You can go," he said, firm. "It is yours."

She leaped up and began hugging him, clinging, kissing his cheek, his neck, laughing and crying and pressing her body against him. Feeling his response she cried, "We can leave Lucía with Tío. We shall be so happy."

He gripped her arms to push her away, but she pulled him down on the bed, wrapped her legs around him, held him by the hair, making him dizzy with her skilled caresses.

When he could free his mouth to speak, he said, "No, dammit. Take the money, for it's all I can give."

She stopped moving beneath him. Relaxed her hold. Expecting to be taken off guard, attacked, he cautiously got to his knees above her, stepped onto the floor.

She sat up. "Wait." She gathered the scattered coins and put them into the sack. Her face was blotched but her eyes were dry. "I don't want your money."

"You wanted it enough to get Pablo killed."

"I was angry."

"You still are."

"I had reason!" Her stormy eyes overflowed.

Gently, he said, "I'm afraid there would always be a reason."

She flung the sack against his chest, and he caught it. "Coward!" she yelled as he escaped into the hall, slamming the door behind him. Through the panels he heard her wails rising with those of Lucía.

Pausing to settle the gold sack in the front of his shirt, he heard Mateo's heavy tread approaching.

"Señor, bienvenido," Tío greeted, but lacking spirit. "My Tinita sounds very unhappy. Does this mean you are leaving?"

"I must, Tío. Already I have delayed too long."

Nodding him into the bar, Tío said, "A drink, before you go."

"I helped myself, while you were resting." Trouble picked up the empty whiskey bottle and offered silver, but Mateo refused to accept it.

"She needs a man, a good man. Are you sure—"

"My horses are tired, but they're worthy stock. I would like to trade them for those in your corral."

"Ah, no, I cannot do that."

"I'll give ten pesos extra."

Eyebrows taking on a bargaining angle, Mateo led the way to the corral leaned on the top pole. He considered the jaded gelding and the bay, made a sound of regret with his mouth.

"Fifteen pesos. In gold."

The eyebrows shot up. "Hombre, you cheat yourself."

"I need fresh mounts."

"You do, truly. Twenty-five pesos in gold buys those two mustangs."

"No trade?"

Tío rubbed the back of his neck. "They are never ridden and eat too much. Take them, and welcome."

The transaction made and his food sack stuffed with everything Tío could fit into it, Trouble put his saddle on the strongest mustang and led it around the lot. When he mounted there was an attempt to buck but he clamped his knees until the dust settled.

Leaving with Bay, the black gelding, two fresh horses, provisions, weapons and ammunition, and the sack of coins riding against his ribs, he felt strong and determined. He had done everything he could for Tinita. He had found a priest to bless the low mountain called La Nariz. Nothing remained between him and Panadero except country.

Chapter Nine

The storm-soaked bits of wood smoldered, filling Luis's eyes and nostrils with smoke and threatening to extinguish the small fire. He gave up trying to feed it anything larger than kindling and when that was gone, he sat hunched and brooding, watching the sparks flicker. No coffee, meat, or beans. He chewed a stale tortilla.

Daybreak came with a stiff wind blowing out of the southwest, scudding masses of dove gray and dark blue clouds across the upper sky, while the paloverde and mesquite remained as still as death, promising another hot morning.

Outside the overhang, the mules moved restlessly, but there was no sound from the mare. Had she broken her tether? Died in the night?

Fighting weariness, Luis stepped into the open and surveyed the rocky hills. Among the wands of ocotillo and paloverde he spotted her wet rump and felt relief that she was standing.

Breaking camp, every move was an effort. His head pounded and he thirsted for one little copita. Even cheap wine would be welcome. The water in his canteens was two days old. None of the animals wanted to start without their ration of grain, but with thirty kilometres to cover by nightfall, he gave them a few cuts with the whip and set out.

He tried to turn his thoughts from his empty stomach to those pleasant daydreams of boarding an Orient-bound vessel with a pretty young companion, dining at the captain's table with influential and wealthy men whose company would enhance his own reputation, sipping a rich port in the heart of Spanish wine country.

Memories replaced his dreams. Marieta. Disturbingly attractive. And the damn boy looked just like her, only macho. More macho than he had any right to be.

The gold. He must think of it.

It would be there, untouched. No other soul knew of the treasure, save for Trouble. Certainly that pious pendejo had never tarnished himself by spending bloody booty. Excitement rose, but a dart of fear tainted his joy.

She would be there, too...where he had left her, under the dirt.

"It was quick. So quick, she never knew. She bent her head over the gold, and I put the barrel here—" He touched one forefinger to the hairline behind his left ear. "Excellent weapon. Forty-five. Heavy powder load. Forty grains. She didn't feel it."

The desolate countryside, once esteemed for its remoteness, now provoked uneasiness. "It means nothing."

Spurring the mare, dragging the reluctant mules, he pushed hard, intending to cover as much ground as possible before the heat gathered force.

It was nearing noon, overcast and oppressive, when he came in sight of La Nariz. He had to rest the mare before crossing the flat, but in half an hour he reined in, dismounted in a bosque, and tied the reins and lead rope to some cottonwoods. As he started up the hillside, one of the mules let out a strident protest, and he stumbled back to quiet it with a few mouthfuls of corn. Not that anyone would be within hearing. Only coyotes.

His scalp prickled, as though he were being watched. Making a circuit with his eyes, he saw nothing moving, other than a few bees and the flutter of leaves. The mountain seemed bigger, the plain more vast, than he remembered.

Boots sliding on the shale, he climbed the slope and finally stood at the opening. Giving another careful look around to be assured he was alone, he threw the trash aside and lowered himself onto hands and knees. The mouth of the cave was narrow, hemming him in, and the entranceway longer than he'd supposed. When he was able to stand, he realized he had left the lantern in the pack and had forgotten candles.

No matter. He couldn't become lost. Gradually, as he felt his way forward, daylight filtered in behind him and he could make out the shape of the crude chamber, the mound of earth concealing the gold. Nothing amiss. A few roots poked out of the dirt, streaks of water trickled crookedly down the walls. The damp odor of decay unsettled his stomach.

He wished for a jug of pulque. The poor man's drink, it had not passed his lips for over a decade. "Demonio," he muttered. He had forgotten to replace the shovel; but reaching the sacks should be easy. The ground wasn't packed by use, and they were on top of the bullion.

His gaze roved to the grave. The surface did not seem changed. Sunken a bit. Perhaps he was mistaken about her rosary. He fingered the cross in his pocket, the silver Cristo hanging in agony. Perhaps the boy had felt the need of religion. He used to pray in the chapel with his mother. Maybe he had never been here at all. The detested boy, who might have been his child, was dead, whether deserving of that fate or not.

Shaking himself, Luis stiffly crouched before the shelf and clawed at the caked earth. He had imagined quickly digging out the coin, disposing of the bones, making a deal for the bullion, arriving in triumph at Casa de Panadero and enjoying rich foods and fine wines, happy music and fireworks at his fiesta. Haste, however, was not possible. His muscles were sluggish, unresponsive, and his knees grew trembly. Uncovering the sacks one by one, he laid them in a row.

...three...four...

His eyes strayed to the shallow grave. Marieta's black hair had been long and silky, a mark of her Castilian blood. Or was it Andalusian? She was an aristocrat.

...five, six, seven...

Lighter than the Indio, darker than the average Creole. The child had inherited that tawny skin and the small, white, even teeth that the village girls admired so much.

...eight...nine...

Marieta, crossing the back lawn at sunset, carrying her prayer book and rosary, the boy running barefoot beside her. They had tried to persuade him to join them, but he always found an excuse to refuse.

...ten...

How different their life together would have been, had she appreciated the finery he risked his life to give her. Eleven...twelve...

...thirteen, fourteen, fifteen...

. . . Sixteen...seventeen...eighteen...nineteen.

If only she hadn't found his map. They might still have been together, had children, been the family he had wanted them to be.

Nineteen.

He sifted the cold dirt, scrabbling against the bullion until his fingers were lame.

There were supposed to be twenty. He was positive of that. He counted again. What could have happened to it? The bars remained. Understandable. A man needed a pack animal, to carry even one bar any distance. Anyone finding twenty sacks full of gold coins would take them all.

Drops of sweat clung to his forehead, broke loose, raced chinward. "Air is bad in here."

Blindly making a last search, he cursed himself for leaving his treasure unguarded, unchecked, for so long. He'd been a fool to wait, when he should have returned in his prime, when years of indulgence did not hamper clear thinking. It had to be here. Gasping from frustration and exertion, he lay down beside the row of nineteen sacks to rest a moment. His eyelids closed. A flash, like lightning, flipped them open.

¡Marieta!

Dressed in blue, her hair drawn to the nape of her neck with a matching ribbon, she sat on the sunken grave, the toes of her slippers modestly peeking from the hem of her skirt. She had no face.

No face, but glowing eyes, alive and taunting.

His jaw worked, the scream in his throat choking him. Scrambling on hands and knees, he plunged through the mouth of the cave and down the embankment, gouging his flesh on sharp rocks and ripping his clothing on thorns. A steady rain was falling, cold and hard upon his back. After a minute he realized she had not followed. He sat up, turned to look back, to be sure. The mouth of the cave gaped like a toothless bruja.

He shuddered. "Brujería." Witchcraft.

Once he had found shelter in a village, and had eaten a bowl of frijoles and drunk several cups of strong coffee, he began to doubt what he had seen. He'd been exhausted, suffering the lingering effects of the crudo. Tomorrow he would go back. All the sacks would be there, and he would proceed as planned.

The more he thought of it, however, the less sure he was that he had the stamina to continue. He had no business connections in Chihuahua, and finding a buyer for the bullion could take weeks. He was loathe to leave any part of the gold at La Nariz, yet the dank stench of death hung in his nostrils, and the more he tried to force Marieta out of his thoughts, the more firmly rooted she became. Tales told around campfires and repeated by his peónes warned against touching dead bodies, or entering caves said to contain treasure. Until now, he'd believed those legends were circulated by men such as himself, to keep away greedy fortune-hunters.

Wakeful in a rented room, trembling as from a fever, he didn't feel well enough even to ride back and fill the saddlebags. He wanted to be home, with Sofía to hover over him and bring fragrant food from La Vieja's cocina. In surprise, he experienced a twinge of regret at having pushed her against the door. He wished she were here to rub his back. He wanted Manuelo to see to the stabling of the mare and the mules, the putting away of the gear. He longed for his bed. After weeks of sleeping on gravelly earth or blanket-covered boards, his mattress would seem like a cloud in heaven. Cielo. Paraíso. Was there such a place? The priest in Nogales thought so.

He supposed he had played the fool, gaining wealth and position by murder and theft, though there had seemed no other way to attain the things he sought, for himself and for Marieta. There was no end to the shedding of blood. Like links in a chain, the men hired for murder must be murdered. He worried over the dangers ahead, not only the treacherous route through the mountains, but from men who lay in wait for him.

Manuelo was a threat, he'd sensed that more and more over the years; so was Felipe García, with his hunger for riches and knowledge of the reward. If either of them went to the authorities, he was finished. He must—

No. It would end. García had been satisfied. If the man did return, Manuelo had the authority and power to cast the bandit into prison. Power... That was what Manuelo possessed which frightened him. He must discover a way to control the segundo, make that power work for himself. Manuelo was an ally to be cultivated.

The feverish activity of his brain slowly relaxed. He'd panicked unnecessarily. One of the men who rode with him in the pack train robbery must have taken an extra sack. Or perhaps he himself had done so, years ago, and miscounted. A night's rest...

In the corner, halfway to the ceiling, a pinpoint of light attracted his attention. It didn't bob about in the graceful arcs of a firefly but hovered unblinking, like a tiny yellow star—or a devil's eye.

Sitting up with a jerk, Luis knew he wasn't dreaming. Something alive was in the room with him.

His tongue was like a piece of tough beef in his mouth, his heart thudded, his limbs refused to move.

The lights became faces of his dead enemies. Faces that he had not seen in over fifteen years. Among them were Marieta and Trouble, laughing at him from the depths of the night. Laughing while blood ran from their eye sockets. The faces exploded into a shower of red and yellow and white, like fireworks, only silent. The showers covered him like a swarm of bees, and he shrieked.

With a bound he found himself outside beneath the scorpion-ridden ramada, trailing his blanket, shivering until his teeth chattered. He sought the innkeeper and ordered his stock to be brought. He sent a niño into the room for his things. The boy returned, carrying his saddlebags. "The satchel," he urged. "Go back for the satchel." It contained his clothing and money.

When everything was done, he mounted the jaded mare and took up the mules' lead rope. He set out westward, toward the mountains. Away from La Nariz, leaving behind the gold. And, God willing, the ghosts.

II

"¡Diosito! Are you injured? Ill?" Drunk? Sofía ran to Manuelo and knelt at his side. He lay face down in her big hammock on the kitchen patio, limp as if dead, and her heart lurched in terror.

He stirred, opened his eyes, grasped her trembling hand in his strong brown fingers. "Está bien, querida."

Sitting up, he gave her a reassuring smile. Don't panic."

With a shaky laugh she said, "Panic is what I do best." Always with good reason, she added silently.

It had been three days since she watched him disappear from the smoky circle in the willow grove. Doubting, she had gone forward, walked among the smoldering hot spots which sent up lingering wisps like discarded cigarillos. She found no trace of shucks or white paper to prove that ordinary objects had caused the sight. The hillside behind his casita, sloping on one side to the river and reaching to a distant line of piñons, was dotted with small slender trees, no underbrush. Even running, he had not had time to hide anywhere. He had not passed her on the way into the hut, and when she checked anyway, the hut was deserted.

Where had he gone? How had he gone?

That evening at supper, when Manuelo took his place beside her after being out of the house all day, she had caught faint whiffs of burnt wood, and something more subtle, like incense. It was not the copal of the church censor. Something else. Something wild. She didn't dare question him, for fear of knowing the answer.

Each night, she had wakened to find him out of their bed, and in other circumstances she might have suspected he was with some woman in the village who was younger, prettier, more charming. Each time he returned, sometimes before morning, sometimes like now, late in the day, he was gaunt and withdrawn. He had not sought the marital union since their wedding night, but when they lay together he held her close, murmuring, "Sofía, trust me. Trust my love for you."

"I do," she kept assuring him. "I love you, too." And, at those times, she did. But a part of her feared him.

The corners of his eyes crinkled in a wan smile. "I'm tired, querida. Would you bring me a cool drink?"

Sofía hesitated, almost saying, *So you can disappear when I turn my back?* but she didn't want him to know she had witnessed whatever he had been doing in the field behind his hut.

She carried a gourd of chilled fruit juice to him and he drank it in long swallows. His eyes were more bloodshot than usual, and the faint odor of smoke lingered.

At the top of the ridge overlooking Casa de Panadero, no grass relieved the jumble of bare rock. Since sunrise, propped on his elbows under the tent of his blanket and blending into the surroundings like a brown lizard, Trouble had watched the home compound.

Every three hours the guard at the front gate changed hands. Peónes, vaqueros, and horse wranglers came and went freely, leisurely, without purpose. Was El Patrón ill? Unable to bluster about, giving orders? Was he in Nogales, paying another bounty hunter to go looking for the hated heir to this sprawling estate? Or had he returned to La Nariz?

If so, they had missed each other, due to timing or his looping by Mateo's to give Tinita the gold. What had the old man thought, discovering a missing sack? How long, before he stopped searching for it, and rode into the yard, itching to punish whoever happened to cross his path.

Until he was sure of the situation, Trouble postponed settling on a battle plan, other than getting rid of the old man, or dying in the attempt. The Mexican Colt lay holstered companionably along his hip. The ridge was too far from any of the buildings for a handgun to do much damage. He hadn't shot anything other than game with Walker's rifle, still carried on his saddle, so had reservations about firing it into a place where innocent people might be hit. He toyed with the idea of sneaking into the house, leaving some sign that he was alive and had come back. Would that spook the old man, or only alert him?

He was puzzled to see two women stroll out on the kitchen patio, in pale green and rose gowns of a style that neither Sofía nor La Vieja, nor any of the criadas was likely to be wearing. Only the wife or daughter of a businessman dressed so expensively, and no woman of quality would set foot in the servants' area. Who were they?

Presently they went back into the house, and he dismissed them as unimportant.

On his left, willows marked a bend in the Río Sangría. He wished he might strip off his clothing and plunge into the shady river, letting its current carry away trail dirt and weary anger.

The rushing of water over rocks reminded him of a night in his childhood, when he fled to the cliff to escape the old man's fists and cruel accusations. He had waited, listening to the river and the churning of his heart, for Mamá; and when she failed to join him, he'd crawled to the edge—this spot—and peered over. In the lamplit doorway were two moving shadows, like players behind the curtain of a traveling show. Dishes flung by someone in anger crashed into fragments on the well-trod ground. One of the cane chairs bounded out as if fleeing for its life, only to stumble to a halt in a posture of prayer.

He remembered how at last all the shouts and cries and motion ceased. Even now he tasted the bitterness of that fear which had seized him. Death in the village, animals and Indios alike, was common; and despite his tender years, he had understood the fragility of existence. In that horrible silence, he was alone until Mamá called to him from the darkness. He'd rushed to the comfort of her arms. But on that night, on this ridge, a terrified child witnessed the murder of his mother, years before it happened.

Lifting a canteen, he allowed a small swallow, making it last. Along the arcade, ollas filled with drinking water were suspended from roof vigas by hemp cords. Liquid in those jars kept cold by evaporation. Knowing they were there, out of reach, increased his thirst, though chewing a fragrant herb kept his mouth moist.

With Panadero gone, the great house would belong to him. Land, livestock, crops, storerooms. Everything. Even the families across the river.

He hadn't seen Manuelo yet. If he were patient, some opportunity to speak to the mayordomo alone would present itself.

Studying the grounds, he considered the problem of getting inside without drawing notice. Not the front gate, guarded by unfamiliar men. The wagon portal stayed open only during the day and served heavy traffic except at siesta; possible, but risky, as many glass doors and windows faced that direction. Not everyone slept the hot hours away. The back entrance was connected by path and footbridge to the village. Who could he trust? By now, Walker's death might be common knowledge, and a reward such as don Luis offered could tempt even friends.

Growing up, Trouble and his compadres had tracked anything that had feet. Rabbits, mice and chipmunks, lizards and geckos and tortoises, coyotes and foxes and bobcats. Once they'd even dared each other to stay on a fresh trail of a puma, and he'd gone close enough to her den to hear the cubs mewling. He and his friends tried to run down deer, but, aside from an occasional rabbit or quail trapped or killed with a rock and roasted over a campfire, their only prey came from don Luis's flocks of fat hens.

Dozing in the noon heat, he remembered Mamá's stories of her girlhood in Spain. "The patios," she would tell him, "were paved with pink tiles, and our bedrooms were warmed with thick carpets from the Orient." Her dresses were all silk, and, instead of the rough plain rebozo that covered her head when they went to the Indio market, a silver comb held a lace mantilla over her black hair. Her brothers often took her to the countryside for a día del campo—a picnic beneath spreading trees, a whole day spent in sunshine cooled by ocean breezes and full of music and games. Whenever he asked her, "Where is Spain, Mamá?" she always sighed and answered, "Far, far away, mijo. Too far ever to return."

He had imagined that Spain was like Cielo, Heaven, and her family just like the pictures he'd seen of La Virgen and El Niño. If Father Navarre were right, Mamá was with them now, waiting for him. Dying held no terrors, so long as he thought of that.

Toward evening, crop workers and horsemen began straggling in from fields and cattle range, stowing gear, calling to one another before going into the bunkhouse or crossing the bridge to the village. After dark, dogs would be set loose. They might not remember him, or be different beasts that had never known him.

When the westering sun was half an hour above the mountains, he slid down the hill to his horses. He gave them the last of the grain, a drink from a shallow backwater of the Sangría, and changed his saddle to Walker's gelding in case he must leave in a hurry. The black was long-legged, rested. And it could be tied with a slip knot.

Taking nothing but the bag of gold in his shirt and the Colt strapped to his thigh, he ventured through the brush to the wall and pulled himself up enough to see over. Across the little patio, glass doors backed by filmy white curtains gaped open. Moments passed. Then, stealthy, he continued along the wall toward the kitchen yard.

Casa de Panadero dined much earlier than customary in other households, so preparations for supper would be over. In the comedor, the patrón would be enjoying tender beef from his own herd, sauces and breads which were La Vieja's pride, wines from the cellar where once the young wife and her child cowered among root vegetables.

Placing his hands on top of the wall, Trouble sprang across, landing noiselessly on the flat stones of the servants' patio. A door opened directly into the despensa, the pantry. He tried it, and when it yielded, he closed himself inside.

Two female voices moved about in the kitchen beyond. Neither Sofía nor La Vieja. The figures seen in the patio earlier, wearing pretty dresses. Why were they in the cocina?

176

His presence would frighten them into fits if one of them happened to open this door.

The dark little storeroom was poorly ventilated and uncomfortably hot. His throbbing temples cried out for Manuelo's headache remedy or Sofía's lavender-soaked handkerchief. Presently the voices faded. Likely they were returning to the dining room, where the French windows would be open to catch cool evening breezes. He opened the pantry door and tiptoed across the kitchen.

Around the doorpost, he could see the west patio, with its wrought iron settees, soft with cushions. A number of heavy glazed clay macetas placed in the corners spilled out an abundance of fragrant blossoms, and he remembered the last afternoon he had spent there, talking with Sofía while the rain fell. Over a year ago—almost two. The day he found that damned map.

In the adjoining comedor, there was a babble of chatting and laughing. He hadn't expected a house full of people; only don Luis, Sofía in her mouselike posture on his left, Manuelo across from her, a few house servants. The angle of the doorways made it impossible to see anyone. What would happen if he walked in and took his chair at the table? No doubt the riding whip was waiting. Or the dragoon, cleaned, oiled, and chambers loaded.

Then he realized he heard no males. Was don Luis not in the room? Nor Manuelo? The old patrón would never allow women to dominate the conversation. He must be away, either Los Pobres to do the job himself, or to retrieve the treasure at La Nariz.

Pondering his next move, Trouble was startled by Sofía coming suddenly into the hall, pulling the door shut behind her. Before he could react she raised her eyes and saw him. "¡Ay, Dios mío, Ramón!"

In a couple of strides he was beside her, his hand to her mouth. "Silencio, por favor."

Instead of calling out or running away, she caught him into a fierce embrace. "¡Dios, gracias!" Then her hands behind his head pulled him to her, her mouth claiming his, forcing his lips apart and giving him no small shock.

When he could draw breath, he cried softly, "¡Sofía, qué bienvenida!" What a welcome.

"I thought you were dead! I thought you were dead—" She clung to him and began crying, muffled against his shirt.

Not caring to be discovered, especially like this, he shook her slightly. "Where can we go?"

Where can we go? The urgency of his words and the clean taste of his mouth and the feel of him, alive in her arms, stunned Sofía.

Her first thought was her bedroom, but with so many girls in the casa it might as well be a mesón. Any place at this hour was subject to people strolling through, except the bath house, and even that wasn't completely safe. The barns were far from suitable and hay dust made her sneeze. Her tía's casita in the village was occupied by cousins. And there was something more than El Patrón's command that had always made her shun the library.

"Don Luis's room!" she cried, breathless. "We can use it." His fingers on her elbow jerked her to a stop. "It is all right, he is away."

He stopped her again. "What about the hut? Is anyone living there?"

"No—"

Voices behind the closed door grew louder, and as the diners pushed back chairs, he grabbed her hand and led her down to the wine cellar. The place was dark and cobwebby, and the stone floor stained and unpromising underfoot. At the bottom of the steps he said, "Where's the old man?"

"We don't know—"

"Nor when he is to return?"

"No."

"And, Manuelo?"

She hesitated. "He is always very busy, with duties. But usually back, by night."

"Is there a lantern?" He searched about in the dimness.

"Do we need one?" She felt more than saw the sharp, questioning look he gave. Then he found a lantern and after a couple of tries had it burning.

"There used to be a tunnel—" He led her toward the end of the long, narrow cellar, past racks of don Luis's imported wines. Coming to a small door, he lifted the latch and shoved until it creaked open.

"I didn't know this was here," she said, following him along an almost airless passageway, lit by the wavering flame. They stumbled over the uneven earth floor which turned and twisted as if laid out by diggers unsure of their bearings, or compelled to veer around solid rock. The walls, like those of a mine, had been shored up with timbers. A few had cracked, settled, making her aware of tremendous weight overhead.

"¡Cuidado!" he warned, holding the lantern away from three small kegs lined along the route.

"What is it?" She looked about, fearful.

"Madre de Dios, he should not be keeping these so near the house."

"¿Porqué no? It's only wine."

"Perhaps. I'm sure that's what he told everyone. But I wouldn't let a spark fall into one, if it is opened."

She had no time to press him for an explanation, for they came to a ladder. His hands on her waist boosted her up, and after a confused moment she realized there was a trap door. She pushed, and a wooden square fell back, letting in a draft of musty air. She sneezed.

Clambering up the rest of the ladder and into the barn, she wondered if Manuelo would be at the hut—or behind it—deep in a ritual the meaning of which she preferred not to know.

Ramón put the trap door back in place and covered it with straw. His breathing in the dusk sounded as if he were controlling excitement. He smelled of leather and fresh sweat and the smoke of campfires, but the odors were not offensive. They were alluring, hinting of the life he'd lived in distant places. A life she had hoped to share . . . She grasped his wrist, her other hand caressing his forearm beneath the shirt sleeve. "When García came and said you were dead, I—"

"Who is García?"

"A greedy, vile mestizo. He told don Luis that he saw you kill the one called Walker, and that he had killed you."

"Panadero paid this—García—the reward?"

"Sí, he showed don Luis something. A small object, I don't know what. Little enough to be held in the closed hand."

Ramón stood thoughtful, not returning her caresses. In the dark stalls the more prized caballos which were kept in at night moved about, hooves striking against boards or adobe. Distant voices, from across the river, drifted on the currents of warm air. "Where have you been? I have missed you so!"

"The old man didn't say where he was going? You cannot guess?"

"No, he would not say. He expected to be gone for a month, or more. Already it has been three weeks."

"Then, aside from accident or illness, he might be home in a few days."

"Sí, and we are to hold a grande fiesta—"

"Fiesta! To celebrate my death, I suppose."

She fought down a sneeze. "Ramoncito, you have no idea—"

He took her hand in his but instead of spreading a bed of clean hay in some concealed corner, he guided her out a side door and along the riverbank. She hurried beside him, bound for Manuelo's casita. She prayed that the man she had so recently married would not be there. "Slowly," she whispered, tugging at Ramón's arm.

They stopped, panting lightly, and peered at the dark open doorway. Moonlight filtered through the willows, dappling the ground in front of the hut. She strained her eyes for any movement, ears for any sound, nostrils for wisps of scented smoke.

He whispered back, "If no one is using it, why are you afraid?"

How could she tell him that she couldn't be certain Manuelo wasn't standing right beside them, listening to every word? Pulling his earlobe, tiptoeing, she placed her lips close to his head. "Do you know any charms against brujos?"

He jerked slightly as if to look at her and she sensed he was less surprised than he pretended. "Have you seen a brujo?"

"Maybe."

"Why would he hurt us?"

She shrugged. "Jealousy. Some reason of his own."

"Who? Do you know him?"

Did she? She knew his name, at least the one he was called. She knew the passion which his passion could arouse in her. She knew the thousand kindnesses he bestowed every day on villagers as well as everyone in the household. She knew he had been Ramón's friend.

"I am not sure...."

"Don't be afraid," Ramón said, leading her forward.

Chapter Ten

No moonlight fell inside the hut, though the single window space overlooking the river provided enough illumination to make out shapes. Sofía was relieved that the small room contained only the cot, a table on which was an olla and gourd, and against one wall a longer table holding an assortment of empty vessels. Arm around Ramón's ribs, she said, "The bed covering is fresh. And the water."

He moved toward the olla. "Are you in the habit of coming here?"

"Only in the day, when the house is so busy and noisy."

He drank two gourds of water and she waited just inside the doorway, her heartbeats drowning out the songs of night crickets. Manuelo would be looking for her—unless he knew already where she was, and who she was with. No one else would think to seek her here, but it was the first place he would come. Yet she couldn't leave.

Ramón sat down on the edge of the cot and began working off one of his boots. She knelt to help, as she had done so many times for his father. The thought of don Luis was uppermost in his mind, for he said, "Has the old man been treating you well?"

"Except for his hatred for you, I have no complaints." She took hold of the other boot, prolonging the removal while she built her courage. As the minutes ticked by and Manuelo didn't appear, the possibility that he was unaware of them grew. If he assumed she had gone to the hut alone, to rest from the fiesta preparations, would he not simply work on the account books or read, before sleeping? He had been too tired for anything else since the night of their wedding.

Ramón touched her hair. "You never understood why El Patrón wanted me dead, did you."

She caught his hand and held it to her face. "Nothing matters except that you are alive, and here." Peering through the gloom, she added, "Why did you risk coming back? Why not send me a message?"

His silence beset her with vexing questions. She laid her palm against his chest, where his shirt was open. Fingering the chain he wore around his neck, she realized it had been a rosary. "You have lost the Cristo," she murmured.

"It isn't lost. It's—"

183

He seemed to change his course. "It must be what García showed to prove he had killed me. Bastard found out about Walker, and went into my house looking for something to convince Panadero to give up the money." He lay back on the cot, brooding, knees drawn up in an M.

Moving to sit beside him, she asked, "You have a house? Where? Where were you, all this time? Have you been——" She dared not say aloud the thing she feared: with a woman? but ended, "——happy?"

His hand lazily ran up and down the arm bracing her as she leaned over him. "Happy? Dios, Sofía, I do not know what 'happy' means."

Emboldened by his touch, she lay down in the curve of his arm, savoring the warmth of his chest, and after a moment, she kissed his neck. "I do. It is loving you."

He tensed, as if he might shove her away. Then he was drawing his shirt tail out of his jeans. In the darkness, he removed an object he'd been carrying inside the garment—a sheathed knife or a small pistol?—and slid it beneath the pillow.

He was willing to accept her caresses! How far did she dare go? With trembling fingers she unbuckled the gunbelt, saying, "We shall be more comfortable without this."

He placed the weapon out of their way but in reach. "I'm very tired, querida. Don't expect too much."

Already she was receiving more than she could have hoped for so easily, so quickly. He held her in a close embrace, his kisses tasting of wine, and there was nothing grudging or hesitant about them. She guided his other hand into areas that had hungered for his attentions since she first saw him flirting with other younger girls on the village streets.

Pressure on his shoulder woke him. Coming up from the pillow with the Colt in his hand, he jammed it into someone's belly.

"¡Ramón, Diosito mío!" Sofía cried in fright.

Shaken, he released the cocked hammer. "Next time, speak first."

Trembling, she sank down beside him. "Sí, I shall."

"What time is it?"

"Near morning. I had Gerardo feed your horses and move them to the arroyo behind this casita."

"Gracias." He stepped out of the doorway and relieved himself. The moon was low in the western sky. What might the day bring? The night had been a surprise. He'd always known Sofía liked him, that her constant watching had not been for Panadero alone, but he'd underestimated the depth of her feeling. Taking her with him would be more of a problem than he'd anticipated.

"Can you eat in the dark?" She was unpacking a basket on the long table.

He carried a chair over and sat down. "I can try."

Cold tortillas, rolled into suggestive little rods. Cold frijoles in a small dish. Cold beef in bite-size chunks and tasting of peppers and onions. A bottle of white wine. He sampled it. Chablis, the only kind he liked; the kind Luis passed over in favor of port. "You remembered."

She didn't ask, *What?* "I have lived on memories for more than a year."

He laid aside the taco of beef. "Sofía—"

"Shhh!"

In the dimness he saw her make a quieting gesture.

"¿Qué está?" he whispered, thinking she had heard something outside.

"Eat," she told him. "It's almost dawn."

Did she suspect that he didn't return her affection in the way necessary for a lasting commitment? He hoped she did, so he would be spared the saying of hurtful words. Finishing the meal, he rinsed his mouth with the wine and swallowed. "Would you care for some?" He offered the bottle.

Coming close on soundless bare feet, she drank from it. Presently she said, "What are your plans?" While he wavered, unsure, she set aside the bottle and entwined their fingers. "You can tell me...over here."

Undressing each other, he had misgivings about the wisdom of indulging her, especially when he was feeling the effects of more wine than he was accustomed to. If Panadero—or anyone else, for that matter—discovered them, there would be no time for regrets or plans or defense. A blast or two from a pistol, and Sofía, at least, would die contented.

Earlier urgency past, he paced himself, savoring the moist heat of her body, the knowing caresses of her tongue and hands. She was as lithe as a younger woman, and the satisfaction they achieved went beyond expectations. He could almost love Sofía. After a long while, he said gently, "You haven't told me about Manuelo."

She tensed and seemed to stop breathing.

"You think he is the brujo, don't you?" In the growing light, he saw the flush of ardor drain from her face. Her eyes were fearful, her voice guarded.

"Why do you say that?"

Leaning above her, he continued to stroke her skin, more to soothe now than to excite. "When I asked about him, you were very nervous. Have you seen something unusual?"

She bit her lip. "He—has been . . . making advances. If he found us here, I don't know what he might do."

"His friendship means a great deal to me. I like to think mine is of equal value to him." Trouble slipped his arm beneath her head, grasped her thigh with his free hand. "Let him be angry if he must. It is not like you are married."

With a little whimper she hugged him tight and began to cry, silently, her tears trickling over his collarbone. Her muffled words sounded like, *I thought you were dead, I thought you were dead.*

The heat and light of daybreak reached the point that she was compelled to leave him, or Manuelo would come to find her. "You have not told me what you intend to do." Dressing, she let her eyes touch him though her hands were busy with petticoats, hooks, and buttons.

He sat up, rubbed his face and hair as if to restore his wits. Reaching for his jeans, he stood to pull them on. Hands resting on his hipbones, he blew out a long breath. "Damned if I know."

Hugging him hard and long, hoping it was not the last time, she tiptoed to kiss his unshaven cheek. "Keep out of sight until we know who our friends are."

She ran up the long hill, through the gates, across the patio and into the casa. Pausing just inside the open glass doors, she held her breath and listened. There was no one stirring; it was too early. She hurried down the hallway to the bath house, where water warm from yesterday's sun could not remove her sin and fear, but would wash away the traces of Ramón's lovemaking.

Instead of the customary chocolate and pastries in their rooms, everyone gathered in the comedor for coffee and meat, determined to enjoy don Luis's finery as much as possible before he came home. On her way from the bath house, Sofía tried to avoid them, but Manuelo spotted her and called, "Mi amor, have you eaten?"

Turning, she smiled and shrugged, still toweling her hair. "I hoped we might have something later, together." Had he wakened when she slipped out of their bed, to take Ramón supper? Had he followed, lurking in the darkness, and listened to them? Did he know what she had done, or was his lack of suspicion genuine? He appeared unarmed, but she knew he carried a knife in a sheath at his back, beneath his clothing; she had seen him remove it.

He glanced over his shoulder to be sure none of the girls was in sight and came to her. His embrace was gentle, his kiss urgent. "Tonight," he murmured. "I am strong again."

She hid her face against his chest, conscience wrenched by guilt. "Tonight," she whispered, then broke away and hurried into her room.

When she emerged after an hour, she was told that he had gone to tend a village child with a stomach complaint. Her stomach felt none too well. Coffee and a pastry might help. She was on her second cup when he came through the cocina door.

Swinging a chair around, he sat with his arms on the back. "We must talk."

Her heart jumped. Had he heard something in the village? Had someone seen her running with Ramón to the hut or going back to take him food? Manuelo might enjoy toying with her, aware all the time that the vows she'd said before a priest and before God were already broken.

"Unless I am mistaken," he went on, "don Luis will be home in a matter of days, a week at most." He picked up her limp hand and held it in both of his. "I don't want him touching you, ever again."

She swallowed, feeling as though the pan dulce she'd eaten were lodged in her throat. "I don't want him touching me, either," she said faintly. "Do you mean to leave now?" How could she leave with Manuelo, when Ramón had just come home! "Are we going soon? Where will we live?"

"For now, let me say only, be ready. There are still some things I must finish."

What things? she thought, but shrank from asking.

During siesta, when Manuelo lay in the hammock to catch the breezes, she stole into La Vieja's pantry and put items in a sack. Careful of the kegs in the passageway, she hurried through the tunnel and along the river to the hut.

Ramón was waiting, pacing. He looked older, weary; but nothing could spoil his attractiveness or dull her need to be with him, to experience their intimacy again.

While he ate she sat on the bed, wiping her sweaty palms on her skirt until the material was damp.

"I could use clean clothes," he said, around a bite of cheese and bread. "Can you send a trusted niño with some garments from my wardrobe?"

"There is Gerardo..."

"Sí, have him bring them here."

He drank from the new wine bottle. Catching her uncertainty, he said, "I am able to keep him from seeing me."

"Are you?" That wasn't reassuring. Did he mean that he could disappear, as had Manuelo, before her eyes? Dios, maybe she was bewitched, not by the segundo but by him. That would explain the raging desire, the willingness to do whatever he asked.

He seemed to read her mind, for he gave a one-sided smile, a fleeting frown. "Ah—you think I use the dark forces?"

"¿Cómo no? You know what I am thinking."

"Sofía, your heart shows on your face. I pray others are too occupied with themselves to notice."

She felt her cheeks flush. He had finished eating. Why didn't he come to her? He sat with an elbow crooked over the knob of the chair back, one ankle resting on his knee. "You still do not smoke."

"No."

Regarding him closely, she was disappointed to recall that he had never said he loved her. At the moment he appeared not even to want her. "What is going to happen?" she blurted, desperate.

His jaw tightened, his chin lifted. Averting his eyes, he said, "I'm going to kill the old man, before he kills me."

She jumped up and ran to him, knelt at his side, and clasped his near hand. "Oh, but don Luis believes you are dead! He will not send any more men."

"So I should thank Señor García, instead of shooting him."

"You don't have to shoot anyone—you are free." *But I'm not*, she thought with a pang. Aching to confess

190

everything and throw herself into his arms, she rested her cheek on his thigh, reveling in any contact.

"I can never be free," he said, his hand smoothing her hair, "until the old man is dead. No matter where I am, or how the years may pass, I'd be eaten alive, wondering if he had learned of García's deception. If one day I would look up into the barrel of a gun, and not hear it fire."

"Oh, Dios mío, Ramón, don't talk like that."

He fondled her shoulder thoughtfully. Then he said, "I need to talk to Manuelo."

Her throat closed. "Please don't."

"Why not? I have no fear of him. I told you, somos amigos. Compañeros. Even if he were a brujo, he would never use his powers to hurt me."

"Things may—have changed."

He leaned to see her face, but she stood up. "I have to go, siesta is nearly over."

"What things?"

Dipping from the olla, she drank a gourdful of water. "Promise me you won't leave, or come to the house," she begged.

"I promise." He looked mystified. "If Panadero returns, you will tell me, won't you?"

She chewed her lip. "I will come again when I can."

"Tonight?"

"Not tonight." She left without looking back. She knew if she did so at this moment, she would not be able to return to Manuelo. Ever.

II

The mare came up lame just east of Bavispe, where Luis planned to have supper and spend the night. The afternoon storm had caught them in the open, drenching him to the skin so that even a westering sun of blinding intensity failed to dry undersides, causing chafing at his crotch, the backs of his knees, his armpits.

Climbing down, he transferred the saddle to the mule unburdened with the pack, and mounted. Not accustomed to a rider, the animal pitched about, shaking like a dog emerging from a stream. A few hard blows to its head put it in a more docile mood, though insistent spurring was needed to start moving in the right direction.

Drained by continual watchfulness, expecting attack from a wild animal or band of thieves, drained by rigors of the trail unnoticed in other times—heat, hunger, thirst, biting insects—even with many stops for rest, Luis longed for his bedroll at dusk. Yet in the chill darkness of mountain and desert, sleep eluded him.

Like the unceasing grinding of the arrastre stone that separated silver or gold from ore, his thoughts churned and tumbled, always going back to the things he had done, admittedly evil things. Lying, cheating, stealing, whoring. Murder.

Perhaps Marieta had not come to the cave to harm him, but to warn him. In life, those entreaties to stop drinking, to stay home and be a faithful, loving husband, to go with her to Mass and confess his sins—those whining appeals had only served to enrage. No man he knew behaved the way she asked of him. "I am not a mujer!" he remembered shouting. "If you want fine things again, to be accepted in homes of people who wear shoes and eat with forks and sleep in beds, then, leave me alone. What I do, I do for you. Always for you."

Even as he said it, he knew it was he who hungered for fine things and to be accepted by people whose position he envied. Aside from her beauty and innocence, Marieta Cordero's status and obvious breeding had made him actually marry her instead of simply stealing her from her family and using her as he wished. Over the years he'd almost forgotten the scheming necessary to place him as hacendado of Hacienda de Panadero, lord of north Sonora.

Worth the lawlessness, the ruthlessness, to be able to ride over his land and know that all those cattle, goats, horses, crops, families of workers, belonged to him; that he was strong enough to defend his holdings against whatever threat came. That men feared to cross him in the slightest matter. Behind all his self-assurance lay the promise of the gold. With enough money, a man could crush every obstacle, every enemy.

Now, there was a bitter taste in his mouth that didn't result from drinking gypsum water from a canteen. Where did it come from?

The mule carrying the pack brayed, the sudden loud noise like a knife in his ear, and the one he rode heaved a breath and gave an echo. Bavispe was in sight.

III

Trouble lay on the cot in Manuelo's hut and watched the willows sway in the wind. The quick, hard shower coming down now cooled the afternoon heat, causing air currents that sent dead leaves and small twigs whirling past the open doorway.

From his hiding place he had watched activity on the hill all morning. Peónes leaving the house with morsels prepared in the cocina. Niños racing about without orders or supervision. La Vieja coming to the edge of the grass to throw down scraps for a flock of chickens. Criadas continually passed over the foot bridge to the village and back, sometimes carrying bundles. He wondered what they were stealing. When the rain began, everyone disappeared indoors, and lanky curs foraging in the home compound found places of shelter.

He tried to rest, to doze, but vivid fragments of his life thronged his head. Mamá, baking treats in the old ovens; families in the village, the visiting priests who came to say Mass and hear confessions. The building of Casa de Panadero. Boyhood amigos. Manuelo. Sweethearts. Father Navarre, the casita in Los Pobres, the two bounty hunters dead in the unblessed corner of the campo santo. The men sent to rescue him, pretending to be Rurales. Walker's fascination for the Mexican Colt, Walker dying. Who was García? Where had he gone, to spend the fortune paid out for the life of a man he'd never met. Tinita. . . .

He leaped up and went to stand in the breezy doorway. The rain had stopped.

From the direction of the barn, Sofía came through the willow grove toward him, a parcel in the crook of one arm and a basket swinging by its handle over the other. Close enough to speak, to give him the basket, she said cheerfully, "Hola. Here is comida."

He lifted the corners of a cloth. Two roasted ears of corn, another bottle of wine, flour tortillas, a chunk of piquante barbacoa, and a lidded container of camote con fruta. The last dish, made of sweet potato and apple, spiced with brown sugar, orange juice, butter and cinnamon, had been a favorite when he lived in the casa grande. "You haven't told La Vieja about me, have you?"

"Oh, no. She talks too much." Laying the parcel in a corner, she told him, "Here are the clothes." Then she sat on the bed and watched him eat. "I'm sorry, but the chicas finished all the frijoles and the biscuits."

Sucking the last sweetness out of the second corncob, he picked up the spoon. An ornate "P" was scribed on the little flat silver shield at the tip.

"Of all the things I've missed, those biscuits rank high. One cannot get them, in Los Pobres."

"Easy to make, if one has milk and flour, and a bit of butter."

"In Los Pobres, milk and flour and butter are luxuries."

"Where is Los Pobres?" she asked, but he was chewing and neglected to answer.

"You are not—" she began.

He waited, eyebrows angled to encourage completion of her thought.

"You really don't intend to kill don Luis, do you, Ramón?"

She appeared distressed. He ate another bite of the camote. "Would you be sorry to see him dead?"

"I would be sorry that you killed him."

"But you don't have tender feelings for him?"

Her face softened. "I have tender feelings for you."

He scraped the bowl, licked the spoon. "Sofía, maybe we should—"

"I know what you are going to say. Please, don't." She stood up, wringing her hands, and went to take the wine bottle out of the basket. "Let me have just these few hours."

And then——what? he thought; but he drank a little Chablis, and they made love again. It was a new feeling, to be truly loved by someone who had no false motive.

IV

Camping in the foothills above the Río Bavispe, Luis despaired at how little progress he had made that day.

Each day, it seemed, he grew less able to endure the rigors of the saddle, the discomfort of sleeping on the ground after a meal of cold tortillas rubbed with a bit of red pepper, a peon's supper. He lacked the will to warm the frijoles bought in Bavispe, or chew the jerked beef in his food sack. Wrapping in his blanket, he lay down in the shelter of an overhang and hoped for no night rain.

He had been sleeping fitfully, dreaming of pleasant times with Marieta, when a far-off rumble of thunder brought him fully awake. The mules stamped and snuffled, swinging their hind ends and pulling at the tethers as if a puma lurked nearby. The mare stood almost on top of him, and he could feel her trembling, hear the panting of her fear.

Struggling out of the blanket, he was reaching into the saddlebag for his pistol when a terrible rumbling came out of the center of the mountain and overtook them, rolling the earth up on its side, crashing down a few pines rooted in the crevices. Boulders and lesser rocks toppled from the heights into the depths.

The mare leaped over him and disappeared into the darkness. Brays of the mules mingled with his hoarse wordless shouts and, amid a cascade of dirt and limbs and camp gear, he tumbled to the bottom of an arroyo and lay stunned.

Jerking, shuddering ground threatened to split apart beneath him; his single thought was of falling into a chasm and ending in the fires of Hell.

Someone was yelling, "¡Dios mío! ¡Dios mío!" and a part of his mind wondered who else was caught in this temblor de tierra, earthquake, rendered helpless by the relentless powers of nature, or God, or other supernatural force.

Gradually there was a stilling of the movement, pebbles ceased to bounce around him, and in the silence he realized he was alone.

He remained in the arroyo until daylight. When he ventured to climb out, the changed terrain was bewildering. Where the feeder stream to the Río Bavispe had been, was a plain. Where the plain had been, boulders lay tumbled in heaps. Where pines and crags had stood, now a crevasse opened. He tottered to the edge and peered over. At the bottom, rushing water and boulders the size of Casa de Panadero turned him back, shaking.

One of the mules lay dazed in a level space, eyes half closed. Not far away stood the patient mare, legs splayed as if it expected further upheaval. The satchel had come to rest a wagonlength from where he'd cowered for hours. The saddlebags had lodged against a broken tree at the bottom of the slope. His pack and the mule which had carried it—cooking gear, food sack, ammunition—were gone.

After as thorough a search as he could muster, he picked up what was left, put the saddle on the mule, and tried to locate a way out of the rubble. The trail had disappeared, but in about a league he came out of the disturbed area and, the mare following, headed toward a settlement known as Esqueda.

Not much farther. In two nights, he would be home. The room Luis found stank of pigs and damp earth, but nothing disturbed his sleep for the first time in weeks. Groggy, needing food, he asked the keeper of the posada to recommend a place to eat, somewhere he might have savory vegetables, blanquillos, and a cut of beef he could chew.

He didn't feel bewitched now, only tired. Hunger and thirst appeased, he pushed back from the café table and felt for a cigarro and a match. Staring through the smoke at a stained adobe wall, he was struck speechless by a pair of gleaming eyes watching him.

At first there was no recognition, only fear. Then gradually a face became visible around the eyes. It was a woman. Marieta? Sofía? The mother he'd never known? His abuelita, the grandmother in whose home he'd grown up? Some tía, an aunt, come to shout accusations as they had so often done?

No—it was La Virgen herself. There was the bullet hole in her forehead, the one he'd put into the framed picture of her that used to hang in the old house, before Casa de Panadero was more than a dream in his brain.

Aren't you ashamed? she said, though her lips didn't move. Aren't you sorry, for the crimes you have committed, against God and man? Do you not wish for peace? Does not your spirit yearn to be pure?

Glancing about, he realized none of the other travelers enjoying their supper could see or hear her, else they'd fall on their knees and begin offering up prayers. When he turned back to the wall, he expected the vision to be gone, nothing more than imagination, a result of eating rich food after weeks of trail rations, of inhaling too much smoke and drinking too much mezcal.

She was still there, her sad eyes boring into his soul. Again he heard the sweet voice reproaching him: You have not forgotten those men you killed, the ones you cheated, the lies you told. You have not forgotten putting a hole in the back of your wife's head, the same way you put this one in mine. You remember every hurt, every evil thought, every woman you used and dishonored. Aren't you ashamed? Aren't you sorry?

If he did not escape those accusing eyes, he would die. Limbs refusing to move, he struggled to rise, to flee, but his foot tangled in the rung of chair, overturning it, flinging him into the arms of a man who cried, "¡Cuidado!"

The sweet, sad voice followed him into the night.

You grieved those you should have loved, took away life from those you ought to have protected. Aren't you ashamed? Aren't you sorry?

His will broke, and in his heart Luis cried, *Yes!*

V

Manuelo's slight form seemed to fill the doorway. "So. You are back."

The Colt steady in his hand, Trouble finished sitting up and rubbed the sweat-dampened hair out of his left eye. "Are you surprised?" He felt foolish, holding the gun on his friend, but Sofía's fears had planted a doubt.

Manuelo leaned his back against the doorpost. "I am not wearing a pistol."

"You carry a knife."

"Put away your weapon. No one here will harm you." He stepped into the yard, made a welcoming gesture. "Come up to the house."

The invitation was tempting. Through the trees, past the wagon gate, Trouble could see the marble fountain, almost smell the mist-splashed tiles. By rights, the house was his. Though built with blood money, and for base motives, its simple elegance always thrilled him. Desire to claim his inheritance coursed through him like a quickening pulsebeat. Foolish, to care so much about a pile of rocks and mud with a bit of ornament around the edges. He laid aside the gun, wiped his palms on his jeans.

"The risk is too great. Once it is known that I am alive, the old man's offer has the power to make enemies of friends."

"How long do you intend to hide in this old casita?"

"I came to kill Panadero."

"You may have that pleasure—or burden—in a few days. I shall take everyone to the grotto for a picnic. Then you can come inside, without danger."

Trouble buckled on the gunbelt, slid the Colt into its holster and tied the thong. Pulling on his boots, he warned, "If you lie, I will have to deal with you, as well."

Teeth showed beneath the segundo's mustache. "Oh? You think I have reason to trick you?"

The charms of Sofía crossed his mind, and, no doubt, his face as well, for a glint of sunlight showed him the knife, appearing in the brown hand as if by magic.

Manuelo came back into the room with the air of expecting to hear a confidence. "You have something to tell me?" Unspoken words hovered in the space between them: to confess?

Hand trembling near the Colt, he said, "No."

The smile was self-mocking. "You don't have to say it. I knew, long before you, how Sofía feels."

Trouble's fingers closed around the bone grips and blood pounded in his ears, but he calmed his jerking nerves.

The segundo continued, in his unemphatic way, "I love Sofía very much. I can forgive her this—attachment—she has for you" Suddenly he stabbed the knife point into the wooden bed rail. "so long as there is no more intimacy, between you."

"You have my word."

"Gracias." Manuelo reclaimed his knife.

They walked upslope toward the casa grande.

Chapter Eleven

Occupied with dread and longing, Sofía startled half a dozen of the girls who were lazing about in the comedor by snatching away a platter of pastries and screaming, "Clean the house again. Don Luis will be home any day, and will kill us all if he finds such disorder."

"Relax, Sofía, things look fine to me."

"Sí, you are getting old and bossy. You have forgotten how to enjoy life."

"It is siesta now, amiga, we cannot work in this heat."

Her fists clenched. Old. Bossy. Is that how people thought of her? How Ramón saw her? He knew her feelings for him; was he only being kind, giving her what she most desired only because he felt sorry for her?

The dread increased. Unless Dios intervened, he would kill his father. Then—what? She yearned to run away with him, leave all her mistakes behind. Yet, in spite of the turmoil of her heart, a part of her knew that whatever place he made for her in his life wasn't likely to be permanent. He was young, handsome. Women loved him. She loved him.

Manuelo came in through the patio door, saying, "Queridita, gather everyone, including La Vieja, and let us go to the grotto for a día del campo."

"A picnic?" she cried, "With don Luis and a hundred guests arriving within the week, and everything to do over?" Besides the dust and disarray in the house, the imported fruits had either spoiled or been eaten, and the paper lanterns had been pilfered for the celebration of someone's saint's day. She grasped the back of a chair. "Are you loco?"

"Can you think of a better way to get everyone out of the casa grande for a little while?"

With fear and suspicion, she searched his face. "Why would you wish to do that?"

He smiled. "Ramón wants to look at the house."

She felt blood drain from her cheeks. "How—how did you find him?"

Manuelo's fingertips stroked beneath her ear. Though he appeared quite tense, there was no reproach in his voice. "I did not have to 'find' him. Your eyes told me the boy is alive."

She forced words out over her dry tongue. "You must be wondering why I didn't tell you—"

"No importa. I have spoken with him, and he understands." He caught at a passing niño and said, "La Vieja is packing the baskets. We are all going out to the grotto."

The child raced away, spreading the news, and shrieks of joy sounded in several parts of the house. La Vieja's antojitos, snacks, whetted even jaded appetites.

Manuelo stood turned away, arms akimbo, thoughtful. What had they said? Had Manuelo made accusations? Threats? Had Ramón admitted, or denied, the joining of his body with hers? Defended himself by revealing her failure to mention her marriage? What must he be feeling now? Amusement? Shame? Anger? Relief?

Manuelo reached out and took her hand. His grasp and voice were gentle. "Sofía. Are you sorry you married me?"

Suddenly hot, faint, sick, she forced herself to look into his kind eyes, and found the courage to say, "I think, when all of this is over, I shall be glad."

He cupped the back of her head in his hand and kissed her lips gently.

Manuelo was gone only a few minutes before emerging from the back of the house, surrounded by laughing girls and capering boys, the old cook and Sofía trailing. Arms full of white things to be laundered, they crossed the footbridge and went downriver. Manuelo carried two large baskets, and an older boy carried two more.

Trouble stepped from behind the sheltering hedge and let himself in through the glass doors.

Silence. Breezes roved the halls, ruffling a leaf here and there in the flowerpots. No bootsteps, no commanding voice of El Patrón Grande.

Yet, in the comedor, he clearly heard the shouts and accusations that had embittered meals eaten at the long dining table. The silver service was still the centerpiece. The china cabinet, with its German crystal and set of Minton, sat where it always had. The three glass doors leading to the patio were now hung with white lace curtains drifting in the wind. To his right, a wrought iron gate led to rooms which had housed servants and were probably being used by the criadas here for the fiesta.

The crude, unpainted adobe wall of the old casita joined floor and ceiling like a growth drawing life from its surroundings. Its tiny, barred window was covered with thick vines planted in earthen jars. Someone used to keep that cut back; no longer. He pulled the tangle aside enough to see into the library.

Dark. Dreary. A line of pale light around the door leading into the main hall did little to illumine the shelves or furnishings. Evil events had occurred in that room, when it was nothing but a poor man's choza. An evil day, too, when he found that cursed map.

Controlling anger, he swept aside the curtain of silver beads on leather strips. Crossing to the main hall, he peeked into Sofía's bedroom. It was furnished with a washstand, bed, dresser, and small rug. Her few dresses hung on pegs along one wall. Not considered worth giving a wardrobe.

The connecting door that led to Panadero's room stood half open. Or, half shut.

Inlaid woods floored the central hallway, polished to a sheen by criadas with rag mops. More than once he'd run barefoot down its length, holding back sobs of rage, escaping the old man's taunts. Taking off his boots, he walked to the other end, pausing at Manuelo's small room. Along with the basic furniture, there was a cherry wood pigeonhole desk covered with the neat clutter of an organized, busy man; a glass-doored bookcase filled with dark clothbound volumes; a wardrobe in one corner; and a gilt-framed mirror. Here, not in Sofía's room.

The sala never changed. Since those long-ago workmen left, and the room was furnished, nothing had been moved. A rug or two had worn thin, but similar ones were found to replace them. The piano waited forlornly beside the wide front doors. Bypassing Panadero's small office, Trouble came to the old man's bedroom.

He hesitated before pushing the door fully open and stepping inside. Cream colored walls, filmy white curtains. He had never set foot on the thick carpet, nor looked out the French doors to the flower-tangled jardín. Never sat in the deep horsehair chair in the corner.

Now, he walked around his father's massive walnut bed, an uncanopied tester with an Aztec design carved into the headboard. A dresser and wardrobe carved to match. An ornately framed mirror hung over the dresser, and several small boxes sat upon the dresser cloth. Various shapes and sizes, lacquered red or black and decorated with mother-of-pearl birds and butterflies, the boxes seemed out of place. They were not expensive nor uncommon. Had they belonged to Mamá? If so, why did the old man keep them?

Resisting the impulse to open any of them, he turned to consider the notion of leaving something to startle and worry Panadero. He took the sack of coins from his shirt and placed it on a heavy antique Spanish chest blocking the French doors. Studying the effect of dusty leather against polished ebony, he lay on the too-soft mattress, fingers locked behind his head, knees drawn up, the coverlet cool against the soles of his feet. The Aztec carving seemed to lean over him, so after a minute he stood up and smoothed the traces made by his body.

Perhaps on the bed itself. He tossed the bag onto the old man's pillow. Not quite the best spot, either. Jouncing it in his hand, he eyed the dresser. Better. Among the shiny, feminine boxes, the drab brown sack hid in view, like a rattlesnake coiled in a clump of desert primroses. Much better. When the old man went to the mirror to preen, he would get a shock.

Returning to the central hall, Trouble dreaded going to his room. But the stair treads drew his feet upward, banister sliding like satin under his hand. On the landing, he remembered awakening that morning so many years ago to find Mamá telling him God would take care of him.

He remembered too, the circumstances under which he had last closed the door with the china knob. Thrilled with discovering the map, he was on his way to La Nariz to find whatever treasure the old man so jealously guarded.

"You gave me many reasons to hate you," he said. "I wish I could hate you. If I did, killing you would be easy."

Dresses, rebozos, hair ribbons, jewelry, slippers— strewn on his bed, draped across his chair, even piled on the floor. Who, he wondered, now dreamed of handsome chicos on the same pillows once dampened from his crying? His small bookcase had been raided, so that a few of the lesser volumes leaned against the sides. His mirror was dimmed with an accumulation of face powder.

He descended the stairs and sat on next-to-the-bottom step, staring at Panadero's closed door, sorry for the men he had killed, and for the one yet to die.

At last he stood up, ground the heel of his bare foot in the teardrops beaded on the polished wood, and put on his boots. He retrieved the sack from El Patrón's dresser. Then he went down the steps to the wine cellar.

Leaving the lantern at the mouth of the tunnel, he hunkered in the gloom and set about cutting through the wax seals with his pocket knife. He pried up the lid of the first keg. No wine odor. His fingers plunged into a dry substance. Black powder, used in making ammunition and fireworks, and for blasting. Fifty-kilo kegs lined with waterproofing. Three of them.

A sound at the top of the stairs brought the Colt into his hand, but it was Manuelo who came down the steps, followed the light, and suggested, "Let us sample the patrón's special wine."

"If you mean this, I'm afraid there is not enough wine, special or otherwise, to make either of us borrachito."

Manuelo peered into one dark keg, then took a pinch between thumb and forefinger. He didn't seem surprised.

"Why does he keep black powder so nearby?"

"Whatever the purpose, it must not require haste. These have been here for a long time."

"Years?"

"Since you left, and no one was able to find you."

207

Pressing the lids shut, Trouble said, "Oh, they found me."

The bloodshot eyes studied him in silence. Trouble rested his hands on his hips. "I trust that everyone enjoyed the día del campo."

"The grotto is always nice. And the linens and shirts for the fiesta got washed." A smile creased his cheeks. "Would you care to eat something? I can bring a basket."

"Sí, gracias."

He blew out the lantern and when Manuelo returned, they sat on the lower steps and shared baked chicken, soda biscuits, and a bottle of Panadero's Médoc. Presently, he said, "Let us have the fiesta. Invite those whom the old man wanted, and everyone in the village, down to the last grandmother. I want to see ricos mixing with our people. I want a fiesta at Casa de Panadero to end all fiestas."

"You mean, without El Patrón?"

"Sí, without him! Before he can return and forbid it."

Manuelo gave a doubtful shake of his head. "He is a harsh master, as you well know, with fists of iron and ready to use them, and if he—"

"Leave him to me. You and Sofía make things ready for tomorrow night."

Thigh-to-thigh on the step, they passed the bottle back and forth, while the air vents to the outside grew dim as the sunlight shifted. Presently, relaxing from the wine, Trouble said, "He murdered her, you know."

"Who?"

"My mother."

"¿Doña Marieta?"

"Sí. Doña Marieta. His wife."

Manuelo took a mouthful of wine, savored it before swallowing. "I heard that she ran away with another man."

"And you believed it?"

"She was said to be beautiful. It was easy to believe. Remember, I never knew her."

"I believed it, too. But I ought to have known better."

"You were a child."

"I grew up."

"If she was not unfaithful," Manuelo asked, soft, "why would he kill her?"

"Because he's a selfish, ignorant bastard with nothing good in him. Don't waste your time trying to understand. He has no heart. He is ruled by greed. I'm surprised he paid García the reward. Parting with that kind of money must have hurt like hell."

"People say that he built this house for her."

"He built this house for himself." Trouble set the empty bottle on the floor, wishing they had an olla of cold water. In the silence, he became aware of household noises not far above their heads. Stone columns bore the weight of the massive structure, but the wide, smooth planks of the central hallway lay on a support of rough-hewn boards, so that only a thin layer separated the dim, quiet cellar from the life going on upstairs.

Manuelo packed chicken bones, empty containers, and greasy napkins back into the basket. "How do you think you will feel, after you have killed him?"

Tomorrow at this time, if all went as planned, the grounds would swarm with pretty señoritas practicing entertainments of song and dance, and jovens cutting grass, hanging paper lanterns, setting up long tables and chairs in the patios. Making ready for guests, feasting, music. He dared not show himself, but from the ridge, the bounty hunter's rifle at his side, he would watch for Panadero to ride in. Though he loathed the dishonor of laying an ambush, there was no other way to be certain it was the old man who died. "Free," Trouble said.

Even as the word left his mouth, he realized he could never be happy nor free, within these walls. Tormenting memories tainted the contentment he sought.

The casita at Los Pobres waited, beckoned. Long, relaxed evenings in which to read, days spent planting herbs and vegetables, exercising his horses, visiting with Padre. He could be happy there, if no casa grande enticed with its beauty and elegance, tricking him into thinking he would forget.

An idea began to form, and he laughed.

"¿Qué piensa?" Manuelo asked, his manner suspicious.

Trouble grew warm with excitement. He would make fuses. There was a coil of hemp rope in the barn. He had noticed it when he and Sofía paused there a few days ago. Firecrackers, for the fiesta! Fat, squat, fifty-kilo firecrackers.

Three of them.

Trudging up from the grotto beside La Vieja, trailing the girls, her arms laden with washed and air-dried linens for the fiesta, Sofía trembled from an excess of heat and anxiety. Where was Ramón? Would he sleep in the house tonight? What lay ahead, for her? Manuelo's discovering him destroyed any hope of being intimate with him again.

Squeals of rivalry for first in the bath house were cut short as Manuelo appeared and announced, "¡Señoritas! There has been a change. We are going to begin the fiesta tomorrow night at dusk, and all of us—sisters, brothers, cousins, everyone—all have been invited."

The surprised girls cheered and danced about, hugging each other.

Shouting over their babble, he went on, "I trust that anything which has been neglected shall be taken care of by the time don Luis's honored guests begin to arrive."

Criadas bumped into each other, hurrying to tell the news. In half a minute, she and Manuelo and La Vieja stood alone in the main patio. "¡Caramba!" the old cook said. "The mole must be started."

When the señora had hobbled along the corredor to the kitchen, Sofía blew tendrils of hair from her face and said, "What do you think will happen, Manuelito, if Luis comes and the fiesta is over? His food eaten, his flowers carried away. The band, paid for music he did not hear?"

"He will be too busy to think of it, with Ramón back."

"Is—is he still here, in the house?" Impossible, to hope for a quiet evening, just the three of them, reading in the sala, sipping Chablis. Someone might walk in, see him, and word would spread. Or she would drink too much, say too much.

"Wherever he is, he'll be safe. Until tomorrow night, or the night after. Don Luis must come home. Es su Destino."

II

Felipe García leaned on the bar in a cantina in Santa Cruz, marveling how quickly his money was spent. Fine clothes, nights in elegant hotels, rich food and champagne for the expensive women met in high-class bordellos. A blooded horse, a silver-encrusted saddle, a bridle with gold medallions. Boots of exotic leather. Cigarros that didn't strip the hair off his tongue. A narrow-brimmed sombrero of lightweight felt. A Swiss pocket watch, three gold rings set with rubies. A new sheath for his stiletto.

A wallet that was now flat.

He'd supposed that two thousand pesos would last forever; it was more money than he or anyone else in his family—except his tío Alejandro—had ever seen at one time. He'd enjoyed everything, in abundance. Discouraging, to face the fact that those more fleeting pleasures were at an end, unless he put his wits to work.

His first tequila of the evening was creating familiar sensations when, in response to movement at the door, he glanced around.

Luis Panadero stood on the threshold, hesitating, a leather satchel hanging at the end of one arm and a saddlebag on the other. He did not present the dapper, robust figure he had cut at his rancho, only a few months ago. His clothing was wrinkled and dirty, as though he'd been sleeping out. His hair had grown to an unbecoming length and gray stubble covered his jowls. He appeared exhausted. What was such a person doing here, in this low-class cantina?

Not knowing whether the old man had discovered his trickery, García jerked his stare away; but Panadero had spied him.

At his elbow, the hacendado greeted, "Hola, señor," with what seemed to be genuine friendliness. Clearly, he still believed the boy to be dead. García's neck muscles relaxed.

"Ah, don Luis, mi amigo. ¿Cómo está? May I buy you a copita?"

"Sí, gracias. Whiskey, if you please."

Breaking his last double eagle, he bought a bottle and guided Panadero to a nearby chair. He poured their drinks, and was startled when the old patrón gulped his down and held out the glass for another.

Whatever had happened, García must take advantage. "I do not wish to intrude into private matters," he began with seeming deference, "but I think there is something wrong? May I be of assistance?"

Panadero closed his red-rimmed eyes. When he opened them, they were distant with recalling, and he drew a long breath. His words were almost too faint to be heard in the noisy room. "There was a great temblor, un terremoto, in the middle of the night, in the Sierra Madre. Cliffs and ridges fell, valleys disappeared. I was there. The mule, the pack, were lost. It was like the end of the world."

"It must have been frightening."

"Like lightning bolts inside the mountains, breaking them apart. The other mule died later. The mare—" Don Luis feebly waved his hand. "Outside . . ."

"It is my pleasure to feed and stable your mount." García stood, moving the bottle closer to the hacendado's empty glass. "I will also find a comfortable room for you, if you desire."

The fretful face slowly relaxed into submission. "Muy bien." Luis grasped the bottle, began to pour.

Putting the mare next to his own horse, he paid for sleeping spaces in an uncrowded common room in the nearest clean posada, and went back to the cantina. The old don was still there, most of the whiskey inside him.

Gripping an elbow, he helped Panadero to rise. The old man was gaunt, but heavy with the weight of dejection. "Come, we'll have a hot supper, and then sleep. Do not worry, don Luis. I shall take care of you."

Having García at his side filled him with a strange sense of un viaje de pesadilla—a nightmare journey, in which he had lost all control of events. Why had this man appeared now, in the dark of the moon, like a—like a brujo—his grinning, swarthy face and unnaturally bright eyes outwardly those of a friend; but, hiding—what?

Then it was not Manuelo whose spirit dogged his backtrail in the mountains, whose coyote familiar smelled out the route he had taken to La Nariz. It had to be García, the man who had come to Casa de Panadero with Marieta's little cross; the man who had killed Trouble.

No—*he* had killed Trouble, by paying for his death. He remembered, he admitted it.

"The devil sent you," he gasped, pulled along faster than he felt like walking, toward a place he didn't want to go.

"Don Luis, how you insult me." The teeth beneath the mustache gleamed under a smoky streetlight. "You have drunk a bit too much, no?"

The fingers hurting his arm directed him through a low doorway into an earth-floored room. Candle lit, damp—¡Dios mio! He was in the cave—

Snores of sarape-wrapped men and the odor of burning shucks of many cigarettes pulled him back from the abyss. Guiding fingers pushed him toward a corner, onto a petate, and the bandit came to rest beside him. Offering a cigarro, the fortune hunter said, "You appreciate a good Havana before sleeping, I am sure."

Dared he sleep? A sharp pain in his side took his breath and he labored to regain it. He glanced down, looking for blood, for the knife García must have thrust between his ribs. But the man's hands were lax, wrists propped on drawn-up knees. There was no knife. Only the glowing tip of a fresh cigar, and the puff of smoke issuing from the man's thin Spanish lips.

Luis felt his shoulder muscles relax. "You...did not know...Marieta, did you. You were not...here, then."

"Marieta? No, I have only lately come into this norteño country. My tierra is south of Arispe." The speaker crossed his ankles, friendly. "Mi abuelo—my father's father—sailed from Andalusía. He met my mother's papá on the ship, and the two families became friends."

"You were born here. You are gente razón."

"Sí, creole. As were you, Luis?"

He was silent, thinking of his Apache grandmother, his father. More Indio than not, though it didn't show in his face. His grandfather from Cádiz, that was where he got his looks. His ambition.

Damn ambition, and Indian blood. The mix had not turned out well. Nothing achieved had ever been enough. He would have given anything, done anything—and did— to be the hidalgo he appeared, but knew in his heart that he wasn't.

"Señor García."

"¿Sí, amigo?"

"There is a priest in Nogales. Padre Xavier. Do you know him?"

"No. I regret to say that my—travels have left me little time for priests."

"Nor mine." He inhaled deeply of the cigar smoke, let it out gradually.

Brujo or not, it was best to have a strong compañero along to ride for a médico if he became truly ill, someone to see that he reached home in safety. The rigors of the trail, after weeks of fear and the burden of hiring bounty hunters, had spent him. Set him to seeing fantasmas, ghosts, and suspecting innocent people.

Manuelo's service had never wavered. If not for that little segundo, if not for Sofía and La Vieja and all the others, Hacienda de Panadero would not be the magnificent estate which covered thousands of hectares, grew crops and beef and horses, employed a hundred men, gave shelter to a village of two hundred souls. Souls who had often forced him to do things Marieta would have hated. He wished she were here, to forgive him.

That might vanquish this killing sense of regret and guilt, if such a thing were possible. Perhaps it was possible. Nudging García awake, he said, "I have business with the padre. In the morning. I shall be grateful to have you accompany me."

Chapter Twelve

"Fresh flowers must be brought." Sofía had been up since the dark hours of the morning, driven to wake La

Vieja and start the old cook on preparing tamales, readying the mole de guajolote, stewing the chickens for enchiladas. Two pits, one for beef, one for pork, had been tended most of the night by men from the village. "Have you tasted the barbacoa? Is it tender?"

Manuelo sat beside her in the west patio, drinking a cup of coffee. He seemed to be listening; but with him, one couldn't be sure. Several girls straggled about with mops, complaining, while others joked and laughed and fashioned paper lanterns. A couple were in the bath house washing their long black hair. She pressed her throbbing temples. "Are you sure the musicians are coming? And the ice—it must not be unwrapped and chipped until the very last momentito."

"Chuco will get the flowers. The barbacoa is tender. The fish did arrive, and the band assured me they will be here this evening. Juan and Juanito know how to handle the ice. Sofía, mi amor, stop fretting. This is a party—enjoy it."

"Diosmio, easy for you to say. Men have a way of disappearing just when they are most needed." Ay, did she really say that? She darted a look, but Manuelo's face gave no sign that 'disappear' had special meaning for him.

As the morning wore on, chicas flew upstairs and down, leaving tasks half finished and implements scattered. She picked up an oily rag from the piano, giving a few swipes at streaks the duster had missed. Manuelo directed the setting up of tables in the main patio and the courtyard. He spoke sharply to the grass-cutters for scything too close and creating bare spots in the lawn that was don Luis's pride. He showed the boys which trees to climb, what branches to adorn with the lanterns. She watched him with a growing sense of appreciation.

Savory aromas wafted from the pits, braziers, and ovens. Crusty breads, cheeses melting in cazuelas; from Guaymas and Mazatlán came dried shrimp for crema de camarónes, and dried mackerel for ceviche; mounds of shredded lettuce, guacamole, ten-kilo barrels of tomatoes being peeled, cooked, sliced, and diced, along with sweet and picante onions, spices and herbs, and a dozen kinds of peppers for salsas rojo y verde. The slap-slap of tortillas in the making. Bowls of red, green, and purple grapes, platters of sliced mangoes, baked bananas, melon chunks resting in wine. La Vieja's cocina was busy, hot, closely supervised.

For norteamericano tastes that might be scorched by spicier foods, Manuelo had suggested deep-fried chicken, string beans and arroz con leche. Flan, pan dulce, and tartas of fruit paste. Two niños were roasting corn ears in the shuck. And of course there would be frijoles, fried in small flat cakes in the manner of north Sonora. If nothing else went right, there would be enough to eat.

Sofía felt sick when she realized that in hours, fifty rich ranchers and businessmen, along with wives, marriageable children, and possibly other relatives, were actually going to begin arriving, and that she must greet them. They would consider her strange for not knowing where don Luis was or when he might return. If Ramón knew, he had not told her; and he wouldn't be at her side when the visitors questioned her about the absence of their host.

In the afternoon, she vacillated between anticipation and dismay. Even Manuelo's calm failed to calm her. "Will you stand with me to welcome everyone? And shall I seat them in the patios or at the tables? Are the fireworks in a safe place? I saw niños standing around the shed earlier."

"Roberto is guarding the shed. Seat the ladies in the sala, while the gentlemen have a cigar in the courtyard. Our band will play for the girls to sing a few little corridos, and for couples to dance the jarabe before the food is served."

"You are sure those mariachis will be here?"

He led her out to don Luis's walled jardín and made her sit in a cushioned chair. "If you stir for one hour, I myself will lock you in your room until this whole fiesta is over."

However, the niños chosen to be servers had to be scolded for sneaking bits of food, and prompted in their duties until she felt confident that they could manage the trays of dishes, goblets, rum punch and bottles of wine without mishap. More of the girls abandoned work to take a bath, go to the village for something deemed important, or make a last-minute alteration in a dress. She even caught three of them stealing her perfume. At least they took only the scent, and not the little crystal bottle which Luis had given her in a rare moment of affection.

Then the mariachis arrived. Five of the six were young and handsome, and took delight in strutting in and out of the house in their tight black trousers, short coats, and highly-polished boots. They flirted with the girls and also sneaked bits of the foods, causing the niño whose job it was to fan away flies with a palm frond to giggle and grab a slice of mango. He saw Sofía coming and crammed the fruit into his mouth, dribbling juice down his chin and onto his white shirt.

The village band struck up something loud and lively out by the barbacoa pits, and the girls dashed away, pulling the cornet player and the guitarist with them. Through the open glass doors, she noticed men and women, children and strange dogs, streaming into the yard, starting to munch tacos, corn ears, and flautas. So many dark-skinned people dressed in calzones and rebozos, barefoot or wearing sandals, trampling don Luis's grass and in some cases, flowerbeds.

"Manuelo, come quickly! They are ruining everything!"

He joined her, saying, "Don't be alarmed. I shall speak to the jefe about keeping order."

"Oh, why would he want to mix everyone? Our people cannot enjoy themselves with ricos ignoring or insulting them, and the ricos—! What will they think, having to eat at tables with peónes and campesinos?"

Manuelo grasped her hands and held her still. "Don Luis's ricos inside, others on the lawn. That way, all may see and hear the entertainments, without annoying each other. If Ramón expects more than that—" He shrugged.

Hope rose in her that Ramón would come out of hiding and mingle with the guests—perhaps only among the lanternlit crowds of Indios and mestizos, perhaps disguised as one of them—and she could find opportunity to link her arm in his, to suggest that he would be wise to leave Hacienda de Panadero tonight.

"¡Ay, the guard dogs!" Gerardo always let them free at dusk, and if not told ten times not to do so, he would open the pens this night. She started down the back corredor to find him.

Striding beside her, Manuelo said, "To ease your worry, let me show you something."

Wire enclosures at the rear of the barn held half a dozen mastiffs with jaws strong enough to rip off a hand or foot, though to Sofía's knowledge no one had ever been foolish enough to trespass on hacienda property and risk being attacked. The dogs patrolled the walls enclosing the home compound, which included Manuelo's hut and the fields beyond on the north, and all of the corrals wherein were kept the select breeding stock. The ridge to the south lay outside the wall, as did the Río Sangría and the village. Next to the doglots was a storeroom for the chunks of meat which they were fed.

"Mira." Watch. He laid out on the ground a portion for each animal. From a small cloth bag carried in his shirt the same way Ramón had carried some object the night he came home, Manuelo poured a handful of gray powder and, stabbing his knife into each piece several times, stuffed the cuts with the substance.

"Is it poison?"

"Only an herb. If by chance someone opens a pen, the beast inside will have no desire come out. Or, if it does, might stroll about like any other cur."

He tossed the pieces over the enclosures and the dogs tore at the meat.

"Manuelo—"

"¡Sí?" He wiped his palms on the empty cloth bag.

"Where did you learn—to be a—healer? To use herbs, the way you do."

His voice remained patient. "What are you asking me, Sofía?"

She bit her lower lip. "I— You once told me that your tierra is to the south. Are— Are you Mayo? Or, what?" Words began stumbling over her tongue. "It does not matter, really, I only thought, since I didn't know, and now that we are married, maybe you would tell me—" She braced herself to hear what he would say. Yaqui? Seri?

Tales about those fierce Indio tribes were terrifying. Her own Indian blood came from peaceful, civilized Opatas.

He returned her searching look, his head tilted as if he were deciding whether to trust her. "My people are Cora."

Not sure what beliefs Coras held, nor what customs they followed, nor even where they lived, she wished she were bold enough to ask, Are you a shaman, a brujo? For if he possessed supernatural powers, leaving him in order to go with Ramón would mean death for both of them. Another question hovered in her mouth: When you said he understood, was it because you warned him? Threatened him? Cast a spell upon him? She shivered. *I must talk to Ramón.* She had to know that he was all right.

Already the mastiffs were shaking themselves, walking about in the enclosure, lying down and licking the blood off their front paws and jowls. The yellow eyes blinked sleepily.

When she and Manuelo went into the house, two of the girls were putting fresh candles in the chandelier and wall sconces, lighting the lamps, picking up cleaning rags. The serving tables were covered with lidded containers of chilled foods, jars and ollas and bottles full of things to drink, stacks of plates, mountains of napkins, trays of glasses and silverware. The flowers in hanging pots and macetas in corners throughout the casa lent their fragrances to the aromas of brass polish, opened wine, simmered and toasted and fried dishes awaiting mouths.

"Oh, I am so nervous!" The effects of the cooling bath earlier had worn off, but there was no time for another. Manuelo pressed a square of folded paper into her hand. One of his packets of medicine. "Is this what you fed the guard dogs?"

He laughed. "Take it, and find out."

García straightened his stiff legs in front of him and crossed his booted ankles. He'd been waiting for over two hours in the back of the dark church, the mumble of voices from the confessional lulling him into a doze more than once. He and Luis had ridden all day, without comida, siesta, or even a cigarro. Only stops to rest the mare, to relieve themselves in the brush, to gulp stale water from canteens.

"Let us go to a café," he'd suggested, upon arrival in Nogales; but don Luis latched onto his arm, saying, "No, no. We can eat later. The padre first. You have to come with me, stay with me. Ride home with me afterward."

A dozen times he wished he'd gone a few doors down for a tamal and beer; but, not knowing how long this would take, had endured, expecting moment by moment that the old man must finish, step out of the confessional, be his old arrogant self, a man to watch, but also one to respect for his power and cunning.

The bench was torture after so many hours in the saddle. Trail-dirty clothing and vermin picked up in the mesón last night itched skin used to cleanliness. Feeling lean from hunger, he fed himself on thoughts of parting the old hacendado from another sack of money.

The prospect of living in don Luis's casa grande as a trusted bodyguard, or at least securing a post as manager of one of the estancias, outweighed any temporary discomfort. He looked forward to visiting Tío Alejandro at Villa Flora, and saying, "I know you believed I would never amount to anything, but the carefree days of my youth are past and I am now a man of importance, honored wherever I go." So long as his lie about killing Trouble went undiscovered.

Luis shifted on the seat in the confession box. The thing was not made for men his size, but for the devout little Indios and women whose days were bounded by things spiritual, who attended services daily and never failed in their duty to God and Church.

He had shed his light coat early on, dropping it at his feet where it lay crumpled and soiled by his boot tracks. As the narrow door shut behind him, he'd almost panicked in the close space, and jumped in nervous startlement as the padre slid back the panel from over the grate between where he was and where the priest sat. There was no light, and very little air, and with faces a handspan apart he could hear the man breathing. "Bless me, father, for I have sinned." His voice was raspy and he had to clear his throat. There was a brief silence. "I—don't— I have forgotten what is next. I did remember not to eat before coming here."

"You have made a good start. Do not be hesitant about telling me what is bothering you. I am here to help you, and nothing you say can shock or anger me. When was your last confession?"

His tired mind groped back among the years. "A very long time, father. I was a child."

He could hear the priest settling into a comfortable position.

"Have you given sufficient thought to the sins you wish to confess? Try to relate the most grave ones first."

Filling his lungs with the dense air, he scratched a bite in the crook of his knee and gave a sigh. "Murder."

There was a pause. "Do you care to say more?"

"My partners. I killed them. For money. We stole it."

"I see. Theft and murder are grievous sins. But you feel sorrowful, do you not?"

"Sorrowful—" He rubbed his stubbled cheeks briskly with both hands. His eyes felt swollen, burning. "I am tormented."

"It is a great burden, to be guilty of theft and murder, especially against those who were your friends. Was it in a fit of rage, or did you plan?"

"I planned the robbery. It went smoothly. Men were killed then, too." He had given no thought to those packtrain guards, but their yells of terror and pain came back to him now. He supposed they had had families who awaited their return. Was Sofía waiting for him? Standing at the portales, watching the eastern mountains darken with night . . .

"There were . . . women. Many women, when I was younger. And one I have been living with for more than a year. Two years, maybe, I cannot recall."

"Can you sanctify this relationship by marriage?"

Marry? Sofía? Well. Perhaps he should. Those silly dreams of having a beautiful young lady to accompany him on an ocean voyage must have been bordering on insanity. Sofía at least knew his habits and tastes, and certainly wouldn't annoy him by putting herself forward. She was too grateful at being allowed the keys to the casa and given a position of authority over the other villagers. "Sí, I believe we might marry."

"Excellent. And the other women. They no longer interest you? They are in the past?"

"Yes. In the past. All—but one."

"Do you wish to tell me about her?"

His throat closed. He labored to draw in a breath. His palms left damp spots on the knees of his trousers. "She—was—my wife."

"Something happened to her?"

He shut his eyes tight and saw vivid colored pinwheels that brought back the horrible faces which had appeared to him in Barranco. "Something—I did."

The priest waited for him to continue. At last he said, "I—shot her." Tears flowed, surprising him. "I shot the boy, too." He heard the words, frowned in confusion, sorted his thoughts. "I mean, I paid someone to kill the boy. Her son. Maybe, my son. I was never sure."

Another silence. Then the priest said, "Truly, your life has gone astray. There is much to be sorrowful for, much for which to make amends."

"Can I? How can I make amends? They are all dead!"

"But you are alive." The padre's soft voice became vibrant. "And you are repentant. God knows your sorrow. He is willing to forgive. You do not have to carry this burden any longer. You can be free."

"Free." He ran his dry tongue over dry lips. "How wonderful you make that sound."

"Nothing is greater than trusting our savior Jesucristo to forgive you and set you free."

He allowed his mind to drift out of the confessional and over the dark Sierra Madre. A fortune in gold. More gold than a man can imagine. But it was cursed. She put a curse on it. *She has not forgiven me.*

The padre was explaining what was expected of him, to prove to himself and to others that his change of heart was genuine.

226

"Penance—sí. She talked about penance. Punishment. Purgatory."

"Not punishment. Restitution. As you can do nothing except pray daily for the souls of those who are dead, you must do what you can for others. And for yourself. If your heart is truly purified, you will want to live a different sort of life from the one you are leaving behind."

"Yes," he said. "I wish to start over." Stop all those dreams, or visions, or nightmares—whatever they were. To be good, pure, selfless. To make amends.

The narrow door of the confession box gave a little snap and drifted open. A stream of cool air touched the sweat on his face and neck. The priest's voice through the grating said, "Come back whenever you wish. In the morning, perhaps. We can talk more about what is needed. I shall be here to help you."

"Gracias." Luis picked up his coat and stepped into the candlelit sanctuary.

Dark clouds moved across the mountains, and though more rain threatened, the storm appeared to be passing to the southeast. A strong breeze cooled the summer heat, carrying faint aromas of damp earth and greening chaparral.

Leaning in the doorway of Manuelo's hut, Trouble watched young men carry and place long tables in the patios and courtyard. They set out chairs, hung lanterns in the widebranching trees and along the arcade roof. Dancers gathered to practice the jarabe, jarana, and jota. Spirited music and singing criadas left a bitter taste in his mouth.

How would it feel, to be a part of this fiesta, to wander among the crowds, sampling fruits and special dishes that took hours to prepare, from the grinding of the many spices to the simmering in cazuelas over coals for hours to blend the flavors. How pleasant, to kiss the ladies on their cheeks, dance with their daughters under watchful eyes, lounge on the softly-lit patio in the company of gentlemen and sip Champagne, comparing the merits of the blooded caballos out in the corrals.

To be the son of a man honest in his dealings and noble of soul. Not even Padre David had been noble.

"Enjoy it," he said aloud to the small figures in the gardens, lovers coming down to the lower gate to escape the notice of brothers or uncles. A row of niños sat atop another side of the adobe wall, watching, nudging each other in the ribs, laughing. He knew with what anticipation they looked forward to lighting the roman candles and pinwheels later. "Tell your children you saw the biggest fireworks of all, at la fiesta final de la Casa de Panadero."

Nearly dusk, and villagers thronged the tables on the lawns, eating, talking, and laughing in as relaxed a manner as though they strolled or sat in their own plaza.

When they finished the bounty outside, would they storm the casa grande for more? The jefe, the headman with whom all civil matters rested, was a mild if not timid leader whose skills had never been tried. Sofía didn't dare put her misgivings into words, lest Manuelo discover that she had stuffed his remedy into her pocket instead of swallowing it. Being too groggy to act or think clearly, she might miss an opportunity to speak to Ramón.

The singers and dancers making merry in the courtyard with the mariachis surely would exhaust themselves before the rico guests arrived. Turning from the noisy crowds, she passed through the back corredor toward the kitchen, to be sure someone had prepared enough coffee. "¡Dios mío! These tables are not set!"

As she rushed to find hands to employ, Manuelo hurried in, announcing, "The first carriage is coming through the gate."

There was no time to recheck the rooms prepared for those staying overnight—or many nights, as was usually the custom. Only time to pick up the linens and cry, "Help me!"

She and Manuelo spread the six tables, while she shouted to a couple of servers to hurry and place the plates and silverware, goblets and napkins. In moments the patios and comedor and sala lay ready. The boxes of cigarros and decanters of brandy rested on one of the Spanish chests near the glass doors. Clean cushions, plumped and profuse, were in all the chairs. Lamps and candles cast a golden glow over the clean, well-furnished rooms. If only don Luis were here . . . .

The entry-keeper swung open the heavy carved double doors of the zaguán, announcing, "Señor y Señora Macías, de Nogales."

Sweating, trying to tidy her hair, Sofía hastened to stand beside Manuelo and murmur, "Bienvenido, señora, señor. Welcome to Hacienda de Panadero."

After midnight, when cigars and drinks and appetizers, the singing and dances and special requests to the mariachis were over, and the supper—for the most part—eaten, Trouble stepped out of the hut.

Keeping to the shadows, he ran up the hillside to the barn with the trapdoor. He kicked aside the hay, lifted the covering, let himself down into the tunnel. The passage was dark even with a candle, and the air was warm and close—hardly enough to keep the flame alive. Coming to the cellar door, he eased it open.

Across the long, narrow room, Manuelo sat on the bottom step, a candlestick on the floor at his feet. Sounds of spirited conversation, muffled by the flooring. Footsteps of the servers, refreshing drinks or bringing another course or a platter of bread. More distant, music from the village band, playing some sad tune of murder, revenge, and lost love.

"Hola," Manuelo said, on seeing him approach. "Pues, we are in the midst of fiesta. Have you eaten?"

"Later maybe." He took a pail from beneath the steps. Careful not to splash the candles, he fished out three lengths of wet rope.

"I knew I smelled coal oil." Manuelo's eyes were shrewd, alert. "Why is it here?"

Regarding the makeshift fuses with concern, Trouble didn't answer. What if they burned awhile, then went out? Or led the spark into the kegs and merely caused a fire? His appetite was whetted for bigger things.

Rolling one of the containers into the open, he opened it, and with a willow stick cut and brought for the purpose, he jammed one end of a rope into the black powder and replaced the lid, leaving the other end dangling.

Manuelo warned. "If you're not careful, you will blow up the house."

"Exactly."

"You do not mean it."

He studied the joists, determining where the corners of rooms met the main hall. "I mean it."

Manuelo shook his head. "A waste. Not necessary."

"For me, it is. I am sorry. I know you love this house."

"Sí, and Sofía will be broken-hearted."

He prepared and placed a second keg. "There are more important things in life than fine houses."

"Of course. But sometimes, a man may have those things and a fine house."

Trouble pressed down the last lid. "Not this man. Not this house."

Far across the dark plain, Luis saw the tiny yellow lights of home. "Mi casa," he said, gesturing.

García reined in at his stirrup and they let the horses blow.

Half an hour, a bit more, and this journey would be behind him. "Mi tierra. Querencia." My homeland. My home. "Gracias a Dios."

García muttered something in response, but the rising wind swept the words away. It didn't matter. Nothing mattered more than reaching La Hacienda de Panadero. Tomorrow, he would begin making amends.

They rode on, spurring to greater speed, the storm at their backs threatening to overtake them.

Chapter Thirteen

Going up the steps, Trouble opened the cellar door a bit, and listened. The hall was empty.

In the dining room and beyond, already guests were telling stories of ghosts and treasure amid exclamations of pretended fright and soft bursts of relaxed laughter. Still to come were desserts, after-dinner coffee, small favors to remind them of what a grand time they'd enjoyed at Casa de Panadero, and a splendid finale of fireworks.

He dodged back as servers carried trays of used dishes toward the cocina. Other niños came out, their trays laden with glass bowls of flan and platters filled with hot fruit tarts. He could almost taste the crusty pastry shells, the tang of cherry or apple. Manuelo had offered to bring him a basket, but he had been too excited to eat.

"Just a little while," he murmured, "and it will all be over."

Presently Sofía herself came by and he stepped from the landing, calling, low, "Venga acá, por favor."

She ran to him. "Ramoncito, someone might see you."

"How much time to finish the meal?" he asked. "A half hour? More?"

"A half hour," she guessed. "Why?"

"Escuche." Listen. He gripped her arm. "In half an hour—not a minute longer—everyone must be on his way. Tell them the fiesta is done. Bid them goodbye. Nothing else. ¿Comprende?"

"Done? You mean, finished? But a dozen families are to sleep here. Their luggage is in the rooms and clean clothing is in the wardrobes and trunks. The girls will have to pack, and the carriages must be made ready. And still to come are the grand fireworks—"

"Three quarters of an hour, then. No more." He repeated, firmly, "No more. Understand? Make haste.

When every guest is out, you must come directly to the hut. ¡Muy *muy* importante, Sofía!"

"But, Ramón—"

Voices approaching made him step back down the stairway and close the door.

Chewing a corner of her waded handkerchief, Sofía stood at the archway connecting the fiesta dining rooms and the courtyard and watched the tilt of wine goblets in hands wearing diamonds. Minutes ticked by. Upstairs and in the guest wing, criadas were hurriedly folding items and stuffing them back into the cases from which they had come. In the stables, boys were throwing harness on the carriage horses, wheeling the rigs into place, fastening the metal buckles.

Her heart pounded in a disagreeable fashion and she wished Manuelo were here to make the announcement. But he had disappeared before the last course of frijoles was served, and no one seemed to know where he was.

Stepping into the comedor, she wrung her hands, sorry she had not taken Manuelo's remedy. Killed or calmed, either would have been better than this embarrassment. At last she called out in a reedy voice, "Estimados señores, señoras, y señoritas, and our honorable guests from the United States."

A few near, then more farther on, turned curious eyes to her. She felt as though she would faint, but continued, "I truly regret having to tell you that this fiesta must end. Lo siento, es terminado."

Surprised and dismayed cries repeated the word, adding her own silent question: "Why?"

Unable to give any reason, she said, "Your things are packed and the carriages are ready. Forgive me, but I must ask you to make haste. Thank you for coming. Muchísimas gracias, y vayas con Dios."

Puzzlement over don Luis's absence turned to anger. Loud remarks told her they considered themselves the object of a joke, and were offended to the point of staying until the host himself came out to offer an explanation or at least his regrets.

She heard her own polite phrases babbling, while she wondered whether she could push them out of the house and into their carriages in the three-quarters of an hour Ramón had allowed. Part of her mind worried over the change in him. First he wanted the fiesta, then he didn't.

He was sweating, like a high-strung colt being saddled for the first time. He wiped his forehead on his sleeve and went to sit on the step beside Manuelo. Where would they all be, tomorrow night this time? His friend's words kept pulsing through his brain: How will you feel, when the old man is dead?

And Sofía, saying, No more bounty hunters will come.

So long as no one except those two knew he was alive, perhaps he was safe. Los Pobres was far enough away that Panadero's path and his were not likely to cross. He dreaded having yet another man's blood on his hands.

"You are sure about this." Manuelo's tone seemed meant to make him reconsider, not to hear his answer.

"If this house is here, I can never rest anywhere else."

A shrug of acceptance. "As you say, don Ramón."

He looked at the wiry little mestizo in the candlelight, and smiled. "Do you know, you never called me that before."

"I have always thought of you as don Ramón, the hacendado de Casa Cordero."

"That is not meant to be."

"Then, you do believe in Destino."

"I cannot decide what to believe. I think I am making choices, but how can I be sure the road is not already planned for me? ¿Quién sabe?"

"Verdad. Quién sabe."

In the silence, he heard the scrape of chairs being pushed back on the patio tiles, the murmur of surprised and indignant voices. Not much longer. His heart thudded hard in his ears. "Sofía is removing the guests," he said. "I shall trust you to see that our people are safely across the river. By the time the fuse burns to" He pointed to the midsection of the first rope. "here."

He reached for Manuelo's candle. The brown hand blocked his for a moment, then relented. "Sí, don Ramón."

After the door closed, he sat back on his heels to wait. He thought of the disappointed villagers. Some had spent many hours preparing a longer celebration; all had eaten well and enjoyed entertainments, but the fireworks were a favorite part of such a fiesta. They never grew tired of the rockets and pinwheels, the blasts and showers of stars.

"Well, you will soon get your money's worth."

Sofía was relieved when Manuelo appeared beside her, saying to the confused girls gathering in the hall, "Go home, chicas. The fiesta is ended." He rounded up the others, cutting out workers from guests the way Luis's vaqueros separated calves from their mothers.

While those who had cleaned the house, prepared food, served, sang, and danced, were leaving by the back, don Luis's guests straggled in the direction of the gate, mozos carrying luggage. Some tried to stall, lingering to snatch another piece of chicken or finish a drink, but Manuelo urged them toward the waiting carriages.

In the midst of the confusion, El Patrón rode into the yard on a stumbling horse, accompanied by a man who seemed familiar. Both were drenched from a downpour that must have caught them on the plain. She gasped as they came closer. García! Vile man. What was he doing back here?

Don Luis rode right through the zaguán and into the sala, ignoring the dwindling crowd as they reluctantly climbed into coaches, some of them stopping in little groups to chatter and peer over their shoulders in astonishment. Reaching the central hallway, he halted and dismounted heavily. García sprang to catch his reins, and led both mounts out through the portico, past the disordered tables, past amazed guests.

How old he looked! His wet, dirty hair clung to his head. She ran to him. Taking the rain-soaked cloak from his shoulders, she cried, "I shall have José prepare a warm bath—"

"No." Luis waved her aside. "No. I wish nothing more than sleep."

His boots left dark stains as he limped down the hall to his room. She took two uncertain steps after him, but he had closed the door.

Trouble heard the clop of hooves, more than one horse—overhead, inside the house. Impossible. He was imagining things. The brief sound died, and he dismissed it as niños capering about in shoes that felt odd to feet that up until tonight had gone bare.

Gradually, voices and footsteps faded into silence. He felt regret for the piano. To his knowledge, it had never been played.

He lit the nearest fuse. Watching sparks eat along the oil-soaked hemp, he almost set his boot on the small flame, almost backed away from what he meant to do. His hand shook, lighting the second. When it was burning steadily, he struck a new match, touched the last wick.

In the dim cellar, the pinpoints of light traveled away from him, following the paths he had laid out. Escaping by way of the tunnel would be dangerous. If the ropes burned faster than he expected, or someone had chanced to place something heavy over the opening in the barn floor, he could be killed in the explosion or trapped by a cave-in. Manuelo had never admitted to knowing of the passage, and Trouble didn't trust Sofía to think of searching it if that happened. She was going to be much too upset over losing the casa grande and all its finery to be concerned about him.

He went up the cellar steps. Behind him he could hear the sizzle, like meat frying in a pan. The main hallway was empty. The house was empty. Pausing just outside the library—the old casita—he wished he had remembered to take some of the nicer leatherbound books. Such items were hard to come by, in Los Pobres, but no time was left to pore over titles and choose, and he didn't wish to be burdened with volumes of little interest. The door to

Panadero's bedroom, as were those to the other private rooms, was closed. Good. It would make a better impact.

Then he was running down the great central hallway and out into the night.

Sofía watched the gatekeeper bowing to occupants of departing carriages. Friends and their outriders exchanged cries of "¡Hasta la vista!" The mariachis were the last, loading their instruments into a cart with the name of their band painted garishly on the sides. Finally they were gone, and the grounds were deserted.

She wandered back through the zaguán and stood regarding the remains of the fiesta. The masses and garlands of flowers, unappetizing bowls which had held meats and rice and fruits, the dozens of dirty flan dishes and wine glasses, several overturned. Soiled, crumpled napkins, scattered silverware. A few forgotten shawls, a silver-crested cane. What a mess, to be cleaned up in the morning. She would need plenty of help for that.

Don Luis was certain to be furious over what had taken place in his absence. Rested, and strengthened by dulces and brandy-laced chocolate in his room, he wasn't likely to sit idle while Ramón tried to kill him. She shuddered.

The old man had García now, too, to fight his battles. Looking down at the muddy hoofprints, she wondered where those two had been, together. Soon the man would come from stabling the horses, and she did not want to face him alone. Glancing about for Manuelo, she remembered that Ramón had made her promise to come to the hut. Were they there? Or had Ramón decided to run away tonight after all. Did he want to take her with him? or say goodbye . . . .

In the glow from the paper fiesta lanterns, Trouble saw her coming down the long hill. He went to meet her, to hurry her along with a hand on one arm. "Are they gone?"

She nodded, lips parting as if she would speak, but he interrupted, "The musicians?"

"Sí—"

"All the girls? The niños? La Vieja? Every guest?"

"Sí. Ramón, why are you—"

"Then cover your ears."

Like a strike of lightning the explosion rocked the ground beneath them, and she screamed. He grabbed her shoulders.

"¡En el nombre de Dios!" Her hands flew to her head as if the blast had split it and she had to hold the pieces together. "¿Qué pasa? ¿Qué pasa?"

Before the echoes died, the second keg burst, sending roof tiles, bits of timbers and broken adobe, and flames spurting into the air. "I am blowing up the house."

Her eyes went wide. "Oh, Madre de Dios—Luis is in there—" She wrenched away from him and started to run back.

He caught her by the elbow and swung her around. "You told me everyone was out!"

"Guests! You said guests—" She wrung out of his grasp. Instead of running, she sank to her knees, calling on Jesucristo and several saints, words tumbling through her sobs. The third keg exploded and she leaped up, screaming, into his arms.

He held her, gaze on the billowing orange smoke, the fragments of once-loved stuff rising, arcing, raining down. "Where was he? In his room? The comedor? The cocina?"

"He wanted to sleep. He wouldn't wait for José to bring bath water." She began pulling at him, crying, entreating. "Ramón, go! Help him— He must be hurt."

Resisting, he told her, "He must be dead."

She stiffened, eyes wild, accusing. "That is what you wanted and now it has happened! Ramoncito, how could you do this thing?" Both fists hammered his chest, then she rushed into the night, toward Manuelo's hut.

He went forward slowly, awed.

Scattered over the lawn were chunks of rock, pieces of flooring, shards of tile. Uprooted ornamental trees, broken glass glittering in the firelight. Beneath the split columns of the north galería he could see overturned tables and chairs, with their spilled bounty of flowers and half-eaten food. Upper roofs sagged from what support still existed, broken ceiling beams lay criss-crossed here and there. Twisting fingers of smoke sprang out of the rubble. The servants' quarters were standing, but the main house was destroyed. And the evil patrón with it.

Running feet behind him triggered his grab for the Colt and when he swung around with it, a strange man in a trail-soiled but fancy suit skidded to a halt, crying, "¡No dispare!" Don't shoot.

Not expecting to encounter anyone alive, García asked, "How many are hurt? Dead?"

"Probably only one."

"I am not armed. Please put away your weapon. May I be of assistance?" *So close*, he thought. *I had the old man in my pocket, and now this.* What an unpromising development. Was the hacendado dead? Injured? "How did this happen?"

Holstering the gun, the young man pulled a thin rug off what had been a banister and pitched it to him. "Here."

A few lanterns remained lit, glowing from fanciful angles. One burst into flame as he passed, causing him to jerk in startlement. Lifting his voice, he asked, "Are you a guest?"

Tossed over a shoulder, the words were bitter. "You might say that."

Stepping around the broken stone and floor tiles, glass crackling under his boots, García followed into the dark depths. "Why were they having such a fiesta without the patrón? Did they think he was not coming back?"

The boy stopped to douse his sarape in the basin of the fountain, which was still sending up delicate streams that splashed gently in the silence. "It is more effective wet," he said in a dull voice.

"Ah. I see." He soaked the rug and, holding it at arm's length to avoid the drip, hurried to catch up. He hoped he was not called upon to fight the fire raging in a distant wing of the casa. "You cannot save anything." No response. "Let us wait until help comes."

Tripping over piles of smoldering clothing and ravaged books, they made their way through the maze of crumbled walls. Here, the roof had been blown off and heavy timbers lay confusedly about. Dust hung thick in the air currents, ghostly in the flicker of small fires. The boy beat out a few flames in his path, and climbed over the wreckage as if he knew what he sought.

Panadero's bedroom, what was left of it, lay directly ahead. Trouble's breath came fast and shallow. *Would I have killed him?* Now, he would never know.

The man beside him wrenched a burning rung from a chair and held it aloft. "Can you see anything?"

From beneath one of the beams, a hand. Palm up, fingers lax, the bare wrist pitiful. Thinking of the fist which had punished so unjustly, he said, "Under that viga." He started forward, but the man stopped him.

"Allow me— It might not be a body."

Turning sick, and unwilling for anyone to witness a loss of dignity, he cast about for refuge. Across the yard, more lights and excited babble meant others were coming. They blocked the way to the hut and his trail-ready horses. He couldn't stand here, drenched in cold sweat, shaking, about to vomit.

Three swift strides took him through the litter-strewn remnants of El Patrón's little patio.

Over the flattened ornamental iron gate, down the sloping yard, to the lower corner of the adobe wall. He reached the trees before cramping in his stomach forced up bitter liquid. No food—he hadn't eaten since breakfast. When he was able to raise his head, dancing fire-shadows in the lavender-scented foliage around him showed him the bricks of Mamá's chapel.

He put out a trembling hand and touched the rough surface. A few steps away, the black slit of a partly open door offered sanctuary.

Sofía lay curled on Manuelo's cot, weeping. The depth of her sorrow surprised her until she realized it was pity that fed her tears. Don Luis had been so unhappy, driven, that the thought of his spending eternity in that state, with no one except herself to pray for him, nearly broke her heart. She had used some of his money to buy a new suit for him to wear during the fiesta. Now, he would be buried in that suit.

She cried for Ramón, also driven, ready to do murder. Why had he destroyed the casa grande they all loved? He loved it, too. She had seen him touching the carved doors, dipping his hand in the fountain.

Those kegs.

He had warned her they were dangerous. "You knew," she whispered. "You planned this, and didn't tell me." Were he and Manuelo searching through the ruined house, looking for the body? If Luis were injured but alive, would Ramón put a bullet in his helpless head? She sat up, wiped her face, listened for a pistol shot.

Bobbing lights and a growing din of hooves and wheels sent her to the doorway. Departing guests, drawn by the tremendous booms and the thrill of uncontrolled fire, were returning. On the hill, figures scurried back and forth, carrying torches, shouting questions, yelling in dismay or discovery. Past the flames and smoke and charred timbers, instead of familiar roof lines, she saw the dark ridge stark against a starlit sky.

When she could summon the strength, she set out for the village and the comfort of La Vieja's hot herbal tea. Manuelo or Ramón would have to come to her. She couldn't stand going to look for them, for fear of what else she must find.

There was a body, García noted. After the peónes freed it with much wailing and excitement, the mayordomo said, "Take him to La Vieja's house." Watching them obey, the man added, "Well, Señor García. There is nothing here for you now."

The insult stung him. "Don't be insolent. You're not jefe, just because your patrón is dead."

"Don't be deceived. My power never lay in El Patrón."

"I have ridden long hours today and I don't wish to fight. Have you no room for a traveler?" He would have liked a cigarro, too, but thought better of requesting one. The glittering eyes gave him a strange sensation.

"I have never cared for a man who kills others for money, or claims to do so when he is clearly a coward."

"You disappoint me. Where's your hospitality?"

"Come, then. If you pay, someone will give you a bed."

They followed the body to its destination, a casita belonging to a crone who met them at the door and who had cleared her table so that the corpse could be laid out. Though the shack was crowded, she accepted the few centavos García offered for the use of a shuck mattress and sleeping space. For a while he stayed alert, listening for any useful disclosures. However, the babble consisted only of theories as to the cause of the accident and wild speculation about what would become of everyone now.

"What is the name of the majordomo?" he asked, watching La Vieja comb don Luis's hair.

She answered, "¿El? El es Manuelo."

On reflection, he felt sure that the young man with the pistol was the hated son Ramón, called Trouble, and that the majordomo would do anything to protect him. Had they planned to murder the old patrón in this spectacular way in order to make it appear accidental?

If so, they were a ruthless pair, and he must not let down his guard, no matter how exhausted or longing for sleep. Yet, as neither of them had reason to love the self-made hacendado, neither had they reason to care that he, García, had tricked the old man out of the reward.

The housekeeper's endless sobbing finally forced him to exit the casita, and he walked back across the footbridge. He was unsurprised to see villagers carrying lanterns and burlap sacks as they dug through mounds of broken furniture, heavy tattered rugs, kitchen utensils, and scorched clothing. All but a few of the less-well-bred guests had left, curiosity unsatisfied but purses full of small treasures taken for souvenirs. He resisted the impulse to pick up a dented brass cigar box.

Surveying the ruined walls, he felt an unaccustomed awareness of Dios. Ten hours in the saddle had made him resent having to wait supper for Luis to make confession. Had El Patrón sensed an impending death? Why else, with the threat of rain and a long ride yet ahead, would he have insisted on seeking absolution.

"A few more minutes," García muttered, "and I, too, should have been in that casa." Glad that he had searched the old man's saddlebags, though he'd found nothing of value, he went back to the candlelit choza to a tattered mattress in a room full of strangers. The housekeeper sat in a corner, silent, her red-rimmed eyes dry and swollen.

By daybreak, people were preparing food in the yard as well as inside the hut where don Luis lay. Everyone wanted to be at the center of things, and much of the shock had turned to avid gossip and relieved laughter. Scavengers showed off items or traded for those deemed more desirable.

García accepted a plate and found a place to sit in the doorway. He was starved, and the old Indita proved to be a damned good cook.

Shafting through a small high window overgrown with purple bougainvillea, a beam of sunlight in Trouble's eyes woke him. Unbending stiff arms and legs, he sat up. He had not been in Mamá's chapel for years.

Blown sand covered the tiled floor in irregular rows, and chunks of mortar lay near the walls. A faded tapestry draped the altar. In nearly fifteen years, nothing had been touched. A silver candlestick, offering up stubs of melted wax, was still here. Her prayerbook was dimmed with thick dust. The velvet of the prie-dieu bore the imprint of her knees. He thought of all the prayers she had recited, the secret rosary by which she counted Our Fathers and Hail Marys. He supposed the cross lay in a trash mound somewhere. Or, Panadero might have placed it in one of those lacquer boxes, the day García gave it to him in exchange for the reward.

Fingering the rosary chain around his neck, Trouble remembered that she wished him to be devout. Had she lived, and had life at Casa de Panadero not been cursed, she might have guided him into some service for the Church. Now, he could not bring himself to repeat rituals formed by mortals long dead, nor revere saints who had to be bribed with bits of food or coins or burning candles before they acted in one's behalf. His refusal of the sacraments available in the mission at Los Pobres had caused the old padre much despair. If Father Navarre ever learned that he possessed, and meant to read, the Bible taken from the bounty hunter's pack, the old padre would consider him a heretic, and their friendship would end. Surely truth lay somewhere in between.

Going to the doorway, he looked out. A hundred paces up the sloping lawn, the servants' quarters, less damaged than the main house, partly blocked this view of the casa; but voices carried on the clear morning air, and now and then he caught a glimpse of several heads, moving about amid the rubbish.

Manuelo, coming from the willows, hailed him, adding, "I fed your horses."

"Gracias."

"You must go into town and have your name put on the deed. Everything is yours now."

"It was never mine. I want no part of anything that was his. I didn't know that until I came back." He hesitated, unsure how his concern would be perceived. "Is Sofía all right?"

"She will be. In time." Manuelo glanced at him and away. "There is something you should be told."

"What?"

"García is here."

"That fortune hunter? What is he after?"

"He's at the hut of La Vieja, if you care to ask him."

Crossing the footbridge, Trouble suspected that money in large sums was the force that drove García.

The stranger in the stained fancy suit was sitting in the doorway, scooping up the last bite of blanquillos with a piece of tortilla. Motion suspended halfway to his mouth, he said, cordially, "Buenos días. Don Ramón, is it not?"

"Forgive me for being rude, but I must remind you that you have already collected for my hide."

"True. Don Luis was quite generous."

A crowd was gathering, not too close but so filled with surprise at seeing him alive, he could feel their suppressed wonderment. At the far fringe, arms around each other's waist, were Beatriz and Chuco, staring in mute uncertainty.

García set the plate aside and would have stood up if Trouble hadn't halted him with a hand against his chest. "Did you expect to trick him again in some other way?"

"You misjudge me. I chanced to meet your father on the road and, as he appeared in no condition to travel alone, I agreed to ride with him."

"Did he tell you where he had been?"

"No, and I did not inquire."

"Did he have mules? Burros?"

"Only the mare he rode."

As others nodded agreement, García again attempted to rise and again Trouble stopped him. "The mare which you stabled."

Angrily, the man cried, "What do you think I've done? If I had stolen anything from don Luis, would I be here, enduring your arrogance?"

He believed that, to a point. But he was also sure that Panadero had gone to La Nariz to bring home the sacks of gold coins, if not all of the bullion. What had happened to them? Had the old hacendado become so ill or exhausted that he left it all behind? Or had he lost heavily-laden pack animals in a plunge over the canyonside into a chasm?

If he had managed to reach home with a few bags, where were they?

Calling La Vieja out of the hut, Trouble learned that when the body was brought to her, El Patrón was wearing his velvet smoking robe. No hidden money belt, not even slippers. Manuelo, she said, had made sure that nothing was taken from what was left of the hacendado's room. Trouble trusted both the cook and the segundo.

"If you believe I'm hiding something," the fortune hunter challenged, "have me searched."

"¡Armand—Tiburcio! Search him and his horse, and see that he leaves just as he came. Also, bring me El Patrón's saddlebags."

He went back across the river to assess the devastation by daylight.

Sofía was standing apart from small groups of villagers who were going through the rubble like ragpickers. Her hair hung in wisps over her ears, and her cheeks and forehead were smeared with what must be dirt and blood. Her new dress was marred with similar stains and masses of wrinkles where she had clutched the material. Hearing his bootsteps on the rocky path, she turned, started run to him, stopped, and said piteously, "Oh, Ramón!"

"Sofía, have you been up all night?"

"I cannot rest." Her fingers pressed against her lips in a distraught fashion.

Together they watched carts being piled full of salvage. "Has anyone found anything. . . valuable?"

She seemed puzzled. "There was much of value. But everything is being carried away. Even Manuelo could not make them stop."

"I don't mean things from the house."

The bewilderment on her face deepened. "What do you mean?"

He couldn't mention the map without setting off a search for it, in case it had not turned up. And he dared not mention sacks of gold, for the same fear. "When Panadero came last night, did he tell you anything?"

"About his trip? No. He was too tired, and soaked with rain—"

Pent up tears hovered, so he assured her, "No matter." Then he added, as casually as he could, "Didn't the old man have an iron box? One with a big key?"

"There." She pointed. "It doesn't use a key, but a knob with letters and numbers. No one can open it."

He walked over to where the safe lay, one corner cocked up by a chunk of adobe. It wasn't the customary metal-bound chest that men of wealth kept for securing treasures, but a smaller steel box with a dial in the center of the door. At most it might hold five or six bags. Enough to live well the rest of one's life. He kicked idly at the handle.

Stepping amid the litter, he paused to turn over scraps of furniture or fragments of colored glass with his boot toe. Dead flowers were strewn everywhere. All the pots, broken. The dirt, spilled. Most of the books, taken by people who had never learned to read. A few, burned too badly, had been thrown aside. No treads left, the stairwell to the wine cellar was now a dark pit. Where the old ovens once baked fragrant pan dulce and tartas, later concealing the map and the seed of all that came after, nothing remained except gray rubble and blackened roof tiles. The dull ache inside swelled, and tears trickling from the corners of his eyes moved Sofía to touch his shoulder. "Have you seen him?"

He shook his head.

Linking her arm in his, she steered him around the gaping hole, the adjacent heap of roof tiles and vigas.

"The padre in Nogales will do as you wish. Only tell him."

"Whatever is customary." Out of calling distance, he could see the segundo talking with a peón and his wife, who carried a baby in her rebozo. "Manuelo is a good man. I'm leaving everything to him."

250

"Everything?"

"Sí. He may build here, if he likes. Name the place Casa Vásquez."

Steps faltering, she turned her face away.

He grasped her chin to make her look at him. "Sofía, what are you keeping from me?"

She swallowed, bit her lower lip, refused to meet his probing eyes. "We are—married."

The word seemed to stop his heart. Those nights he'd made love to her in the hut by the river, he knew of Manuelo's fondness for her, but had no idea it was serious. First Tinita, now this.

Her lashes overflowed with tears. "After García came."

"When you thought I was dead."

"Sí." It was a whisper.

He placed his hand over hers where it rested on his arm. "He is a good man. I'm glad you have each other."

A boy bringing Panadero's saddlebags and a satchel skirted the remains of an arcade, but Trouble motioned him to wait. Barefoot, the niño climbed onto the high, curved surface and waved to someone only he could see. The way he carried the bags, they were not heavy.

"I shall always remember the happy times, Sofía."

"I, too."

They resumed strolling through the rubble. Presently, she said, "What are your plans?"

Pausing in what was once the main hallway, he leaned his head back. Instead of ceiling and a glass chandelier, far overhead were puffy clouds in a dome of brilliant blue. "I cannot stay here." He felt her tremble.

Lips crimping, she asked, "Because of me?"

"No...because of me."

Distant cries of joyous people wafted into their silence. A village dog barked. In the morning sky, a laughing falcon soared, its *eek eek eek* resounding from the cliffs.

"Where will you go?"

He turned to regard the plain that stretched into a blue haze to the south, and thought of his casita. The promise of solitude, of peace. Evenings spent with Padre under the ramada, listening to the doves, not worrying that a paid killer might lurk in the chaparral.

The road still hung dust from the last of the salvage carts. Across the Sangría, rugged mountains turned from lilac to azure. This afternoon, summer rains would wash over the parched earth, bringing life to the spiny ocotillo and brittlebush. In Los Pobres, his spring-irrigated garden plot must be rank with unused squash, tomatoes, corn.

He raised his eyes to the brooding rockcliff where, on a long-ago night, he had trembled at the edge while a man supposed to be his father ripped apart the universe.

Sofía must have thought he hadn't heard, for she said again, "Where will you go, Ramoncito?"

"Somewhere beyond that," he told her, "I'll be free."

The End

Continue reading the Cordero saga in Book 2 of
Tierra del Oro

México, 1883. A story of greed, hidden treasure, magic, and legends, told against the grandeur of the Sierra Madre.

A young man's longing for peace turns into a search for love, an adventurous mustang hunt turns into a quest for treasure, and friends are not what they seem.

Look for

Legend of the Sierra Madre

Chapter One

Los Pobres. 1883.

Far across the valley, set between low brown hills to the east and distant blue mountains to the west, the village lay hot and uneventful beneath the westering sun. A surge of expectation made Ramón whisper, "Home."

He craved rest. Solitude. A drink from his spring.

His casita stood on the near point of the ridge, above a brush-choked slope that had provided cover for Panadero's killers. He reined in. The black gelding flinched as the horses trailing on a lead crowded into it. Dust drifted up from their hooves, floated away on a little breeze.

No need to clear the chaparral now. Don Luis was dead, and the reward would not be paid again.

Memories faded, stopped hurting, in time. How long, before he could think of the horse he rode as his own, before he slept free of *malos sueños*, bad dreams.

He flicked the gelding with his heels.

The planks and wood shingles were losing their raw look, weathering, blending into the background of earth and rocks, shadowed by a gnarled mesquite.

Tomorrow, or the next day, if this drought broke, he'd replant the corn, beans, and squash that had gone neglected in his absence. He would visit the booths in the market, buy the healing herbs which Manuelo favored, and grow them. He looked forward to long evenings spent relaxing in a cane-bottom chair shaded by the priest's brush ramada, drinking unconsecrated wine and listening to happy cries of village children in the near distance.

Patting a handful of masa, Juanita leaned to place the tortilla on the hot griddle. Through the broken window she glimpsed movement, a rider on the plain, and watched him draw near the village. The low-crown sombrero and dark clothing suggested a mestizo of the middle class. He led two horses, and rode in the relaxed manner of a rico landowner. Though rock-walled casa grande down the street had been deserted for many years, he might be going home to it.

In the month she had lived here, she'd avoided meeting the families in the better neighborhood. Pride was too great and shame too fresh, to face the curiosity of strangers.

"There is a casita," Father Navarre told her, "where you may stay." He led her up the rocky hillside to the single room and lit the lamp. "It belonged to a young norteño whose father sent men to kill him. Two are buried at the edge of our campo santo, but the last one took him."

She had placed her traveling bag on a flat-topped trunk under one window. A door opened beneath a shed at the back. Foodstuffs and utensils were arranged in an orderly fashion on shelves. A pot and two cups on the table smelled faintly of coffee. "Gracias," she had said, glad for the old man's kindness but happy to be alone when he returned to the mission church.

As her body changed, she pushed Guillermo from her thoughts and into a dark cell like the prison in Hermosillo, pretending the baby she carried belonged to the young man whose hands had built and furnished this house.

Small square table with two chairs, a stand to hold a basin over which hung a clay olla of drinking water, a wooden tub for washing, and a strange little stove in place of a charcoal brazier or oven. A young, handsome man called 'Trouble,' who had slept in the bed where she now spent nights tormented by anger, whose pillow her bitter tears soaked.

Whenever she ate from his dishes, or read the books found in his trunk, or placed her lips where his lips had touched the tin dipper, she could forget the way Guillermo, a man she once trusted and loved, had spurred his horse and left her with the dust of Los Pobres swirling around her bare feet.

Forget his baby, at least until it was born sometime around navidad. To take its life by means of deadly herbs or a curandera's magic was a mortal sin, a thing she shrank from doing. Mamá and her sisters would be horrified.

Hoofbeats in the yard jerked her thoughts back to the rider. Through the front window space, she saw him dismounting in the yard.

¡Madre de Dios! Why had he come here? with the bell tower marking the church, and the whole town, tiny as it was, from which to choose a destination.

Seeing his face and slender build, checked cotton shirt and denim trousers and dusty boots, dark curling hair and alert glances—she knew him. Knew he was the norteño called Trouble, who was not dead.

The flutter of a white curtain at his north window startled Trouble, and he dismounted with reins in his left hand and the bounty hunter's .44 in the other, at his side but cocked. Keeping the gelding between himself and the house, he looked for tracks in the yard and found only those made by the padre's sandals and a small bare foot, though larger than a child's.

Could Father Navarre be keeping a woman here? The thought had scarcely formed when a pale girl wearing a loose dress came to the doorway, saying, "No dispare, por favor." *Don't shoot.*

He put away the pistol and nudged the horse's head out of his line of sight. She appeared to be about seventeen. "Damn, he likes them young."

A flare of anger in her eyes told him she understood his meaning if not his English. More formally, in Spanish, he offered, "Forgive me, I did not mean to insult you. But you surprised me. This is my house."

She was no Indita. No servant nor woman of the night, kept for the padre's pleasure. Her features, light even for a mestiza, showed a quality bloodline, like an expensive filly. Her voice fit her appearance as she spoke. "Father Navarre said he thought you had been killed, and so allowed me to live here. I am Juanita María Martínez Muñoz. Please do not make me leave."

A beautiful young woman was the last thing he had expected, or needed. "Of course you must leave."

He led his stock around to the shed, stripped off the saddle, and stowed the gear. As he worked, the leather bag of gold coins tucked into his shirt lay heavy against his ribs, reminding him of the cave at La Nariz, where a fortune lay concealed beneath a few handspans of earth alongside his murdered mother.

The brown aroma of beans simmering with chiles and tomatoes, and the acrid smell of a burnt tortilla, brought back the sweaty anticipation he'd felt as he waited on the cellar stairs for guests to finish feasting, fuses in the kegs and matches in his hand. He heard Sofía's screams mingled with strains of leftover fiesta music throbbing through his brain. The ruins of La Casa de Panadero lay heavy on his mind. His fist clenched at the memory of another hand, protruding from beneath a fallen viga, stilled forever in the flickering firelight.

In nightmares he saw the flames and chunks of rock, adobe, and roof tiles spouting upward, the columns of smoke against a starry sky. He hadn't wanted to know where the man who nicknamed him 'Trouble' was buried. Manuelo had shouldered that duty.

When the horses finished rolling in the scant grass, he took them for a drink. Run-off from his spring ponded in a rock basin two wagon lengths across at its widest part, and chest-deep. Old willows leaned over the water. He slung one leg across the sturdiest trunk and sat watching shadows lengthen on the rippled surface.

His thoughts wandered to Tinita's curly coppery hair and amber eyes. Her warm lovemaking. The child and husband she had neglected to mention.

In time, he knew, he could forget her sort of treachery; but it would take longer to get over Sofía. Brought to the casa grande by Panadero, she was older than Trouble, a friend who had lived in the same house with him for over two years; yet she'd kept her marriage to Manuelo secret until after she'd gotten him into bed.

He felt his face flush, as much from remembering how much he'd enjoyed her as from a sense of guilt. At least their indiscretion hadn't damaged his friendship with Manuelo. It had destroyed his willingness to trust women.

The horses moved, their muzzles dripping, to snatch mouthfuls of long grass edging the pond. He listened to the crisp, rhythmic sounds, familiar and peaceful.

Determined to be rid of the padre's homeless girl, he tossed a stick into the pond and slid off the willow trunk.

Juanita heard the clops of his horses, saw him pass the open doors. He went into the shed and, from the tinny noises, she imagined that he dipped grain from barrels into pans for his stock.

Heart thudding, she ladled beans from the earthen pot, scooped the last tortilla from the griddle and added it to the stack, poured a cup full of fresh water. She had set them both a place, but fear of what he might say or do caused her to return the extra plate to the shelf.

The padre called him Ramón, but said he was known as Trouble. The English word meant 'to make unhappy, to distress.' Who had given him that insulting nickname, and why?

Padre had hinted at a dark past, some great sadness. Had his sweetheart died? Only a little older than she, still he must have had many girls in love with him. She didn't care to dwell on what sort of woman was free to satisfy a man's appetite without an aunt or older sister hovering at her elbow. She had been stupid to believe Guillermo's lies, to leave her tierra at Bacabachi.

When he came in at the back door, he paused, looking about as if to see what might have changed. Then he went to the wash basin, splashed water over his face, dried on the clean cloth and hung it back on its peg. He sat down to the filled plate. "You can't stay." Then he fell to eating.

She sat on the trunk and clasped her hands to lessen the trembling. She had daydreamed that Trouble was alive, young, handsome. Gentle. Kind. In her dreaming, they had shared meals, talked of many things, laughed together. Touched each other.

He was handsome. Dark, clear-cut Spanish features. Assured manner and pleasant voice. The wounded look in his eyes—all these wrenched her with a longing to be near him, to experience the things she had imagined. She couldn't leave, now that he was here with her. Besides, where would she go? Not home, to the sympathy of her mother, the ridicule of her sisters.

"The food is good. Gracias."

"Padre says you come from the border country. That you are educated and speak much English."

He regarded her for a long moment. "It was the custom in the house where I lived to eat the last meal of the day early, like norteamericanos, or campesinos who work the fields. Did Padre tell you this, or is it your custom as well?"

Was he interested? Or fishing for information? Before she could respond, he gestured for her to join him. Trying not to appear too eager, she took the chair across from him, saying, "Eating late bothers me because—" Ay, no, don't say that. He would learn of the baby soon enough.

He wasn't listening. "There must be some place you can go. Padre can find a family—"

"No. I cannot accept the charity of strangers."

A look of amusement crossed his face. "Yet you expect me to give you my house."

"Only a corner." She had no appetite for the food. She took a sip of water, her hand bumping the cup against her teeth. "While you were tending your horses, I remembered that it was you who built this casita. How easy to make the shed into a little room for me to sleep in, and if I help, it can be finished in no time." For a moment she thought he would say, *What a good idea.*

Then with a scowl he pushed back from the table. "I have no intention of living with someone underfoot."

She watched him go out into the dusk.

....

To check availability of

Legend of the Sierra Madre

Book Two in **Tierra del Oro**

email the author at **rlbhartmann@gmail.com** or
sonora10@att.net
or search Amazon.com by title or author

Forthcoming volumes in the Cordero saga:

Book 3 - Los Pobres

Book 4 - La Puerta del Sol

Book 5 - A Lion Against the Wind

Book 6 - Bitter Victory

Book 7 - Tierra y Libertad

Book 8 - The Horse Tamers

Book 9 - Tesoro

Note from the Author

A friend asked what compelled me to write a series of novels about a mestizo family in México in the nineteenth and twentieth centuries. All I know is, one day I sat down to write a short story that began with the spoken words, "Get Trouble!" and the image of a portly Mexican in a brocade vest, a freshly lit cigar in his hand.

When I came to the final 'The End,' I'd written the entire story of the Cordero Clan, all 4 generations of them.

In striving for impeccability, I often turn to readers and accomplished writers who don't hesitate to question my plotlines, character motivations, and sanity.

My best advice to a struggling writer is this: if your character is a wrestler, let him be a wrestler; he can't be anything else, regardless of what movie or book comes out with a minor similarity. When you begin, don't focus on the little pebbles in the road, but write with abandon the parts you are sure of. They don't have to be in order, or even complete. Write the white-hot scenes when you can; don't try to fill in the gaps as you go. Getting down a first draft, no matter how pitted and shaky, is the first step. Learn to love revision. It's where the beauty is.

She wrote what she dreamed, and from all failures rose like the Phoenix on a plume of fire and smoke, to victory.

www.ingramcontent.com/pod-product-compliance
Lightning Source LLC
Chambersburg PA
CBHW061955170626
46813CB00006B/2652